SNOWY SURPRISES IN THE HIGHLANDS

LISA HOBMAN

B
Boldwood

First published in Great Britain in 2025 by Boldwood Books Ltd.

Copyright © Lisa Hobman, 2025

Cover Design by Alexandra Allden

Cover Images: Shutterstock

A CIP catalogue record for this book is available from the British Library.

Paperback ISBN 978-1-83703-996-8

Large Print ISBN 978-1-83703-997-5

Hardback ISBN 978-1-83703-995-1

Trade Paperback ISBN 978-1-80635-331-6

Ebook ISBN 978-1-83703-998-2

Kindle ISBN 978-1-83703-999-9

Audio CD ISBN 978-1-83703-990-6

MP3 CD ISBN 978-1-83703-991-3

Digital audio download ISBN 978-1-83703-992-0

This book is printed on certified sustainable paper. Boldwood Books is dedicated to putting sustainability at the heart of our business. For more information please visit https://www.boldwoodbooks.com/about-us/sustainability/

Boldwood Books Ltd, 23 Bowerdean Street, London, SW6 3TN

www.boldwoodbooks.com

To Ruby, Wilf and Bertie, my canine children. Thank you for encouraging me to leave the house every so often to get some much-needed fresh air. And thank you for the cuddles, and for sitting with me in my office, snoring as I type. Your snuffles are the soundtrack to my work, and I couldn't be happier.

1

Bella Douglas sipped her mimosa by the twinkling Douglas fir tree – that had come to Skye all the way from her former place of employment Drumblair Castle's plant and tree nursery, no less – and smiled as she inhaled the fresh fragrance of pine. There was nothing to match the smell of a real tree, she decided. It was Christmas morning, one of her favourite times to be in the house she shared with her wonderful police inspector boyfriend, Harris Donaldson, because it always had an extra-cosy glow about it during the festive season.

She wasn't sure how 2024 was almost over already and how this was her *third* Christmas on the island, but in spite of the whizzing by of time, she was filled with warmth and felt sure she probably looked like one of the kids on the old eighties Ready Brek ads; a glowing aura of light around her for the world to see. It could have been the alcohol or the heat from the log burner, but she liked to think it was simply happiness.

Harris had got up before her that morning and had gone downstairs to light the fire and put on a fresh pot of coffee before calling to her to come down. After climbing out of bed, she had paused a moment to look out of the bedroom window and had been greeted with a Christmas-card-worthy vista. Although there was, as yet, no snow, a heavy frost had covered the garden and trees behind their newly built home that adjoined the police station – an old, converted bothy, or farm worker's cottage – and it had glistened in the rising sun as if a pot of silver glitter had been scattered across the ground. An amber glow had tinged the sky, and she was reminded, once again, of how much she loved the isle she now called home.

Living on Skye was quite different from her upbringing in and around the Highland city of Inverness. Back in her youth, she and her school friend, funnily enough also named Skye, had spent many a happy hour at Drumblair Castle, the home of their other best friend Olivia MacBain – now Lady Olivia MacLeod, since her inheritance and subsequent marriage – playing hide and seek in the many rooms and dodging each other in the vast stone corridors. Or spying on Olivia's older brother, Kerr, as he played an invisible guitar along with the music blaring from whichever CD he was listening to in his room. Skye and Olivia would mock him with exaggerated facial expressions, giggling hysterically behind their hands, but not Bella. She would swoon and pine from a distance until he heard them and slammed his door sulkily, chuntering under his breath about his stupid sister and her stupid minions.

Bella had loved Kerr MacBain from a young age, but of course he'd never noticed her – well, not until they were adults and even then it didn't turn out how she had dreamed, in fact she had discovered him to be as horrible as the rumours had suggested.

These days, following online studies, Bella was living her dream as an interior designer on the Isle of Skye where she'd relocated to be with Harris when he was promoted, Olivia was a mum running a successful visitors' attraction at her family seat, Drumblair Castle, and Skye lived with her partner, Ben, in Bella's Granny Isla's old house that they were slowly renovating in readiness for their new baby that was due to arrive in four months. Again, she was reminded of how time flew, and things changed.

Bella missed her best friends very much, but Harris was worth the sacrifice of the distance between them. And at least Granny Isla was only up the road near Broadford. Isla had settled in very well to her new little home in a sheltered housing complex overlooking the water and the small uninhabited island of Pabay. Bella saw her granny regularly and Christmas Day was no different. Her parents and brother were over from Inverness and had insisted on staying at a hotel close to the complex, rather than 'imposing' on Bella and Harris, and the plan was to have a gathering at Isla's for their usual family Christmas dinner. Harris's mother lived in the same complex as Isla so the tiny unit would be bursting at the seams with them all there.

'It'll be turkey on a tray on your lap, but it'll be good to have you all here. I mean I'll put the turkey on a plate too, obvs,' Isla had said with a wink and a giggle when discussing the plans. Her little house didn't have the room for a proper-sized dining table but the whole family had agreed it would be fine. They had made it work the previous Christmas, sitting on the floor, the pouffe and the chair from

Granny's bedroom, so there was no reason this year would be different.

Once Bella and Harris had opened their gifts by the tree that morning, Harris had gone into the police station that adjoined their pretty home – the place that had been her first interior design job on the island, and of which she was incredibly proud. He had ensured his staff had the day off to spend with their families; he was such a kind-hearted and considerate man. It had meant he wasn't drinking – although he rarely drank anyway – and would be on call throughout Christmas, which, in turn, had meant there were more mimosas for Bella to drink. This had further resulted in the alcohol going straight to her head, but it was Christmas, after all.

Bella glanced down at the wonderful gifts Harris had bought for her. The Orla Kiely handbag had been her favourite thing of all. She inhaled a long breath and let out a contented sigh as The Waitresses sang about 'Christmas Wrapping' in the background, and she watched the coloured tree lights slowly fading in and out in a hypnotic wave. She had always had a personal preference for simple white lights, but Harris had loved the coloured ones they had seen when they went shopping for decorations during their first Christmas, so she had put her metaphorical interior designer's hat away and had relented.

Seeing his face when they'd had their grand switch on had made it all worthwhile. 'Takes me back to my childhood,' he'd said with a slight croak of emotion to his voice. He'd cleared his throat and pulled Bella into his arms. 'Thank you for agreeing to the coloured lights. I know you don't really like them.'

Bella had gazed up into his kind chocolate-brown eyes and melted. 'Actually, I have to agree with you. They look lovely.'

He had lowered his face and kissed her tenderly. 'Even if you're fibbing, I still love you.' He had grinned then.

But she'd meant it. 'Honestly, Harris. I've always thought white lights were more classy... more tasteful, you know? But—'

He had gasped and dramatically feigned hurt with his hand over his heart. 'Are you saying I'm not classy?' He had smirked teasingly.

She had giggled. 'Let me finish, Inspector Donaldson. I was going to say *but* I'm seeing them through your eyes now, and I love them. But I love you more.' She had reached up and kissed his lips softly.

'You interior designers,' he had said with a shake of his head and a smile. 'So very picky.'

* * *

No emergencies had occurred, thankfully, during the morning, and even though Harris was still on call for the rest of the day, all was quiet. By the time they were due to leave and head north to Isla's, Harris was still dressed in his police uniform, just in case, but over the top he sported his new Christmas jumper – courtesy of Granny Isla, of course – and was ready to go. Bella had been quite pleasantly surprised by the jumper. Knowing the wicked sense of humour Isla was famed for, she had dreaded what would be displayed on the front when her granny had announced she was knitting them for all the men in the family. But instead, the jumper was a Fairisle design in dark green and white. He looked so handsome and still made her heart flutter.

Her own handmade gift from Granny Isla had been the thing to make her giggle. She had received a medium-sized box wrapped in snowman paper and had ripped off its covering in eager anticipation. On opening the box, she had been greeted with a blonde-haired Barbie-style doll, sporting pink lipstick and blue eyeshadow and wearing a knitted cerise ball gown that was intended as a toilet roll cover. It was truly a sight to behold and a real blast from the past interior-design-wise. Especially considering Bella's impeccable taste to boot! Bella had held it aloft and cringed through her laughter. 'Oh, my word. It's so tacky! I love it!' There had been a note attached to it that stated:

My name is Cynthia and I'm to be used all year round, not just dragged oot the cupboard when your Granny visits! She'll be watching! And I'll be reporting back!
Love Cynthia

Bella had laughed out loud and immediately put Cynthia to work in the otherwise tastefully decorated downstairs loo, where the clash was almost painful to Bella's sensibilities, but it simply had to be done.

* * *

Bella stood before the full-length mirror in their bedroom, smoothing down the Christmas-themed dress she'd found on Vinted. It too was green but with red-nosed reindeer prancing all over the fabric and all manner of other woodland creatures wearing scarves and hats. Granny Isla had insisted that they all wear something Christmassy and fun, just like every other year, and Bella couldn't wait to see what everyone else had chosen.

'I think you get more beautiful every day,' Harris said as he slipped his arms around her waist from behind. He placed a tender kiss on her shoulder and rested his chin there. 'I need to drop you off and then nip up the coast to Dunan quickly. Shouldn't be too long though.'

Bella crumpled her brow. 'Oh? Is everything okay? I thought there hadn't been any issues called into the station.'

He lifted his head and shook it. 'Oh, it's nothing to worry about. I just promised one of the residents that I'd pop in. Neighbourhood dispute thing.' He shrugged.

Bella turned in his arms to face him. 'On Christmas Day? Can't they bury the hatchet for twenty-four hours like most people? So long as it's not in *each other*, that is. I mean, for goodness' sake, they did it in World War I.'

He laughed. 'You can't really compare a historical international conflict to that of two old gadgies arguing about a fence.'

She continued with a huff, 'I believe I just did. You really do go above and beyond. I hope they appreciate it.'

'Aye, I'm sure they do. Anyway, come on, let's get going. The suspense on what jumpers the others have is killing me.'

* * *

Bella watched as Harris drove away from Pabay View before turning and making her way around to Granny Isla's unit. Before she could reach out for the handle, the door flung open, and her mum grappled her into a hug as Beau, her granny's beagle, jumped up at her legs, giving excited yips.

'Ah, Bella, my darlin', I've missed you!' her mum said with a squeeze. She was sporting a very sparkly top with a sausage dog on the front and the slogan 'Dachshund Through the Snow' embroidered in sequins and sparkly thread. Even Beau had a bandana on that read 'Santa's Little Helper' which made Bella chuckle.

'Hey, Mum,' she said as she hugged her back. 'It's only been a couple of weeks. We saw you when we picked the Christmas tree up.' She laughed.

'Aye, well, we'll soon be looking for a house over

here if it's anything to do with me, so it'll only be days in between visits. Although, convincing your dad to retire is taking longer than I thought, which has set my plans back a wee bit.' She huffed.

'But he's always talking about retiring, so I don't get it. I'm sure he'd be happier.'

Her mum sighed. 'Oh, don't I know it. I just want to be closer to you, Harris and Isla. Speaking of Harris, where did he go dashing off to?'

'He promised someone in Dunan he'd call in on them,' Bella replied, knowing how strange it sounded.

'On Christmas Day?'

Bella could see the incredulity in her mum's expression. 'He's very committed to his role,' she said, feeling a little defensive but also simultaneously disconcerted. What was really going on? Why would he take leave of them all on Christmas Day if it wasn't an emergency?

'Ahem, is this a private party or can anyone join in?' Isla asked as she walked through from the lounge, her arms open wide.

'Hi, Granny. Merry Christmas. Sorry, Mum was just asking where Harris was going.'

'Oh, it'll be some police business, I should expect,' Isla replied quite nonchalantly, and Bella felt a little silly for worrying. She did a double take at her granny's outfit, which consisted of a red sparkly top under an apron that, from the neck down, gave the illusion that she was in fact a very busty Mrs Claus, scantily clad in a bikini. Bella couldn't hide her mirth.

'Hi, love!' Bella's dad said as he joined the hallway gathering. 'Merry Christmas!' He hugged her and didn't seem to notice the absence of her boyfriend.

She hugged him back. 'Merry Christmas, Dad. Love the jumper!' She pursed her lips in a pointless attempt to hide her amusement. It was a bright red affair with a rather goggle-eyed penguin on the front standing under mistletoe and in big white letters it read 'Cwistmas Kisses'. Isla had clearly saved the less embarrassing creation for her best friend Maeve's son, Harris, and given her own son something a tad more memorable. Some would call it favouritism, Bella thought, as she allowed a giggle to escape.

Her dad smoothed the jumper over his rounded belly. 'Aye, it's braw, isn't it? A real belter,' he said with a chuckle, obviously quite proud of his festive attire. He put an arm around his mum and gave her a squeeze as she beamed up at him.

'Hey, sis. Look what Granny made me,' Bella's younger brother, Callum, said from the doorway. He twirled on the spot, showing off his navy-blue jumper complete with snowfall and a reindeer in the fore-ground whose antlers were decorated with baubles. It was quite sweet.

'Wow, Granny, you have been busy,' Bella said as she hugged Isla once more.

'Aye, well, you know what they say, "Many hands make light work of the devil,"' Isla said as she walked back through to the lounge, leaving everyone sharing questioning glances.

Bella's dad crumpled his brow. 'Who's this "they" that says *that*?' he whispered, following his question with a chuckle.

Bella shrugged and giggled. She removed her coat and hung it on the narrow dark-wood stand in the hallway with all the others and walked through to the lounge. The Dean Martin Christmas album played from the old turntable by the patio doors; the familiar hiss and crackle of the vinyl as it turned was another staple Christmas memory for Bella. It was Isla's favourite festive record, and in the current track Mr Martin sang about a 'White Christmas' as the fra-grance of cinnamon and cloves from a bowl of festive pot pourri mingled with the delicious aroma of turkey and stuffing emanating from the kitchen.

The wee white tinsel tree Isla had owned since time immemorial stood on a small table at the other side of the patio doors, its coloured lights rotating in a series of rather distracting patterns that could potentially cause a seizure if stared at for too long, and its old glass baubles and trinkets told a story of her granny's life in vivid and gaudy, but fun, technicolor.

'Hello, dearie, you look lovely as always,' Harris's mother, Maeve, said as she reached up to hug Bella. Maeve wore a pair of smart navy trousers, and a navy jumper embellished with holly and Christmas puddings.

'And so do you, Maeve. I love your top.'

'Och, wait 'til you see this!' She reached down and fiddled with something on the hem and suddenly all the berries lit up and flashed.

Bella laughed. 'That's brilliant! Oh, and if you're wondering where Harris is, he's—'

'Dunan, aye, dearie, I know. Now let's get you a drink. Tam!' Bella thought it a little odd that neither Isla nor Maeve were baffled by Harris's disappearing act; they clearly knew more than they were letting on.

Isla's gentleman friend and neighbour, Tam, was seemingly in charge of beverages and was sporting a rather fetching green knitted waistcoat embellished with snowmen – clearly another wonderous Isla creation. *She must have started knitting last January*, Bella thought. With it, Tam wore a smart white shirt and his obligatory bow tie, the colour of which, on this occasion, matched his waistcoat. He was a lovely, well-spoken and immaculately dressed man and she had grown very fond of him since she'd met him on Granny Isla's moving-in day.

'Ah, *bella* Bella, my dear, how lovely to see you. What can I get you to drink?' He had taken to doubling up her name from early on and it endeared her to him even more.

'Hi, Tam. I wasn't expecting to see you, I thought you'd be spending Christmas with your daughter,' Bella said as she kissed him on the cheek.

Tam gave a brief smile and broke eye contact. 'Oh yes, well, she and her husband have jetted off to sunnier climes for the festive season. And anyway, I would've missed my lovely Isla.' A wave of sadness washed over Bella as it was clear from his crumpled brow that he was a little upset about being abandoned by his family at Christmas.

She placed a hand on his arm. 'Well, lucky us, Tam. I'm sure I speak for the whole family when I say we're happy to have you.'

His face brightened. 'Oh, I think you deserve a nice chilled glass of prosecco, *bella* Bella.' He hurried off to the small kitchen at the rear of the unit. 'I'll even pop a raspberry in there for you.'

***

Bella sipped the bubbly liquid from a rather large wine glass as she chatted to Maeve and Tam for a little while about the goings on at Pabay View – the place was like a soap opera, with new couples forming and then splitting up; arguments over who had won the Christmas charity raffle for the third year running, and insinuations that it had been fixed; mumblings of complaints over the types of puddings being served at the Sunday lunch club these days, and how they were clearly microwave offerings, which they never used to be; the drama of the Elvis impersonator who had been booked to sing at the Christmas party but had arrived clearly too drunk to perform and had proceeded to completely muck up the words to 'Blue Christmas'. Dorothy, the manager of the residential home, had sat him down with a strong cup of black coffee and then the residents had done karaoke with his gear while the inebriated man, in a bejewelled white satin jumpsuit and a bad, slightly squint wig, had waited for his disgruntled wife to come back and take him home. And then they had all witnessed the poor, slight woman pack away said gear and struggle to manhandle the would-be Elvis into their little white van while she berated him and told him how she had known he had been too drunk to fulfil the gig, and that she had no idea why he hadn't just listened to her and cancelled like she had suggested.

'You're an embarrassment to the name Elvis Aaron Presley, Graham Armstrong!' she had apparently said as she had slammed the door and driven away.

Bella giggled as she listened to the antics of the residents and thought someone really should write a book about the place.

Then she caught up with her younger brother and listened as he enthused about his plans to move to Glasgow with his friends once he had found a job.

'Glasgow's where it's all happening, Bells. Loads of gigs to attend, plenty of bars and cinemas. I can't wait.'

* * *

After around half an hour, the front door opened, and Bella turned as a flash of chilly air preceded Harris into the living room. In his arms was a huge cardboard box covered in the most stunning traditional holly-print gift wrap. *So, the person who he was visiting wanted to give him a gift*, Bella thought. It all made sense now. It was testament to how well thought of he was already.

'Is everything okay?' Bella asked as he was greeted by everyone.

'Aye, all good,' he replied with a nod. 'Can I just have everyone's attention for a moment?' The conversation in the room fell silent and all eyes turned to him as he gently placed the box on the floor. 'Erm, Bella, I have another wee gift for you,' Harris told her as he stood.

Bella shook her head in surprise. 'But, Harris, you already got me so much!'

'Aye, but this one is extra special. Come on and open it.'

Bella crouched and noticed that the box wasn't actually sealed. She opened the loosely folded cardboard flaps and gasped. Inside was the cutest ball of fluff she had ever seen.

Harris told her, 'He needed a good home so I figured we could be his family.'

She reached in and lifted out the golden retriever puppy to a chorus of 'awww' from her family members. The pale cream puppy wriggled in her hands and proceeded to lick her face and squeak excitedly. Then he peed, which made everyone laugh, luckily he missed Bella's clothing, and Granny Isla dashed to the kitchen for paper towels.

Bella's eyes welled with tears. 'Oh, my word, he's gorgeous. Thank you, Harris!'

'What will you call him?' Harris asked.

'I think he's definitely a Bertie,' she said, cuddling the pup to her body as more 'awwws' ensued and her family gathered around to greet him.

'Bertie it is,' Harris said with a smile. 'Oh, and check out his collar. I got it especially with you in mind.'

Bella glanced down at the red, green and black tartan collar and gasped one more time. 'Harris!' Her eyes widened, and her gaze flicked up to him and then back at the simple yet elegant princess-cut diamond solitaire ring on a white-gold band that dangled from the dog's collar on a tartan ribbon, its facets glinting in the lights of the wee Christmas tree. It couldn't have been more perfect if she had chosen it herself.

'I've had a chat with your dad and got his approval to ask you a very important question,' Harris said as he lowered himself to one knee, his eyes glassy with emotion. 'Bella Douglas, I'm not great with fancy words, as you know, but I love you with all my heart. And if you say yes, I promise to love you for as long as you'll have me. So... will you marry me?'

'Oh yes! Two hundred per cent yes!'

'We told you she'd say yes!' Isla blurted as she linked arms with Maeve, and now everything about their reaction when he'd left earlier made sense. They were in on it!

Harris stood from his position on the floor and scooped her into his arms, being careful not to squash Bertie, and kissed her passionately to a round of applause and cheers from everyone else in the room.

2

A MONTH LATER

The day of the engagement party had arrived and Bella was thrilled to have Skye and Ben, Olivia and Brodie, and her family in Glentorrin to celebrate with them. When she and Harris had video called Olivia and Brodie to tell them about their engagement late on Christmas Day, their friends had been so happy for them.

'You must get married here at the chapel, Bells! It would be our gift to you. And I know it's always been your dream to get married here,' Olivia had said.

She was right. However, Bella had dreamed of one day marrying *Kerr MacBain* in the chapel by the loch, in the beautiful grounds of Drumblair Castle. *Funny how things turn out*, she thought. 'We wouldn't want to put you out, Liv. And you can't just offer us a free wedding. You have a business to run.'

'You wouldn't be putting us out, you dafty. You're my best friend.'

Brodie interjected, 'Aye, we'd be sad if you chose to marry somewhere else.'

Olivia's eyes widened and she held up her hands. 'Unless you want to get married in Glentorrin, of course. We'd totally understand, seeing as it's where your life is now.'

Bella had turned to look at Harris, who had shrugged. 'Drumblair is definitely a dream wedding venue. I'm game if you are.' He turned his attention back to Olivia and Brodie. 'Thanks ever so much, guys. What an amazing offer.'

Bella had been desperate to jump from her seat and perform a happy dance, but instead she squeezed Harris's hand and beamed into the camera lens. 'In that case, we would love to get married in the chapel by the loch. Thank you.'

They had been floating on air since Christmas but had waited until after Hogmanay to gather everyone together at the Coxswain pub in Glentorrin for their engagement party, meaning everyone was free. The party was taking place on Burns Night and

was going to be combined with the usual annual celebration.

There had been a heavy snowfall during the daytime but thankfully everyone had arrived safely and
Glentorrin just happened to look picture-postcard
perfect for the occasion. Even though the festive decorations were gone, Glentorrin in the snow had a
wondrous, magical feel about it. The air was crisp
and fresh, and the village's inhabitants walked
around rosy cheeked and wrapped up in woolly hats
and gloves.

Bella's friends, Skye and Ben, were staying at Morag's B&B close to the pub, and Brodie and Olivia were
staying at the pub, where landlords, Joren and Stella,
were looking after them, while Grandma Mirren and
Grandad Dougie – Brodie's stepmum and dad –
looked after wee Freya, Olivia and Brodie's daughter,
back at Drumblair Castle.

Bella's brother and parents had booked into a holiday cottage on the way to Broadford and had a
viewing lined up at a house for sale near Dunan
during their short stay. It seemed her mum had finally
convinced her dad that retirement would be good for
him after all. Although Bella wouldn't have been surprised if her mum had bribed him with the prospect

of being near to future grandchildren. Even though that was a long way off yet, Bella was keeping everything crossed that they liked the house. Their own property was now on the market, so she knew they were definitely serious about a move. And it would be wonderful to have all the family so close by again.

The Coxswain was heaving, as if everyone in the village had turned out to celebrate the engagement of their newest residents. It was a traditional pub that sat on the corner near the entrance to Glentorrin. The exterior was painted white, and the swinging sign outside depicted the old lifeboat and its crew. The interior walls were clad halfway up with dark oak panelling and there was usually a roaring fire in the grate at one end of the bar that gave the place a warm and cosy feeling in the winter months. A row of shiny tankards hung above the bar and behind it, in between the optics, was a pinboard full of photos of the villagers and the musicians that had played live music there over the years. The walls were painted a pretty sage-green and covered with framed artwork, much of which was painted by Reid MacKinnon. There wasn't a huge amount of space, but somehow the residents of the village often managed to hold ceilidhs in there by pulling the tables back and stacking them against the walls. This evening would be no different. The Coxswain really was the social hub of the village.

On this occasion the fire had been allowed to die out because of the number of bodies crammed into the place but it was still almost as hot as a sauna. Bertie the pup had fallen asleep under the table, by Bella's feet, in spite of the noise in the place and he lay, quite happily, on his back with his tongue lolling out; his favourite position. Stella had made her renowned haggis, neeps and tatties – the obligatory fare for Burns Night, and of course Caitlin, the owner of the village bakery, had surprised them with a beautiful cake.

Bella was delighted at how quickly Glentorrin had come to feel like home and how willing the villagers had been to welcome them into the fold. She felt like she had always lived there and the friends she had made felt like she had known them for so much longer than the couple of years they had lived there.

Since their relocation, Harris, who had been missing playing with his band Coppercaillie, had managed to form a new band with some men from the village. The band consisted of Bella's friend Millie's fiancé Dex – a mechanic who used to roadie for bands and spent a while as a guitar tech for The

Darkness – on guitar; her friend and Lifeboat House Museum owner Jules's husband Reid on piano – he was also the owner of the art studio in the village; and Caitlin the baker's husband, Archie, who owned the outdoor gear shop and campsite, played an instrument called a cajon which, Bella discovered, is a sort of box drum that's sat upon and played like a bongo. They had called themselves 'The Glentorrin Four', which Bella had remarked sounded like a notorious criminal gang, but it turned out the name had been deliberate, considering Harris's job; such was his sense of humour.

The band had been practising in the village hall so they could play at the party and Bella was excited, if a little trepidatious, to hear them. In order to advertise their first gig, Reid had designed some very arty posters that featured band photos taken by his teenage son Evin. In the shots, the guys were down by the water's edge in a variety of poses. Bella's favourite shot was a rather silly one where Evin had asked them all to jump up in the air and make daft faces. He'd snapped the picture at exactly the right moment and in Bella's mind the photograph totally encapsulated the men's personalities. The other shot chosen for the poster was one in which the band were wearing sunglasses, regardless of the fact it was winter and freezing cold. *Very Britpop*, Bella had thought, smiling when she had first seen the final prints. This evening, seeing the posters up in the pub took her back to a recent conversation she'd had with the other women about their partners and their new venture...

* * *

'So, girls, what's it like to be living with the members of a boyband?' Morag had asked when they had gathered at Jules's house for their first book club after Hogmanay. Her husband Kenneth, who ran the village shop, was the only man from the close-knit group who wasn't in the band. He had been asked if he'd like to join but he had said he might scare audiences away with his lack of musical talent so would stick to watching them.

'I'm fighting for the mirror on a morning these days.' Caitlin laughed. 'That's no different from normal though, to be fair. I do have a rock star *and* two girls to compete with.' The other women joined in with her laughter. Her teenage daughter Grace, and stepdaughter Sophie, were growing up fast.

'It's when the groupers start to come round that you'll need to worry, eh, Bella?' Isla had said, winking

at her granddaughter, who got the joke immediately.
Isla had once talked of pop stars having group*ers* instead of group*ies* and it had made Bella giggle uncontrollably for ages.

'I think we can all rest assured that they're not
quite glamorous enough for that,' Jules had said.
'They're more dad bod than boyband.'

Isla scoffed. 'Oh, I don't know. They're all as good-
looking as that Robin Williams singer you youngsters
all used to rave about. The one who sang that song
about Angels. I liked that song.'

Jules had almost choked on her gin and tonic. 'I
think you mean Rob*bie* Williams, Isla.'

'Aye, that's what a said,' Isla replied in true Isla
form.

'I tell you what though, have you seen Take That
lately? They're all maturing like fine wine if you ask
me,' Ruby said. A former Hollywood actress, she had
moved to Glentorrin to be with her now husband
Mitch. Mitch had stepped in to manage the band
which the women translated as, 'I'll go to their re-
hearsals and drink beer with them at the Coxswain
afterwards.'

'Oh yes, Howard from Take That is just lovely,'
Morag added. 'He was always my favourite.'

The rest of them turned to her. 'Fancy a toy boy, do you, Morag?' Bella asked with a teasing smile.

'Och, I think I'm past all that,' Morag replied. 'Although a girl can dream, eh? Just don't tell Kenneth I said that.'

'Our guys are as handsome as Take That already,' Millie said dreamily. 'Although it's to be hoped they're not going to start attracting groupies. I've heard some terrifying stories from Dex about obsessed fans from his days on the road with The Darkness.'

'Aye, you'll not want any panties being thrown,' Isla said with a giggle. 'They used to do that to Tom Jones, mind. Now he's a handsome man. And he's more my age.'

Bella nudged her with her shoulder. 'I thought you only had eyes for Tam, Granny!'

'*Dinnae* get me wrong, Tam's wonderful, aye. But you heard what Morag said!'

'All joking aside though,' Millie said. 'Dex is loving playing again. He's so enthusiastic about it. It's really lovely to see.'

Jules nodded. 'Same with Reid. He's only ever played classical stuff on the piano, so he's really enjoying learning new songs on his shiny new keyboard. And it's great for them all to spend time together. Men don't often have close friends.'

'I'm all for it,' Bella agreed. 'It means I get to watch whatever I like on the TV for an evening. Or better still, drink wine with you lot.' They all laughed again.

'So, what did everyone think of the book?' Jules asked, holding up a copy of *O Caledonia* by Elspeth Barker, trying to get the meeting back on track. 'I felt quite sorry for the main protagonist, Janet. She seemed to be somewhat neglected and sidelined. Did anyone else think that?'

Bella had opened her mouth to respond but Isla had blurted, 'Speaking of watching what you want on TV, I have to tell you a story, ladies, about something that happened recently,' she had said, ignoring Jules. 'It'll make you chuckle.' She giggled to herself briefly and then continued, 'Me, Gladys, Maeve and a few others at Pabay View were watching a film starring that Jamie Doorknob, I forget what it was called, anyway, it got me thinking about other things he had been in. And I remembered *Fifty Shades of Grey*, although the book was better in my opinion—'

'Isla!' Caitlin had exclaimed, wide-eyed. 'You dark horse!'

Isla had waved her hand and snorted. 'Oh, hen, I've been on this earth so long now that nothing fazes me any more. Anyway, so I told Gladys she should read it, but I warned her it was a *vera* spicy book and that she should hide it from her son and grandkids when they came to visit. But...' She'd started to giggle again, and her face had coloured bright red. 'But she came to me the other day and said, "I don't know what kind of books you're usually into, Isla Douglas, but spicy is not a word I'd use to describe this one." So, there I was thinking *oh my goodness, she's really offended, and she'll never look at me the same again.* Anyway, she thrusts the book into my hand, turns on her heel, and walks away in a huff, and I look down at the book. She'd only gone and bought *Fifty* Sheds *of Grey!*'

The women howled with laughter and Bella, once more, realised how lucky she was to have Isla as her granny.

* * *

Back in the present, Joren, the owner of the pub, tapped the microphone, pulling Bella from her reverie. 'Ladies and gentlemen, I'd like to welcome this evening's entertainment to the stage. There's not an arrest warrant in sight so please give a warm hand to the Glentorrin Four!'

The place erupted with whoops and cheers as

Harris took the microphone from Joren and placed it back in its stand, and the other three men took their places behind him in the tiny allocated space.

'Hi, everyone. Thanks for having us and for being here to help me and my beautiful fiancée celebrate our engagement. It goes without saying that we're so happy to have you all here and we're especially grateful to those of you who've travelled a fair distance just for us... and Mr Burns, of course. I also want to thank the guys up here with me for agreeing to start up a band. We're the oldest teenage garage band you'll ever meet.' A rumble of laughter travelled the room. 'And we don't even practise in a garage.' He grinned. 'Anyway, I'd like to dedicate this first song to the woman of the hour, Bella Douglas, soon to be Bella Donaldson. The sooner the better for me.' More mumbles and awwws could be heard. 'Although I've been told to be patient because apparently these things take a while to plan.' He shrugged and then continued, 'I met Bella in Inverness when her granny and my mum decided we should be a couple. I have to say I'm grateful to them both every day of my life for not giving up when they knew we were right for each other before we even did. Bella is the light of my life, she brings out the best in me and I can't quite believe I get to marry her.' He cleared his throat as his emotions almost got the better of him. 'Anyway, this first song was originally released by a very cool young guy called Benson Boone. The lyrics are pretty awesome at saying exactly how I feel about Bella. This one is "Beautiful Things". Bella, I love you more than my own words can express.'

Bella's heart skipped and a wide smile spread across her face as Dexter played the opening chords of the song on his guitar and Harris began to sing, keeping his gaze fixed on her. Her heart soared as he smiled, the lyrics falling from his lips as if he'd written them himself. The feeling was mutual. She couldn't quite believe she had fought her feelings for him for as long as she did. But nothing was going to stop her marrying the man of her dreams now.

Olivia slipped her arm around Bella at one side and heavily pregnant Skye did the same on the other side as they all sang along to the chorus. Harris wowed them all with his voice which had always been good but had somehow got even better, and at the end of the song the applause was enough to tear the roof off the place.

* * *

The night was filled with dancing, laughter and music and Bella had loved showing off her stunning diamond ring to everyone who asked to see it.

Olivia joined Bella where she sat stroking Bertie. He was at the bitey stage and every time her hand loomed towards him, he bit her finger.

'You monkey,' she said to the ball of fluff as she giggled. His little teeth were rather like pins.

'He's so bloomin' cute,' Olivia said as he rolled onto his back, and she rubbed his belly. 'I have a question to ask you, Bells.'

Bella lifted her chin. 'Oh? Go on then.'

'Can I design your wedding dress? If you haven't already chosen one, that is.'

Bella's eyes widened. 'No, Liv, that's just too much. You're providing us with a venue and—'

'Please?' Olivia stuck her bottom lip out like a sulking toddler. 'You can pay for the fabric if that helps, but I would love to design something wonderful for you. You deserve to look stunning on your special day, and I'd be so honoured.' Bella didn't know what to say so she didn't speak and Olivia filled the silence. 'I've already done some sketches,' she said with a cringe. The scenario was reminiscent of the time Bells had put together a mood board for the interior design of the stable block apartments at

Drumblair Castle, never really expecting Olivia to use them.

'You have?'

Olivia nodded. 'Want to see?'

Bella's heart tripped over itself with excitement. 'Absolutely!'

Olivia took her phone from the pocket of her dress and pulled up the drawings she had produced of the most stunning wedding dresses Bella had ever seen. If she had been talented enough to design something herself these images were exactly what she would've drawn.

Her eyes welled with tears. 'Oh, Liv, these are gorgeous.' She wiped at her eyes and giggled. 'Look at me getting all emotional at a 2D wedding dress.'

Olivia nudged her with her shoulder. 'It can only mean one thing. You want me to design your dress.'

Bella grappled Olivia into a hug. 'I definitely do.'

* * *

After the haggis had been carried in to the sound of bagpipes played by a friend of Evin's, everyone sat to eat and listen to Burns poetry being read in an open mic kind of way. When it came around to Harris's turn, he read the poet's most famous love poem.

'Of course this is for you, Bella,' he said before he began.

> 'O my Luve's like a red, red rose
> That's newly sprung in June;
> O my Luve's like the melodie
> That's sweetly played in tune.
> As fair art thou, my bonnie lass,
> So deep in luve am I;
> And I will luve thee still, my dear,
> Till a' the seas gang dry:
> Till a' the seas gang dry, my dear,
> And the rocks melt wi' the sun;
> I will luve thee still, my dear,
> While the sands o' life shall run.
> And fare thee weel, my only Luve,
> And fare thee weel awhile!
> And I will come again, my Luve,
> Tho' it ware ten thousand mile.'

* * *

When he was finished, the room erupted in applause and Bella thought her heart might burst with the love she felt for the man who was unabashed about showing his feelings for her. This was real love. This was what Robert Burns had been writing about.

Once they had finished their food and no one else

was left to get up to read, the tables were pulled back, and a duo called the Toilichte Hens – which loosely translates to Happy Hens – took to the makeshift stage area. One of the two women played the fiddle, and one played an accordion and between them they started the ceilidh.

As everyone danced, Harris slipped his arms around Bella's waist and kissed her. 'Are you having fun?' he asked.

She nodded. 'It's been the best night. I couldn't have asked for anything better. And watching you read Rabbie Burns and dedicate it to me was ridiculously sexy.' She felt her face heating with a flush of desire.

'Hold onto that thought, Bella Douglas,' he said with a chuckle. 'I can't wait to marry you.' His eyes were filled with as much love as she felt inside.

'I feel the same. We're quite lucky, really, when you think about it.'

Harris shook his head. 'Nah. Not lucky, just meant to be.' Once again, her heart melted as she gazed into his dark eyes. 'And we get to wed at the most stunning location. Now that's the lucky part.'

'Absolutely. And Liv is going to design my wedding dress.'

Harris's eyes widened. 'She is? Wow! I've no words

for what her and Brodie are doing for us. They really are the best friends.'

Later, Bella sat with her arm linked through Isla's as they watched everyone dancing. 'Granny, I have a very important question to ask you.'

Isla turned in her seat to smile at her granddaughter. 'Anything, my sweet girl. Ask away.'

'Would you be my maid of honour?'

Isla's brow crumpled and tears welled in her eyes. 'Och, dearie, I *wasnae* expecting that. Surely you'd rather have one of your young friends for that job, not some old *yin* like me?'

Bella took her hand and squeezed it. 'Granny, you're my best friend, you're the one I'd like to take the role. If you'd like to, that is.'

Isla sniffed and reached up to wipe her tears away. 'In that case, I'd be absolutely honoured, and wild starlings couldn't keep me away.'

Bella giggled. 'I'm so glad. The only thing is... The colour scheme isn't purple or lilac.'

Isla huffed. 'In that case you can ask someone else.'

Bella tilted her head. 'Granny?'

Isla giggled and nudged her. 'Och, okay, seeing as it's you I'll wear whatever colour you like. I'm just touched and honoured that you asked me.'

'I'm touched and honoured that you accepted.'

* * *

Bertie got lots of attention and cuddles throughout the evening and Bella shared stories of how he loved to run off with socks and had discovered a love of carrots after one had fallen on the floor while Harris had been cooking. She had reminisced how the pup had ended up with an orange face after that particular encounter.

Ben and Skye left around ten o'clock as Skye was worn out, and once she had gone, Bella sat chatting with Olivia and Brodie while the band packed away their gear.

'We have a business proposition for you, Bells,' Brodie said as he sipped his whisky.

Bella tilted her head in intrigue. 'Ooooh, go on, tell me more,' she said as a ripple of excitement travelled her spine. The memories of her first real taste of interior design, working on the rental apartments at Drumblair Castle, were still some of her fondest and she hoped this was going to be something similar.

'How are you fixed for time just now? Design-wise, I mean,' he asked.

Bella narrowed her eyes. 'It's pretty full-on just

now. But mainly small residential jobs apart from a vintage fashion shop interior I'm working on... Why do you ask?' She hoped she knew the reason but didn't dare presume.

He glanced at Olivia and she grinned as she took over the conversation. 'Okay, so you know the distillery is up and running back at the castle?'

'Ooh, I do, it's very exciting.'

'Well... we've decided not only to *make* the drinks and sell them in the castle gift shop but to open the place up to do tours and talk about our whisky and gin-making journey. The front of the building is a blank canvas right now seeing as it was only going to be used for storage and it lends itself perfectly to becoming the reception and shop area. So, we're going to need a stunning and welcoming interior to be created, and I wondered if you knew anyone.' She had a glint of mischief in her eyes.

Bella pursed her lips. 'Hmm... the trouble is, all my fellow designers are pretty chocka just now...' She tapped her chin, feigning concentration and trying not to smile. 'But there is this one designer I know who would absolutely jump at the challenge.'

Olivia smiled. 'Are they any good?'

Bella nodded slowly and narrowed her eyes. 'Oh, they're incredible. World renowned in their own back yard. They completed a house in Glentorrin for the police inspector, no less.'

Brodie smiled and Olivia's grin widened. 'Sounds good! I'm guessing they're modest and unassuming too?'

Bella laughed out loud. 'Now that's something I can't promise. In all seriousness though, you guys, I'm in! And... I'll do the design for free.'

Brodie's brow crumpled. 'What? No, you can't do that! You have a business to run.'

Olivia shook her head. 'He's right. Absolutely not!'

Bella sighed. 'You are hosting our wedding and making my wedding dress. It's the least I can do. Please?'

Brodie and Olivia shared glances. 'We'll discuss the payment situation on another occasion. But you'll do the design anyway?'

'Of course I will!' Bella said.

'Yay!' Olivia said and clapped her hands. 'I'm so glad! I didn't want to presume you'd do it because I know things are taking off for you, and I'm so happy about that, but selfishly I hoped you'd make time for us at Drumblair.'

'Of course I will! Do you have any specific requirements?'

Olivia shook her head. 'Nope. You have carte blanche. I trust you. I know you'll come up with something my mum and dad would've been happy with so just go for it. We're aiming to open it up to the public for tours in June so hopefully that will give you plenty of time.'

The fact that Olivia trusted her with her parents' legacy was so touching. Bella clapped her hands this time. 'Don't worry. It's definitely doable. Thank you so much for this, Liv. I have so many ideas! I'll get to work right away.'

* * *

Later that night, Bella and Harris returned home with their sleepy puppy. Bertie was being crate trained and although he cried sometimes when he was in there he was doing really well. After they had let him into the garden one last time and cuddled him on the kitchen floor, they made sure he was tucked up safely and went upstairs.

As they got ready for bed, Harris came to stand before Bella. 'Are you happy with me, Bella? I mean truly happy?'

She smiled widely and put her arms around his neck, closing the gap between them. 'It's a bit late to be asking me that, isn't it?' she teased. 'We just had an engagement party.'

His face remained serious. 'But we're not married yet. Nothing is legal. So, if you're having doubts...'

Her heart skipped in her chest and a niggle of worry gnawed at her mind. 'What? No, I'm not having doubts. You make me happy, Harris. And I can't wait to be married to you.'

'No regrets?' There was something akin to sadness in his crumpled brow. 'Because life's too short to be with the wrong person. So...'

Bella frowned. 'I have no regrets at all. Why? What's brought this on? You're worrying me.'

He shook his head and smiled briefly. 'Oh, it's nothing. Just the alcohol that's gone to my head. I'm such a lightweight these days. I drink so little that when I do it frazzles my brain.' He kissed her forehead, but Bella sensed that something was amiss.

'Is there anything you want to talk about?' she asked, running her fingers through his hair.

He shook his head. 'Nothing at all. Let's go to bed, eh?'

He released her and climbed under the duvet, holding it up for her to climb in and snuggle up next to him.

* * *

The following day, Bella met with Olivia and Skye for coffee while the men went walking with Caitlin's husband, Archie, who was determined to showcase the stunning scenery around Glentorrin, even on a cold and frosty winter's day. Harris had forgone the walk as he had paperwork to do, something which Bella had tried to encourage him to leave until Monday, but he'd said there was no time like the present.

The sky was dull overhead as they walked from the car park in Portree and there was a real nip to the air. Skye and Olivia chatted away as they walked quickly, their breath clouding before them as they put the world to rights, but Bella was somewhat lost in her own thoughts.

They found a table in Bella's favourite café that overlooked the harbour with its brightly coloured houses. Seeing them was enough to lift her spirits on the bleakest of days usually but worry was niggling at her after what Harris had said the night before.

'Are you okay, Bells? You're quiet,' Olivia said as they waited for their coffee and cakes to be delivered to their table.

Bella smiled and nodded. 'Yes, yes, I'm fine.'

Skye tilted her head. 'You do know that we can tell when you're not yourself, don't you?'

Bella forced a laugh. 'Okay, *Mum*. Seriously I'm fine. Just a wee hangover, that's all.'

Olivia shook her head. 'Nope. Not buying it. Come on, Bells. We're your oldest friends. If you can't tell us what's troubling you, who can you tell?'

Bella sighed. 'It's just something Harris said last night after the party.'

'Which was?' Olivia asked.

'We'd had such a lovely night and there were no signs that anything was wrong until we got home. But when we did, he asked me if I had any regrets and said something about life being too short to be marrying the wrong person. I'm worried he's getting cold feet.'

Skye raised her eyebrows. 'Harris? Cold feet? Pfft, he's got the warmest feet of any man I know.' Olivia turned to her with a questioning look, so Skye elaborated. 'What I mean is, he absolutely adores you, Bells. There's not a chance on earth that he has cold feet. Are you sure he's not worried *you've* got cold feet?'

Bella's heart sank. 'But why would I? He's everything to me. And I've never given him any reason to think anything else.'

Olivia reached out and squeezed Bella's arm. 'Don't forget he'd had alcohol, and he rarely drinks so maybe it was just the red wine melancholy. It happens a lot to people who don't usually drink much. Maybe he was just feeling so much love for you that he was overwhelmed?'

Bella shrugged as the waitress brought a tray with their drinks and three plates with luscious deep cakes covered in thick chocolate frosting. Bella's mouth watered as the rich aroma of coffee and chocolate mixed and reached her senses. 'I hope that's all it was. We can usually talk about anything, so it's knocked me sideways.'

'Look, give him a couple of days and approach him again. I think you'll find that it's absolutely nothing to worry about.' Olivia was always so positive and optimistic and at that moment it was just what Bella needed.

She took a deep breath and decided to change the subject. 'Enough glumness. I have a favour to ask you both.'

'Ooh, that sounds intriguing, go on,' Skye said, jiggling in her seat.

'Do you need to pee, Skye?'

Skye cringed and held up her finger and thumb.

'Little bit. This little monkey likes playing footy with my bladder.' She patted her bump.

'Go on then, I'll wait 'til you get back.'

Skye waddled off to the loo and Olivia watched her. 'It's so exciting that she'll be a mum in April. Her little boy is going to be adored,' she said.

'I know. Have they chosen a name yet?' Bella asked.

'Apparently but she's keeping it quiet for now. Although you know what Skye is like with us. Can't hold her own water... literally.' She giggled. 'I bet we'll know before we head home today.'

* * *

A few minutes later, Skye returned and sat down once more. She narrowed her eyes. 'What? Why are you looking at me like that?'

'We were just talking about you being a mum to a little baby boy soon.'

Skye smoothed her hand over her bump and smiled. 'See, Theo, me and Daddy aren't the only ones excited to meet you.' She snapped her head up and widened her eyes. 'Dammit. Pretend you didn't hear that.'

Bella and Olivia burst out laughing and both stood to hug their friend where she sat in her chair.

'What a lovely name,' Bella said, placing a hand on Skye's bump as her eyes welled with tears.

'It's gorgeous,' Olivia said, doing the same.

'Ugh, me and my big mouth. Anyway, what did you have to ask us, Bella?' Bella and Olivia sat down again.

'Okay so... I was wondering if you might be my bridesmaids for the wedding in December?'

Skye and Olivia shared smiles. 'Absolutely!' they said in unison.

3

The following day, Harris and Bella said their goodbyes to their friends, hugged and then waved them off. Bella was even more sad than usual seeing Olivia and Skye leaving but she couldn't quite put her finger on why. But when the door was closed, Harris silently disappeared into the police station and was gone for hours. She tried to tell herself it was fine because it was Monday and that's where he should be. But the nagging feeling deep inside of her wouldn't let up.

Bella had cleared her diary in order to be able to see her parents and brother after their house viewing and they arrived mid-afternoon as she was curled up on the sofa with the latest book club choice and

Bertie snoozing at her feet on one of the cushions at the end.

'So, how did it go?' she asked eagerly as she carried a tray of mugs of tea into the living room and handed them out.

Her mum was grinning like the Cheshire Cat. 'Oh, Bella, it was gorgeous. It's called Rowan Cottage but it's quite big really. You always imagine quaint and charming when cottage is mentioned. It needs work but as you know, your dad's quite handy so that shouldn't be a problem.'

Her dad shook his head. 'Aye, nothing like retiring to do more work.'

'And we just happen to know an interior designer,' her mum said with a smile.

'Oh, and the neighbour has two golden retrievers. Absolutely beautiful. Reminded us of Bertie. They were ever so friendly.'

Bella sipped her tea. 'Oh, of course, the house was in Dunan! I bet you met Bertie's mum!'

'I said to your dad that I wondered if they might be related,' her mum replied, the wide smile still fixed in place. 'The house has an Aga too. I've always wanted an Aga. No clue how to use one but I'm happy to learn.'

'And what about the garden, Dad? Big enough for you?'

'Oh, it was grand, aye. I could see myself pottering about happily. Plenty of room for a veggie plot and a shed. There's already a wee greenhouse for my tomato plants. Might need to get a wee dug too.'

Callum huffed. 'Great, you wait 'til I'm leaving and then you decide to get a dug,' he said with a shake of his head. 'I've wanted a dug for ages. I bet you end up with a golden retriever too. I might have to come to Skye instead of moving in with the lads.' He winked at Bella. 'My room at Rowan Cottage is a decent size too, sis.'

'Erm, how come you've chosen a room when you're starting a new job in Glasgow next month and you're moving in with your pals?' Bella asked, raising her eyebrows.

'I'll still need somewhere to sleep when I come home to visit. I'll be doing that plenty if they get that house and especially if they get a golden retriever dug.'

Bella's mum huffed. 'And that translates to, "I'll be bringing my washing home for Mum to do."'

Callum laughed. 'Aye, well, I can't leave you with nothing to remind you of me, can I?' He chuckled.

A flutter of excitement landed in Bella's stomach

at the prospect of her parents moving to be closer. 'So, what will you do now?'

Her mum sighed. 'We have to sell our house now it's on the market and we've no idea how long that might take, so there's no guarantee that Rowan Cottage will still be available when we're ready to buy.'

'But we're going to go home and get pushing the agent all the same,' her dad added.

Bella's dream of having her whole family close by felt like it was within reach. 'I'll keep everything crossed for a quick sale.'

* * *

A while later, when Bella was washing their cups, her mum joined her and picked up the tea towel to dry them. 'Is everything okay, love? You don't seem yourself.'

Bella smiled. 'I'm okay. Just a bit worried about Harris.'

'How come?' A crumple of concern appeared between her brows.

'He's been a bit quiet since the engagement party. I'm not sure why but I'm concerned at the timing. Maybe he's changed his mind.'

Bella's mum scoffed. 'About marrying you? Have

you seen the way he looks at you? No, it's got to be something else. Just talk to him, love. That's the best thing you can do. Communication is key in a marriage.'

Bella nodded. 'You're right. I'm going to. I need to get to the bottom of it because this feeling is awful.'

Her mum reached out and squeezed her arm. 'He adores you though, Arabella. That much is obvious to everyone. Try not to worry.'

* * *

Even for a couple of days after that Harris seemed a little distant; didn't talk much and had an air of sadness about him. He was still affectionate, held her at night and kissed her goodbye when she left for work, but Bella could sense that there was something not quite right. It was as if he was going through the motions, like a robot following its programming. She had been working her way up to asking him what was wrong, but every time she was about to do so, his phone would ring, and he'd be called away on police business. There just hadn't been a fitting time.

On Thursday morning, Bella spent a few hours putting together some ideas for the Drumblair distillery and in the afternoon, she went to Sconser to visit potential new clients. They were a young professional couple who had bought a rundown house, and it needed totally gutting. They had so much enthusiasm and lots of ideas for what they wanted to do with the place that it should have been rubbing off on her. After all, she saw herself and Harris in them and their excitement for their new life together but instead of making her happy she felt a little lost. Sad even. Possibly a tiny bit envious.

The house was a little further north than Rowan Cottage, the house her mum and dad had viewed, and on the way home she imagined calling in to see them as she passed the now empty house. A twinge of sadness tugged at her though. Everything was amplified; missing her friends, missing her mum and dad and she knew it was all because of Harris's change of mood. Although she wasn't technically alone, she somehow felt the weight of loneliness, nonetheless.

On the way home, she made a detour via Loch Ainort viewpoint and pulled over. She wrapped her coat and scarf tightly around her body and climbed out of the car. She filled her lungs with the fresh sea air and even though there was only a light breeze, it numbed her lips and nose with its icy fingers as it touched her skin. She walked down to the water's edge and watched the sea birds diving into the water fishing for their supper. Their lives were simple, she thought, search for food, build a nest, bring up chicks. The only worry they had was finding the food to feed their chicks... and of course predators. Okay, so they maybe had things just as hard, but they didn't have to deal with emotions, did they? Nor did they have to worry about whether their partner had changed his mind on the future he had offered. Because at that moment in time she felt like her relationship was suddenly hanging by a thread. What if he was working out how to leave her? Trying to find a way to say it was all moving too fast? Or that perhaps he had realised he only loved her as a friend, nothing more.

She couldn't do this any more. The ice-cold temperature she was experiencing from the weather should remain outside and not be seeping into her heart. She shouldn't be accepting it from her fiancé either. It wasn't fair to be kept in the dark when whatever he was trying to hide from her was making her miserable anyway. So, whatever it was, and however hard it would be to hear, she needed to know. With renewed determination, she climbed back into the car and returned home, prepared to get to the bottom of things no matter how much it hurt.

* * *

Bella found Harris sitting at the kitchen table, staring at a mug of coffee. She walked over to the countertop by the coffee machine and removed her coat, placing it and her bag down.

'Is the coffee fresh?' she asked. He didn't answer but Bertie jumped up at her legs, wagging his tail; he was excited to see her, at least. She crouched to see the pup who was growing rapidly but still a cute ball of fluff. He wiggled and wriggled as she said hello to him, rubbing his belly when he rolled onto his back.

'Harris.'

As if coming out of a trance, he turned. 'Yes?'

'I was asking if the coffee is fresh?'

He stood and poured his full mug down the sink. 'Sorry, I'll make a fresh pot.'

She reached out and touched his cheek. 'It's fine, I'll do it. Are you feeling okay?'

He rubbed both hands over his face. 'Aye, just tired. I'm off to go shower and see if that wakes me up.' He turned to leave the room, and she took her opportunity. It was now or never.

'Are you sure that's all it is, Harris?' She felt the stinging of tears behind her eyes. 'Because you've been pretty distant since the engagement party, and I'm worried you've changed your mind about us.'

He paused for a moment, then turned and stood there, just staring at her, a look of disbelief on his face. And then, as if a realisation had hit, he quickly walked over and pulled her close, wrapping his arms around her and holding her tightly as if his life depended on it. She cried into his chest, not really understanding why, but knowing things were definitely not right.

'If you *have* changed your mind, please just tell me. Because I can't bear this silence and feeling as though you're thinking you've made a mistake in asking me to marry you.'

He tilted her face up with his hands, his eyes were red and glassy with emotion too, and it was evident from the dark circles under his eyes he hadn't been sleeping.

He shook his head. 'Don't *ever* think that. I'm so sorry I've made you feel that way. I would never, *ever* think I'd made a mistake with you, Bella. You're my world, don't you know that?'

'But you asked me if I had any regrets the day of the engagement party, a party you were eager to hold by the way, and then you've been acting strange since then. Like you're on autopilot, but not really there.

What else am I supposed to think? You keep dashing off into the station and making excuses to not be in the same room as me. Then at night you cling to me so tightly that I struggle to breathe. It's so confusing. I honestly don't know what to think any more. Apart from maybe that you're trying to figure out how to dump me and you're racked with guilt for wanting to.'

'Come and sit down,' he said, leading her to the kitchen table. 'I owe you an explanation.'

'I think you do,' she said, her stomach in knots and her whole body shaking.

She sat down and he followed suit, pulling his chair close so he could hold her hand. 'On the morning of the engagement party I received an email out of the blue. It threw me when I saw the sender and I didn't read it until the end of the night. And then I didn't know what to think or what to say about the news it contained. So, I just tried to digest it by myself.'

Panic gripped her. Was he ill and he hadn't told her? 'Who was it from?' She was terrified of the answer.

Harris sighed. 'My ex, Alba.'

Hearing this deepened her worry. She remembered about Olivia's brother Kerr's son and how he'd never known the boy existed until his mother decided to announce it years later. Was this going to be another one of those situations? 'Oh. I see.' Her hands trembled in his.

'It's not what you're thinking, I can guarantee that.'

'What was it then? What did she want? Why was she contacting you after all this time?'

He pulled his lips between his teeth for a moment and then said, 'She's going through a *very* rough patch. An incredibly tough time.'

Bella couldn't help the twinge of jealousy, even though she had no reason to feel it. 'But why does that involve you?' The fear of him announcing a child reared its head again. What would she say? How would she cope?

He squeezed her hand. 'You have nothing to worry about, trust me, Bella.'

'Maybe not, but I don't understand why she felt the need to contact *you* when you haven't seen her in years. And isn't she married?'

He closed his eyes briefly and nodded. 'She is... But she's ill. Seriously ill. And her husband couldn't cope with it, so he left. So now she's alone, in pain and scared about the future.'

Guilt gripped her insides. 'Oh. That's awful.'

He nodded. 'It is. She's trying to right some

wrongs before...' He shook his head and sighed. 'She seems lonely and she has no idea what will happen next, or how long she has left where she'll be fully aware of everything, so I guess she's trying to make amends with people in her life while she still can. Anyway, she has lots of regrets about us, me and her, I mean. She was apologising for choosing her career over me and said that she's regretted it for a very long time. She said that she knows I would never have done what her husband has. That I wouldn't abandon her when she needed me the most. I mean, she's right. I would never do that to anyone. Least of all the woman I love.' He used present tense and that stung more than Bella cared to acknowledge; did he still love Alba then? Was she simply second best? But as if realising, he added, 'I mean I would never do that to *you*, because you're the woman I love, Bella.'

He sat quietly, looking at their joined hands, for a moment, and Bella wondered if he was trying to decide how much to tell her. He lifted his face again. 'She warned me off getting married, saying it's not all it's cracked up to be.' Bella silently wondered if this was why he had been distant. Had her words affected him that much? 'She said you marry someone who you *think* you know but you never really know them at all, until push comes to shove and then their true colours wave like a flag. And in her husband's case, a red one. She asked if I would go and see her.'

Bella lowered her head. She knew what was coming. He would meet her and realise he still loved her, that he couldn't leave her to suffer alone, and this would be the end of them. He and Alba had history. It was understandable that he'd want to go to her in her time of need, wasn't it? Or was it more than that?

'Bella, would you look at me?' She lifted her face and gazed at him through tear-fogged vision. But she saw the love he had for her in his eyes. 'I said no. I told her my life is with you. That my future is with you. And that just because her marriage hadn't worked it didn't mean mine wouldn't, because I trust you with my whole heart and I *do* know you, in spite of what she thinks. And I said that as bad as I feel for her, dredging up the past would do neither of us any good. I said I forgave her and was very sorry for what she was going through, and I wished her well. But I said I won't go.'

Bella allowed the tears to spill over. 'But do you *want* to go see her? I would understand if—'

He leaned closer. 'No, Bella, I don't. I'm being completely honest. I just feel sad for her. As I would for anyone in that situation. But what she and I had is over and it's been over since she left.' He chewed his lip for a moment. 'I think... I think it's made me a little scared, that's all.'

More tears came and she let them fall freely. 'Scared of what?'

He reached out and wiped her tears away, smoothing his thumb over the apple of her cheek. 'Scared of losing you. Scared of what my life would look like if you weren't in it. Terrified of you realising that I'm not good enough for you.' His voice broke. 'That's why I've been distant. It hasn't been intentional, but I couldn't get rid of the fear. I think the things she said had the opposite effect on me than perhaps what she intended. I kept imagining waking up to find that you'd left. I've lain awake at night trying to convince myself that you won't go but a voice kept saying *but what if she does*?'

She shook her head and took his face in her hands. 'Harris, have I ever given you a reason to think I'm unhappy?' He shook his head. 'That's because you're the love of my life and you make me so, so happy. You're my best friend, Harris. I'd be lost without you. And believe me when I say I'm not going anywhere.'

He pulled her to her feet and wrapped his arms around her once more. 'I'm so glad. Because I don't know what I'd do. Please forgive me.'

She gripped him just as tightly as he held her. 'There's nothing to forgive.'

'But I've been a horrible fiancé these past few days.'

She pulled back and smiled at him. 'But the rest of the time we've been together you've been amazing. And now that I know your reasons for these past few days I completely understand. It's bound to have been a shock for you. But please, promise me...'

He nodded, swiping at his own tears. 'Anything.'

'No more secrets, okay?'

He nodded. 'Agreed. No more secrets. I can't lose you, Bella.'

'That won't happen if I can help it.'

4

April arrived in a riot of colour as daffodils, tulips and snowdrops sprouted and then bloomed on the island; marsh marigolds sprang up by the water, their vibrant yellow faces reaching for the sun as the days gradually became longer and the temperature on Skye increased, ever so slightly. Then the video call came that Bella had been anxiously waiting for.

'I'm a daddy, Bella!' Ben's voice and expression were filled with emotion. 'Theo is here and he's perfect. He was a whopping nine pounds! Can you believe it?' He looked frazzled on her phone screen. His hair was unkempt, and he had dark circles under his red-rimmed eyes.

'Oh, Ben, that's wonderful!' Bella said.

'Congratulations, buddy!' Harris was sitting beside her on the sofa.

'Thanks, guys. It was a long night and I'm so proud of Skye. She's amazing,' Ben said, wiping at his eyes. 'It was hard to see her in pain like that, but she did so well. Every time I think about it I get emotional again.'

'I think you can be forgiven, you've both been through a lot,' Bella assured him with a smile. 'How is she doing?'

Ben huffed the air from his lungs through puffed cheeks. 'She's resting now. She definitely needs it, bless her, it was exhausting for me, and I wasn't the one giving birth. I don't think any number of antenatal classes can prepare you for what it's really like. But you should see him, Bells, he has this thick mop of brown hair and a scrunched-up wee face but he's so cute. I think he's got a look of Skye, but she says he looks like me. I still can't believe we made him and that we're parents.'

'Aye, the fun starts now, eh?' Harris said with a wide smile.

'I can't wait to see him,' Bella said. 'Make sure you send photos as soon as Skye's up to it.'

'I will, aye. I'm heading home just now for a wee sleep. Then I'm coming back later to the hospital to bring her some food as she's complaining of being hungry after all that hard work. It's hard to leave to be honest and it'll be hard to stay away. Skye's staying in overnight tonight just because the little guy was stubborn and took longer than expected to make an appearance and it took a real toll on her, but she's really happy regardless of all that.'

Bella's eyes welled with tears. 'I'm so glad. Give her our love when you see her later. I'll drop her a message on WhatsApp, but I'll wait for her to ring us, so I don't overwhelm her. Speak soon.'

'Aye, cheers, guys. Look, I'd better get going, or I'll be falling asleep on my feet. Speak soon.' Ben ended the video call and Bella turned to Harris.

'Well, that's two of my friends with wee ones now.'

He tucked her hair behind her ear. 'Do you still see kids in our future?'

'Definitely. I'd still like to have them. Maybe two.' She shrugged. 'But... I hope it's okay that I'm just not in a hurry. How about you?'

He smiled. 'I'd still like to have kids, too, someday. But I'm happy to go at your pace.' He leaned in to kiss her and nibbled suggestively on her bottom lip. 'So long as we can practise plenty.'

She giggled and felt her face flushing. 'Well, they do say practice makes perfect so I think that can be arranged. Just to be clear, do you mean like borrow one and take it for walks and babysit, that kind of practising?' She tried to hold back her smile and failed.

He pulled her into his lap. 'Erm, I think you know *exactly* what I mean by practising, you tease.'

She gazed down at him from her position straddling his legs and traced the line of his jaw with her fingertips. She knew she couldn't love any man more than this. He was her future, and it was even better that he was ridiculously sexy.

A surge of heat and desire swept through her body; she wanted him right then and there. 'We could start now,' she said, swiping the long-sleeved top she was wearing from her body.

His eyes lit up. 'Now you're talking,' he said as he got to his feet, still holding her in his arms, and carried her towards the stairs.

* * *

As Bella lay in Harris's arms she snuggled closer into his side, revelling in the scent of his skin.

'Christmas Eve,' he said out of the blue.

Bella pushed herself up so she looked down at him where he lay with one arm behind his head.

'What about it?' She giggled. 'That was such a random thing to say.'

'We're getting married on Christmas Eve,' he said.

Bella widened her eyes. 'I'm sorry, what? You can't just pick a date, Harris. We need to consult Olivia and Brodie and—'

'Done.' He grinned. 'All the key players have been briefed. It's all organised. I wanted it to be as close to when we got engaged as possible because I'm a romantic sap. And I can't wait to see you in whatever dress Olivia designs for you.'

Bella gasped. 'You've already organised it?'

He pulled himself to a sitting position and chewed his lip. 'Is that okay? Did I overstep the mark? I just... I couldn't think of a more perfect date.'

'Of course it's okay! I'm just a bit taken aback, that's all. I was thinking it would be next year. I'm not sure we can get things organised that quickly.'

'Says the woman who organises things for a living,' he said laughing. 'Just imagine it, Bells. A thick frost on the ground, glistening in the winter sun, lights strung up along the driveway and all around the grounds. The smell of fresh pine from the trees. Beautiful flowers in rich reds and purples, and gold accents everywhere.'

She could see it all, and in her mind's eye it was

stunning. It sounded magical and that's exactly what she had always dreamed her wedding would be.

Bringing herself back to reality, she shook her head to dislodge the distracting images. 'But... we have to think about everyone's Christmas. People might not want to come to Inverness on Christmas Eve. Isn't it a bit selfish?'

He reached out and touched her cheek. 'I checked with your folks, our friends and Liv and Brodie to test the water. They were all excited about a Christmas wedding, Bells. So, unless you'd rather wait until next summer... what do you say?'

Bella's stomach was suddenly alive with butterflies, and she couldn't help the smile that took over her face. 'Then I say *ho ho ho yes*! We're getting married at Christmas!'

* * *

A few hours later, Bella sat nervously in front of the camera on her laptop. It was the first time she had met a client for an initial consultation over a video link. The call was due to start at 3 p.m. Bella's time and it was just a couple of minutes before. In Texas, however, it would only be 9 a.m. The call had arisen following the receipt of an email from a prospective client via her website. At first, she was a little baffled as to why someone from the US would be considering hiring her, but it all became clear.

'Hi there, Miss Douglas?' a blonde woman appeared on the screen before her. She was perfectly made up with immaculate hair and Bella guessed her age to be around sixty.

'Yes, Mrs Somers. Good to meet you.'

'And you too, darlin'. Excuse me lookin' like this but it's early here and I've just come in from my mornin' swim.'

Bella wasn't sure what she meant because she looked as well put together as was humanly possible. 'Oh, no, you look lovely,' she replied, hoping that wasn't too forward. 'So, how can I help you?'

'Well now, as I explained in my email, my husband and I are in the process of purchasing an old hotel over on Skye in a place called *Por*tree.' Her emphasis on *por* made Bella smile. 'And we want to update it seein' as it's been hit by the ugly stick in every single room. I mean, I hated the seventies when we were in 'em, but that place looks like the seventies threw up all over it. Literally.'

Bella laughed. 'I can totally understand. I'm not a fan of seventies décor either.'

'Well, that's a relief to know. Anyhow, I emailed

you the brochure we got before we put a bid on the place with the real estate agent, did you get a chance to look over it?'

Bella nodded. 'I certainly did. I didn't even know the place existed before now so it's an exciting prospect. It's a stunning building. I think it would look amazing if the interior was taken back to something close to what it would have been like when it was built, but with the addition of all the mod cons and today's luxuries.'

'I'm liking the sound of that. Tell me more.'

'Okay, so just as a brief overview, I'm thinking William Morris for the soft furnishing and wallpaper prints, rich colours and sumptuous fabrics, velvet and damask, but juxtaposed with more modern furniture so it's not twee. How does that sound for starters?'

'It sounds wonderful, honey. I've had a good look at your portfolio on your website, and I love the schemes you've already created for other folks, I loved the apartments at Drumblair Castle, very fresh and modern but classy, so I think you're the right person for the job. You'll definitely need to go along and have a look around when the purchase completes. It's going to take a while yet because it's going through probate, or I think they call it confirmation in Scotland, and we know these things can take time.

They're a pain in the *derrière*. But as soon as it's all gone through, I'll be in touch again. My son, Carlton, will be managing the hotel once it's up and running and we'd like him to be involved from the get-go, so he'll be the one you're dealing with once we own the place outright.'

'Sounds good. In the meantime, I'll put some mood boards together and email them across, so you have an idea of what I'm thinking for the place. Of course, once I see it in person it may change a little but that will only be the prints on the wallpapers and fabrics so we can make sure they fit the space we're working with.'

'That sounds good to me, honey. I'll wait to hear from you.'

'Great. Thanks, Mrs Somers. Speak soon.' The screen went blank, and Bella heaved a sigh of relief.

Harris appeared behind her in his uniform. 'That sounded very positive.' He placed his hands on her shoulders and gave her a squeeze.

'It did, didn't it? I'm quite excited about it.'

'I think I know the place. It's been empty for years but it's on the loch and the views will be incredible from there. Great spot for a hotel.'

'I can't wait to go and see it. Maybe we could have a drive up and look at the outside.'

'Sounds like a good idea. We can drive up after we've been to see Mum and Isla at the weekend.'

* * *

As planned, the following weekend they visited Isla and ate the lovingly prepared Sunday lunch with her, Tam and Maeve too. The three golden oldies were like a triple act and there were more than a few giggles to be had. Bertie and Beau ran around the garden until Bertie was completely worn out and then slept at Bella's feet for the rest of the afternoon.

Bella had told them all about the hotel she was going to be working on and that she and Harris were driving up to have a look at the old place.

'Watch out for poultrygeists at that place,' Isla said with an exaggerated shiver.

'Oh, aye, I've heard that they can be *fowl*,' Harris said with a sly wink at Bella.

Oblivious, Isla continued, 'They can if you believe what you see on the TV. Throwing things around. I saw a tick tack video where one had opened all the kitchen cupboard doors when the homeowner had turned her back for a second. Then she turned around again, and it shut them all. Houses and buildings of that age can harbour all sorts of spooks and goolies, you know.' And then she added, rather seriously, 'If you believe in that kind of thing. Which I don't.'

Bella chuckled, not only about the fact that Isla had warned them against something she supposedly didn't believe in, but also because she was now imagining invisible, clucking ghosts throwing items of crockery and cutlery around and banging cupboard doors; she didn't want to think about the *goolies* Isla had mentioned.

Harris chuckled to himself and shook his head. 'Stop it, Isla, or we might *chicken* out of going,' he said.

Bella was trying hard not to laugh. 'We'll be careful, Granny, don't worry. We're only looking at the outside, so I doubt they'll be bothering us, if they in fact do exist.' Bella smirked. 'Anyway, we should get going so we can see the place in the light.'

'Aye, you don't want to be going in the dark, that's for sure,' Isla said... even though she didn't believe in ghosts.

Bella stood and pulled her jacket on. 'We won't see you until next weekend now because Harris is working all week and I'm hoping to head over to Inverness to visit Skye and Ben's wee baby.'

'Oh, bless his wee heart. I must give you a fiver to

take for his piggy bank. Take lots of photos, won't you? And we'll see you next weekend.'

They said their goodbyes and climbed back into Fifi, the red Citroën 2CV that used to belong to Isla but was now Bella's pride and joy.

* * *

They drove up the coast road with the sun still bright overhead, with the windows wound down and Florence and the Machine playing on the stereo. There were daffodils and bluebells scattered in the hedgerows, and birds flitting from hedge to tree and back again. The island was alive and vital, and it was clear that spring had sprung on Skye. The cloudless expanse of blue overhead, combined with the fresh sea air rushing in from outside, put a smile on Bella's face as she drove, singing along with Harris about 'Dog Days'. She had brought her digital SLR camera along to snap some photos of the hotel, figuring that would be better than just using her phone, and her stomach fluttered with excitement.

Once they pulled up the driveway and parked the car, they walked Bertie down by the water's edge and laughed as he dipped his feet into the loch and then ran away again from the cold sensation. He found a huge, gnarly stick that was far too big for him and tried his best to carry it. Bella snapped photos of him as he dragged the thing around, tail wagging frantically.

'Wow, this place is stunning,' Bella said. 'I mean, I knew it was beautiful from the photos but it's even better in person. I can imagine living somewhere like this and waking up to that view every morning.'

They peered in through the windows and the orange and brown colour palette was just as startlingly bad as Bella had expected. Much of the furniture was still in situ and Bella wondered if Mrs Somers had considered selling it. There would no doubt be collectors out there who would snap up the pieces that had sat unused for many years. The most recent owner had passed away and there had been disputes over who should inherit so Mrs Somers had emailed to say confirmation would take much longer than they had originally anticipated.

Bella snapped as many photos as she could, knowing she probably wouldn't visit again until grant of confirmation had occurred and the keys had been passed over, and after Mrs Somers's email, who knew how long that might take.

'Are you still excited to be taking the place on?' Harris asked as he slipped his arm around her shoulders and they both gazed up at the windows. Bella was keeping an eye out for the *poultrygeists* but sadly didn't spot any.

'I am. Although it's bigger than I expected. It could be quite a long project. I just hope I'm up to it.'

'Ah, you can do it, Bella. I've got every faith in you.' They stood in silence for a while, taking in the view and inhaling the fresh clean air.

Harris turned to Bella. 'I'm so proud of you. You knew what you wanted, and you went for it. You've achieved so much in such a short time and it's clear that it makes you happy, which is all I want for you.' The sincerity and love in his gaze made her heart melt.

She tiptoed up and kissed him. 'Thank you, that means such a lot to me. You've been so supportive, and I can't thank you enough.'

'No thanks needed. We're a team. The best team there is.'

The breeze had picked up now and the temperature had dropped. Bella just hoped it wasn't because of the spooks and goolies. She giggled as she thought about that. 'It's getting chilly, let's get Bertie home.'

5

April melted into May, then June, then July and with the passing of the months the weather varied as it was wont to do on Skye. Some days the rain would come in sideways, battering everything with a needle-like icy chill; others it could be hotter than the Bahamas. You just never knew what to expect and Bella loved that about the Highlands and Islands.

On this particular July day, however, which just happened to be Bella's birthday, the sky was a beautiful, cloudless, cornflower-blue. As she drove north to her latest job at the hotel, she took in the vista surrounding her; the mountains were covered in purple heather and the trees lush with verdant leaves. With Fifi's windows down, she could smell wild garlic mingled with lavender. She pulled lungfuls of fresh air in as Harry Styles sang about 'Watermelon Sugar' and she sang along with a smile.

Nothing could dampen her mood. She had so much to look forward to; her wedding for starters, and baby Theo's christening too. She was to be one of his godmothers, which was a role she had been excited to accept when they had visited Inverness in May. She had brought the distillery reception area and shop in a month early and they had celebrated with gin after their visit to see Theo. Everyone loved it, and Bella thought perhaps it might be her best work to date. In addition to all these amazing things, her mum and dad had accepted an offer on their house at the start of July and had subsequently offered on Rowan Cottage. They were now in negotiations, but everything was looking positive.

Yes, today was definitely a good day.

When she pulled to a stop and climbed out of the car, all that could be heard was the sound of birdsong as Bella stood outside the stunning, and vast, Victorian villa that had been converted into a hotel in the 1970s. Once a single, yet grand, family home, the sale on the Iolair-Mhara (or Sea Eagle) had just been completed by new owners and Texas residents, Darlene and Nathaniel Somers, who, according to Bella's research, had amassed a good amount of wealth from oil in their home state. They owned a number of properties around America, but this was their first outside of their home country and Bella wondered what had sparked the purchase.

Following her first video call with Mrs Somers, further video calls and several emailed mood boards had passed back and forth until an overall design had been agreed in order that Bella could bring the beautiful old place back to its former glory. Now that confirmation, or probate, had finally been granted, the work could begin. Standing there on the gravel driveway, Bella couldn't quite believe that this was now her working life. She really was living her dream.

The hotel was an impressive old granite building with a central square turret and a pointed apex at the left side which was then mirrored on the right. The hotel spanned three floors on the inside and an additional annexe building had been built after the Victorian era which had originally housed the laundry and servants' quarters.

A stone canopy, complete with arches, provided shelter for those arriving at the front door and on top of this a decorative balustrade created an upper terrace. When the sun was at its highest point in the sky, as it was today, the visible stonework sparkled as if covered with a layer of tiny diamonds, giving the place an ethereal feel; the kind of place fairies and princesses might reside, rather than *poultrygeists*.

A climbing ivy almost covered the whole of the front elevation, however, and Bella knew that this would need to be trimmed back. Ivy, while pretty to look at, could ruin the integrity of mortar and as this had clearly been there for some time, she was aware that remedial work may also be required. Thankfully Mr and Mrs Somers had enlisted Bella to deal with the *inside* so she presumed someone else would be tasked with taking on that particular job. They had employed their thirty-year-old son to manage the place and informed her he would be her main point of contact from now on.

Across a quiet lane at the front of the property was Loch Portree and behind it was a row of old oak trees that had clearly been there hundreds of years. The location was nothing if not idyllic.

As she stood there admiring the building, a man appeared from inside. He was shirtless and wearing khaki cargo shorts and work boots and carrying a large bottle of water in one hand. He had a muscular physique – the torso of which was covered in a glistening layer of sweat – and blond hair. In his other hand he held a huge set of hedge clippers which,

Bella hoped, answered her concern about the front elevation. She watched as he stopped and placed the hedge clippers on the ground then proceeded to pour half the contents of the bottle over his hair, allowing it to drip down his body like something off an episode of *Baywatch*. *Good grief, love yourself much?* Bella thought. *All we need is some Barry White music and you're good to go, pal.*

'Hey, little lady, you look kinda lost, can I help you?' he asked in a Texan drawl. *Oh, they must have sent over workmen from home, patronising ones too, great,* Bella thought, *strange when there are locals who would have no doubt cost much less.*

She bit back her preferred retort and smiled. 'Hi, I'm actually looking for the new manager, Mr Carlton Somers. Is he here?'

The man walked towards her, smiling. 'Who can I say is here? Are you his lover?' he asked, running a hand through his wet hair. 'If so he's a lucky guy.'

A little taken back by his forthright question, she replied, 'No, no, I'm... I'm Bella Douglas, I'm going to be redesigning the interior of the hotel. I'm supposed to meet with him to show him the approved designs.'

'Approved designs, huh? Who did the approvin' of these designs?' the man asked, frowning, still no introduction.

Bella found his forwardness a little rude for a paid employee, *if* that's what he was. 'Mr and Mrs Somers, the owners. Is Carlton Somers here?'

He eyed her up and down with a mischievous glint in his eyes. 'What if he is?'

'Well, if he is I'd like to speak with him, please.' The man pulled a bottle of sun lotion from a pocket on his cargo shorts and began to smear some on his already tanned skin. *Oh, don't you worry, I've got all day to stand here*, she thought as she fought the threatening stroppy huff. She forced a smile. 'Don't worry, I'll go in and find him myself.' She began to walk towards the entrance.

He chuckled. 'Go right ahead but I doubt you'll find him in there.'

Bella was suspicious of the man before her. She stopped and glared at the half-dressed man. 'Is that because *you're* him and you're playing games with me?'

He grinned. 'I might be. I do like to play games.'

Oh, for goodness' sake, I don't have time for this. She couldn't help flaring her nostrils but bit her tongue momentarily. 'If you are Mr Somers, can you just tell me, please, because I have another meeting this afternoon and I don't want to keep my other client waiting.'

'So, you're already being unfaithful, huh? Not a great start.' It was clear he was teasing by the half-smile on his face. 'It usually takes a lot longer than this for the cheatin' to start.'

'I can assure you, Mr Somers, that this is purely business. Now shall we go inside and go over the designs?'

He wiped his hand down his shorts and held it out. 'You got me. Carlton Somers.'

It didn't take a rocket scientist. She shook the offered hand, feeling the slimy residue of suntan lotion and realising she had nowhere to wipe it. 'Bella Douglas.'

Carlton Somers had been employed, albeit reluctantly from what his parents had said, in the role of manager after he had retired from a career as a catalogue model. It had all felt a little strange, and somewhat contrived, to Bella. He was a handsome man, granted, but why would he go from modelling to running a hotel in a whole other country? She felt sure there was more to his story.

'So you said.' He glanced at her left hand. 'That's quite a rock on your finger. Who's the lucky guy?'

'My fiancé is *Inspector* Harris Donaldson.'

He nodded, looking her up and down again. 'Is he now?' He turned and walked in through the huge oak doors and into the reception area. It was a hideous throwback to when the colour palette took its inspiration from mud. Lots of brown and lots of Formica. *Who could do this to such a beautiful old building?*

He turned his head and asked over his shoulder, 'Can I get you a drink? Some food? I usually order in from a place in *Port*ree. But they're pretty quick.'

'I'm good, thanks. Is there somewhere with a table so I can spread my designs out for you to look at?'

He mumbled something incoherent but from his expression she got an idea of what he was thinking. She felt her cheeks flame. 'I'm sorry, *what*?'

'I said sure, we can go *spread* your designs out in the lounge. The furniture is still in there right now, but Mom has arranged for a removal company to come along this week. Apparently, some folks still like this crap, so someone has bought it, believe it or not.' So, they at least had their dislike of seventies décor in common, if nothing else.

The fifty shades of brown theme carried through into the lounge where caramel faux-leather sofas and chairs sat around a large smoked-glass coffee table on a chocolate-brown and cream swirly patterned rug. It smelled musty and the suspended ceiling was stained with nicotine; the colour of which fit quite well with the scheme, ironically.

'Are you staying locally?' she asked, making small talk, and immediately regretted her question when his face lit up.

'Why, are you gonna come and visit?' When she didn't answer, he added, 'I'm living here for now. But I'm gonna buy a place in *Port*ree eventually, I guess I might as well make the most of my time in this god-forsaken hellhole.'

Charming. 'I see. Well, you might want to look for somewhere sooner rather than later. It may get a little noisy and dirty around here as things progress,' she said, once again regretting her choice of words.

He raised his eyebrows. 'I'm a tough guy, I can handle it,' he said with that pathetic half-smile again.

Bella cleared her throat, if he was trying to impress her he was having the opposite effect. 'Okay...' She took her iPad out of its case and placed it down, then she took out the wallpaper and fabric samples. 'So, the idea is to take the Iolair-Mhara back to its origins with some beautiful William Morris wallpapers and fabrics. These are the ones approved by your parents.'

'Do you know how the place got its name?' he asked out of the blue. She shook her head. 'It was named after a nest of white-tailed eagles that were discovered in the forked trunk of one of the old oak trees in the grounds behind the house, back in the mid-1800s. The eagles returned here, to the same spot for many years after that too. They apparently loved the location on the edge of the loch. Did you see the painting in the foyer?'

Bella nodded. 'The piece by Douglas McKenna? I did. I did some research after your mum and dad told me about it. He was quite local to the area and painted it in 1896. I think it's lovely that it's still here and there's still a connection between the building and its first wild neighbours. Maybe we'll find a more fitting frame and make sure it stays. Make it a feature.'

'Right now, that painting is the only thing I like about the place. Present company excepted, of course.'

'You're not here willingly then?' she asked.

'Let's just say managing a hotel wasn't what I either hoped, or expected, to be doing with my life but... Here we are, the less about the reasons the better, I think. Anyway, show me your grand plans, Miss Douglas.'

* * *

'I like it,' Mr Somers said after Bella had gone through the whole proposed scheme. 'Would've been nice if I'd been allowed to have some input but...'

'Ah, sorry about that. Perhaps if there's anything you really aren't keen on you could speak to your parents and—'

'No, I like what you've come up with. I may make a few additions but overall, you've done a great little job. Well done, you.'

A great little job? Well done, you? You arse. 'Well, I am a qualified professional.'

He raised his eyebrows. 'Wait, you can actually get qualified to decorate?'

Bella's nostrils flared involuntarily. 'Yes. You can.'

'Nice, nice. Well done, you.' There was that condescending tone again. Why did it not feel like a compliment?

Bella stood, fearing she might say something she would regret. 'Right, well, I'll be off. Thanks for your time.' She held out her hand.

He stood too and took her hand. 'Oh, yeah, you have another appointment.'

'I do.' She tried to remove her hand from his grip, but he held on.

He smoothed his thumb over the back of her

hand. 'It was good to meet you, Bella. I can see why your parents chose that name for you.'

'Actually, I was named *Arabella* after Arabella Stuart, the cousin of King James VI. She was a woman who took no crap,' she informed him bluntly as she snatched her hand away. The part about the Stuarts was totally fabricated, she had no clue why her parents named her Arabella and had only heard of the Stuart woman when she'd searched for people with her name out of curiosity.

He chuckled. 'Say hi to your fiancé for me,' he said before turning and leaving the room.

'I'll see myself out then,' Bella said to the empty room as she wiped her hand down her skirt, feeling slimy and in need of a wash. She left the house as quickly as she could, hoping that first impressions were wrong on this occasion.

* * *

Later that evening, Bella stood at the kitchen counter chopping vegetables for a stir fry when Harris came into the room and slid his arms around her waist from behind. 'Hey, sexy. How did it go?'

'Yeah... good. The hotel is stunning from the outside but quite ugly on the inside.' *Rather like its new manager,* she thought.

'Oh? How so?'

'Lots of brown and orange.'

'Ah. I'd forgotten about that. A seventies enthusiast's dream then?' She nodded. 'What's your new boss like?'

She paused for a moment while she contemplated her answer, carefully. 'American,' was what she came up with.

He laughed. 'Interesting choice of adjective. Am I to take it from that that you're not too keen on him?'

'Well, I've only met him today so let's give it time. But what I will say is that I don't like to be referred to as *little lady* and having done a *great little job*.'

Harris sucked air in through his teeth. 'Jeez-oh. How to make friends and influence people in one easy step. I'm surprised you didn't smack him.'

'I was more than a little tempted if I'm honest.' Bella placed her knife down on the countertop, wiped her hands on the tea towel there and turned to face Harris. He looked so handsome in his police uniform. 'You would think that a young guy, in this day and age, would be a little more aware of how to speak to women. Thank goodness you're not a sexist moron.'

He kissed her passionately. 'I'd like to think of myself as more of a *sexy* moron.' He grinned.

She laughed. 'You are silly. And I love you for it.'

He kissed her again. 'And I love you. Right, I'm off to get changed.' He released her and made his way quickly towards the doorway before shouting out in a bad American accent, 'Now you get on and prepare that meal for your hard-working man, little lady.'

She picked up the tea towel and flung it at his retreating form. 'Cheeky!'

* * *

One week later, Bella returned to the hotel to meet with Carlton again for a progress report. The place was cleared of furniture and stripped of the brown and she could hear the teams hard at work in the other rooms. She waited for Carlton in the empty dining room as there was a team in the lounge stripping down the suspended ceiling. She checked her watch for the fourth time since she'd arrived.

He was late.

'Hey, Bella,' he said as he walked into the room shirtless, again, wearing his boots, and in a tight pair of boxers that left little to the imagination.

She averted her eyes and her face heated. 'Hi, Mr

Somers. I can't stay long. We said we'd meet at ten and it's now almost twenty past.'

'Call me Carlton. And yeah, I was working out in my room.' *No apology then? Nice.* 'Can't let the bod get saggy just cuz I'm not working.'

'I can wait while you go put on some clothes,' she said looking him straight in the eyes this time, hoping that her displeasure was evident.

Clearly, he was a little too thick skinned and arrogant to care. He smirked and held his arms out to the sides. 'Didn't you know I'm a model? And because of my modelling career I'm used to undressing in front of people, which means it doesn't really faze me. Anyway, people pay to see this body.'

Modest too. 'Isn't the point of modelling to wear clothes? And in all seriousness, this is currently a building site, so you'd be safer with clothes on. You don't want to be getting splinters, or worse.'

As if he hadn't heard her, he continued, 'Yeah, I did catalogue and website work mostly, but I've done catwalk too. Did a stint for Nina Picarro if you've heard of her.'

Of course Bella had heard of her, Olivia used to work for her in New York, although she wasn't going to tell him that and give him something to latch onto. 'Very nice. Look, it's inappropriate for us to conduct meetings while one of us is scantily clad.'

He tilted his head. 'Awww, come on, what's a little skin between friends, huh? I don't wanna get dressed before I shower, what would be the point in that?'

Realising he had no intention of getting dressed, she pulled her iPad out of her bag. 'Can we please just go through the progress report and then I can leave?'

'So soon? How about I take you to dinner and we discuss the progress there over a nice bottle of red?'

'No, thank you, Mr Somers, you know I'm engaged. And again, this isn't appropriate. In fact, it makes me feel quite uncomfortable and I'm going to have to consider whether I want to continue with the job if you refuse to dress appropriately for our meetings.'

He scowled. 'You're overreacting, don't you think? You're not going to report me to your fiancé, are you?' He held out his wrists and stuck out his bottom lip, chuckling, but there was a slight sinister edge to it.

An uneasy shiver travelled down her spine. 'I don't think I'm overreacting, no. And I can look after myself, thank you. But as I said, you need to dress professionally or at least *to* dress for our meetings if I'm going to continue working here.'

He rolled his eyes like a petulant child. 'Yes, ma'am, sorry, ma'am.'

She ignored his sarcasm. 'You'll be happy to know that everything's on track,' she said, deciding to power on through the meeting as fast as she could and then she'd get the hell out of Dodge. 'Structurally the building is sound and it's all purely cosmetic as we first presumed. Teams will be continuing to work on prepping the lounge for decoration and, following that, the bedrooms, in order that photos can be taken for the new website to give prospective guests an idea of what the place will look like when it's up and running.'

'So, I take it there'll be no dinner date?' he asked, and Bella had to bite her tongue yet again.

6

Another month passed and once again Bella climbed out of her car and assessed the exterior of the Iolair-Mhara Hotel. The August sunshine was hiding behind a bank of ominous clouds and Bella hoped this was not a premonition of how the day was going to go. The overgrown climbing ivy had that had once covered the majority of the front elevation had been trimmed back so the stunning architecture was now more visible, and the true grandeur of the place could be seen. She could imagine ladies in Victorian gowns perambulating, arm in arm, down towards the loch to take in the air, and wondered what the original family who had lived here when it was first built as a home were like. They clearly must have been wealthy. But did they love the place? Were they happy here?

She walked inside and stood in the lounge of the hotel with her iPad clutched in one hand and the index finger of her other poised and ready to go. This particular room was almost complete now with only snagging to deal with.

Back in the seventies, the previous owners had either stripped out or covered over many of the original Victorian features such as cast-iron fireplaces, ceiling roses and cornices, and replaced them with those popular and fashionable at the time, which was sacrilege as far as Bella was concerned – she had never really understood the obsession with seventies interior décor as it utilised some of the most drab colour schemes, shapes and textures, in her opinion. For example, who puts monstrously ugly brown swirly carpet – or any carpet for that matter – in a bathroom? Bella could only imagine the germs and bacteria that had been harboured in the fibres before they were removed, and the thought of that made her feel bilious.

In that state it had held no attraction as a holiday residence as far as Bella was concerned, and she was grateful, firstly that the hotel was under new management, and secondly that the new owners had provided a nice healthy budget and trusted her to redecorate the whole place, returning it to its beautiful origins; a little more akin to the stately family home it had once been. After operating as a hotel through the sixties and seventies it had lain empty for many years after its previous owners had eventually gone bankrupt in the early 1980s. After that it was bought by someone else who chose to let it sit, empty and unused, until now. *There was no wonder,* Bella had thought, *who'd want to stay in such a dismal place, even it was surrounded by the beauty of nature?*

The long driveway that led to the hotel reminded Bella of the approach to Drumblair Castle with its trees and gravel road. And even though the grounds weren't quite as vast as those at the castle they were still picturesque, and she could easily understand why people would want to stay in that location, although she did wonder about its old visitors' thoughts when they stepped through the beautiful ornate oak door and into the vision of brown.

There was still a lot of work to do but gradually seeing her plans coming to fruition in the lounge was the best feeling. It simply never got old. Gone were the gaudy 1970s orange and brown wallpaper patterns comprising of interlinked squares with rounded edges that made your eyes go squiffy if you stared too long, and the decades of cigarette smoke that had stained everything it clung to, and in their place was a wonderfully tasteful, rich colour palette of jewel tones, incorporating many of William Morris's stunning prints on the wallpapers and soft furnishings.

It had been a fun project to work on so far, for the most part, and she was grateful that her interior design work at Drumblair Castle had been featured in the national press, leading to this particular job. As she stood marking things off her tick list, she felt a presence behind her and the hairs on her neck prickled, so she turned around, uneasily.

'Oh, hello, Mr Somers,' she said as breezily as she could before turning to attend to her list once more; she did not wish to engage him in conversation because she was very much aware how that tended to go.

'How many times do I have to ask you to call me Carlton?' the Texan man drawled with a deep, husky chuckle. At least on this occasion he was fully clothed. She hoped he had finally got the message that she wasn't interested in ogling his scantily clad flesh, regardless of whether or not he was or had been a model. His previously brazen behaviour and his arrogance were reminiscent of Kerr MacBain... or at least the *old* Kerr MacBain.

Carlton was evidently a man who was used to getting his own way and had persisted to drop hints that he wanted to wine and dine her after that first time he had asked outright. She had reminded him, countless times, that he had seen her engagement ring and knew she was taken but for some reason it hadn't deterred him. He was clearly a vain man who found the word 'no' to be a gauntlet she had laid down before him. A mere challenge for him to accept, and he had.

Realising she had drifted off inside her own head and not responded to him, Bella felt her face heating in a combination of embarrassment and annoyance. She cringed before turning to face him. 'Sorry, it just feels rather personal to call you by your first name seeing as this is a business-only arrangement, so I always revert to autopilot.'

Carlton pouted. 'Oh, come now, *Bella*, I think we're a little more than just business associates, don't you? We've known each other for two months, surely that counts for somethin'.'

He was sort of right. They had been communicating for two months, but the work had only started in earnest within the last month once the rest of the designs had been approved by his parents. Their subsequent meetings had been short in nature – Bella's decision – and had mainly taken place over video call from her kitchen table. Even that hadn't stopped his innuendos or offers of a dinner date.

Bella forced a smile. 'I'm just trying to be professional, that's all,' she replied, trying to ignore the sense of unease that knotted her stomach when he was around.

He took a few steps closer. 'You still engaged to that police officer?'

She sighed. 'Of course I am. He's the love of my life and I take my commitments very seriously,' she informed him unabashedly. 'And he's an *Inspector* actually.'

He smiled and saluted her. 'Duly noted. But I'm not ready to give up on you just yet.'

Bella turned her back and rolled her eyes. 'Well, you really should. You're wasting your time,' she said as light-heartedly as she could. Memories of being in a similar situation with Kerr when she was working on the interiors of the stable apartments came flooding back to haunt her.

He came to stand beside her, a little too close for her liking, and she took a step to the side and crouched for a moment, pretending to examine the skirting and tapping gibberish onto her iPad.

She heard him sniggering and then clearing his throat and knew he was doing things on purpose to wind her up. It was working but she refused to let it show.

'So, how long before this room is done? It's looking great.' His comment surprised her, considering there was no hidden agenda or innuendo in it.

'I'm glad you think so. It's almost ready to go. I just want the decorators to touch up the paintwork on the skirting boards where they were marked when the flooring was laid. And then it will be ready for the furniture, and following that the first brochure photos can be taken for the new website.' She walked towards the large bay window, and he followed.

'Where do you get your inspiration from, Bella? I have to say you have great taste.'

Your flattery will get you nowhere, she thought. 'All over the place. Books, locations, films, music...'

He turned to her and gave her one of his half-smiles that she was sure other women swooned over. 'You really are fascinating. What I wouldn't give to take you out to dinner and get to know you better.'

Oh, for goodness' sake. Bella flared her nostrils and fought to keep her cool. 'Well, I'm sure my fiancé would be happy to fill you in on the details,' she said with a fake half-smile of her own.

Instead of being annoyed by her response, he chuckled again. 'You're so feisty, I love that about you.' He shook his head. 'Oh, the fun we'd have.' He fixed his gaze on her and she shivered involuntarily. She could almost feel him undressing her with his eyes.

'I'd better get on,' she said, pointing her thumb to a random area of the room. 'Or you'll be complaining it's all taking too long.'

'Never gonna happen, Bella. I'm enjoying your company. In fact, I'm trying to figure out ways I can keep you on once the hotel's done. Only for your decorating skills, of course.' His eyebrow rise, although fleeting, wasn't lost on her.

She smiled briefly. 'Well, I'm afraid I'd need to check my diary. Lots of work coming in just now.'

He pouted. 'Awww, that's a shame. Great for you, obviously, but a shame for me. I'm considering offering on a property I've visited in *Por*tree, you see. It's such a quaint little place, don't you think?' He didn't wait for her to answer. 'I was hoping you'd come and decorate once they accept my offer.'

She continued walking around the room, looking for things that needed to be added to her list. 'You'll need to check with me once you've found a place,' she said as dismissively as she could without verging on disrespectful – he was her boss, after all, for now at least.

'I'll be sure to do that. Are you gonna be working on the rest of the bedrooms next? I'm presuming you can now that the drywall is installed.'

She nodded. 'Yes, that's the plan.'

His smile widened. 'Okay, great. I'll need to meet with you to go over the plans again. It's a while since I saw them and I want to make sure the bedrooms are *especially* good,' he said with a small smile and a distinct twinkle in his eye. 'I'll call you later in the week and we can synchronise diaries.' And with that he turned and left the room.

Bella breathed a sigh of relief. What was it about her that made her attract self-centred, egotistical arseholes? She was so glad that Harris was nothing at all like Carlton or the Kerr MacBain of old. At least Olivia's brother had somewhat turned his life around and realised the error of his ways. Yes, she decided, Harris was the best man for her in every possible way, and she was lucky to have him.

* * *

Later that day, when she arrived home, Bella was greeted by Bertie, his tail wagging like an aeroplane propeller and his funny high-pitched yips that had only deepened slightly as he got older.

She half expected him to take off, he was so excited to see her. He ran away and brought her his tatty rabbit soft toy, something he had started to do when he was having big feelings. It was so cute.

'Hey, boy, have you missed me?' she asked as she crouched before the bundle of fluff. He continued to wag his whole body as she stroked his fur.

'Hey, sweetheart, had a good day?' Harris asked as he walked through to the hallway to join the welcome party. He was drying his hands on a towel which he flung onto his shoulder once he was done.

She thought back to Carlton and his persistence but said nothing about it to Harris and instead nodded and smiled. 'Yes, busy but the place is looking wonderful.'

He leaned close and kissed her. 'I can't wait to see it when it's all done. And the owner's son, is he happy with it all?'

Again, she nodded and forced a smile. 'He seems to be, yes.'

'Good, good. We've had some more RSVPs in the post, which is great. It's all coming together.' When Bella didn't reply, Harris narrowed his eyes. 'Is everything okay? You seem a little off.'

She brightened her smile. 'Oh, sorry, yes, I'm just

a bit wiped out, that's all. Maybe I'm coming down with something.'

He slipped his arms around her and pulled her close. 'Let's hope not, you're heading over to Drumblair tomorrow.'

Bella had almost forgotten about her planned trip to see Olivia and to try on her wedding dress for the first time. Being reminded of this lifted her spirits. 'I'm sure I'll be fine after a good night's rest.'

'Well, come and sit down. Dinner's ready. I've made my lasagne for you because I know how much you love it.'

He was so incredibly wonderful, and she loved coming home when he'd been off work. He always cooked for her and made sure she knew how proud he was of her.

'Oh, lovely, thank you. I'll just nip upstairs and get changed.'

Harris pulled the towel from his shoulder and said, 'Don't be long, I'll get the food served up.'

Bella made her way upstairs and changed into yoga pants and a long-sleeved T-shirt. She stared at herself in the full-length mirror in the bedroom and almost didn't recognise the body she saw there. She really had changed physically since moving to Skye and was losing weight, not intentionally – she had always accepted her curves as part of herself – but simply due to the rushing around she was doing for the several jobs she insisted on working on concurrently; at first she couldn't see it even though her granny pointed it out frequently and with concern. The conversations were tattooed onto Bella's brain...

* * *

'In spite of what you read on the interwebs, men don't like skeletons, Arabella. They like a girl with shape. If you're not careful, you'll end up looking like one of those girls with anaphylaxis.'

Bella frowned. 'I think you mean anorexia.'

Isla curled her lip. 'Anna who?' She waved a hand in annoyance. 'Ugh, never mind, I have no idea who *she* is or how thin she is, but you don't want to be trying to look like her, take my word for it, hen. In fact, I heard a song the other day on a tick tack toe video about big butts. They're all the rage now, you know. People are getting those Brazilian butt lifts, so their bums are bigger, and here you are losing yours. I mean, look at that Jenny from the block woman. And that Nicki Minger. Men love them and they've both got vera ample posteriors.'

'Minaj, Granny, it's Nicki Minaj.'

'Aye, that's what a said. You'll be needing one of those bum transplants if you're not careful.' Images of surgeons harvesting people's bottoms from one person to implant in another sprang to Bella's mind and she scrunched her face at the unpleasant thought. When Bella said nothing, Isla sighed. 'You look better with some meat on your bones, that's all I'm saying, hen.'

Bella forwent the explanation of her grandmother's multi-faceted error this time. 'Granny, I can assure you, with all confidence, that I won't be having buttock *im*plants... any time soon. Or ever, in fact! And I'm not losing weight on purpose. It's just that I'm so busy,' she insisted.

'Aye, well, take some snacks wi' you on the road. You can get all sorts of things *to go* these days. And anyway, why don't they feed you up at that fancy hotel you're working on?'

Bella tried not to roll her eyes but failed. 'Because I'm not there long enough and I do a lot of the design work remotely.' *Mainly on account of the new manager trying to seduce me whenever I see him in person.*

Her granny shook her head and folded her arms across her chest defiantly. 'I'm just worried you're catching an eating disorder. Princess Di had one, you know. But it doesn't make it something to perspire to.

They're not a vibe, you know. They don't slay, in spite of what you may think.'

Bella pursed her lips, this time trying not to laugh. Her granny really did spend too much time on TikTok. 'I can assure you, Granny, I'm not *aspiring* to have an eating disorder. And you can't catch them so stop worrying. But I love you for caring.'

These conversations were a regular occurrence and although they grated on Bella a little she knew they were coming from a place of love, so she tried not to let them get to her too much.

But even Bella was starting to see it more now. She'd even had to contact Olivia and give her new measurements for her wedding dress. Admittedly the situation with Carlton wasn't helping matters. He seemed to think it was all a laugh but she was increasingly unhappy about the way he spoke to her. She had resolved that, if it hadn't stopped, she would contact Mrs Somers and speak to her.

* * *

After dinner, Bella clipped on Bertie's lead and she and Harris headed out to walk the dog. The weather had brightened as the day had progressed and it seemed strange to Bella that the sun had made an appearance as soon as she was on her way home to Harris. It was now descending and painting an amber glow over the pretty village of Glentorrin. It was a mild evening, and others seemed to be taking advantage of the weather too. Jules, Reid and Evin were out walking Chewie, and they stopped to say hello.

'Are you excited about tomorrow?' Jules asked with a bright smile.

Bella nodded. 'I think so. But I'm nervous too.'

'Aye, but it'll be a good kind of nervous, surely?' Reid asked. 'It's not every day you get a renowned designer to create your wedding gown.'

'That's true. And yes, I'm definitely a good kind of nervous. Plus, it will be lovely to see Freya and have a cuddle.'

'How old is she now?' Jules asked.

'A year and eight months! She's growing so fast.'

Jules ruffled Evin's hair. 'They have a habit of doing that,' she said.

Evin's face coloured pink, and he ducked. 'Muuuum, mind ma hair!' he said with a laugh. 'We might see Grace walking Cleo.'

Evin, and Caitlin's daughter, Grace, had been friends for a long time, but things seemed to be heading towards romance these days. Or that's apparently what he hoped.

Jules pulled him into her side and kissed his head. 'Ah, young love,' she said with a wink.

'Evin!' came a female voice from the direction of the bakery and he waved.

'Come on, lad, let's go see Gracie and Cleo,' Evin said as he patted his thigh and began to jog away towards the pretty red-haired girl and her little dog, with Chewie following obediently behind. 'Have a nice time at Drumblair, Bella,' he called over his shoulder.

'Thanks, Evin,' Bella replied.

Reid clapped his hands and rubbed them together. 'So, who's up for a cheeky wee drink at the Coxswain?'

Harris grinned. 'You don't have to ask us twice!'

The alarm on Bella's phone sounded and she stretched out to hit the stop button. Harris stirred behind her and skimmed his hand down the curve of her body. The warmth of his skin reached hers through her satin pyjama shorts and camisole top, and she smiled. There was nothing nicer, that she had experienced so far anyway, than waking up wrapped in her fiancé's arms.

Bella had been excited and nervous, in equal measure, about the arrival of this day for a couple of weeks now. Today would be the day she tried on her wedding dress for the first time. She had only seen the sketches up to this point, and while she absolutely loved them, seeing the dress on her body was something entirely different.

'What time do you have to set off for Drumblair?' Harris mumbled as he feathered kisses down her neck to her shoulder and back up to her ear.

She sighed and let her eyelids flutter closed once again as she relished the sensation of his lips on her skin. 'I should go soon really if I'm going to make the most of the day. I'm meeting Mum at the castle; I just need to let her know what time I'll be there.'

He squeezed her a little tighter. 'But you're staying over, which means I don't get to wake up with you tomorrow, so I have to make the most of you now,' he whispered as he traced shapes on the bare skin of her thigh.

'You can always come with me. It's your weekend off and I'm sure Bertie would love to see his cousins.'

'I've got too much to do. Paperwork, mowing the grass, and I want to make a start on painting the fence before the weather starts to get too bad.'

She turned in his arms to face him and planted a kiss on his stubbled chin, the spikes tickling her lips. 'Well, you can't really complain then.' She smiled. He looked so ridiculously sexy when he was sleepy.

He kissed her, long and languorously. 'I can and I will, so there.'

She pursed her lips and nodded. 'Good argument, Inspector Donaldson, clearly very well thought out.'

He chuckled. 'I thought so.'

'Right, I'd better get up and shower because staying here with you is getting more and more tempting by the second and if I don't go now, I may end up with a half-made wedding dress.'

His eyes widened for a split second. 'Or maybe no wedding dress at all. Now there's an idea.'

She feigned horror, gasping and whacking his chest playfully. 'You're incorrigible, Harris Donaldson. We're getting married in December, so I think a dress is a pretty crucial bit of kit.'

He stuck out his bottom lip. 'Spoilsport.' He manoeuvred her beneath him. 'Maybe get a shower in a wee while, eh? We have our own important stuff to do.' His cheeky, handsome smile and tousled hair were all the encouragement she needed.

'Well, when you put it like that...'

* * *

A while later, after making the two-hour journey in bright summer sunshine through the stunning Highland countryside with its vibrant colour palette of green, purple and yellow, Bella had met her mum outside Olivia's studio and now stood before the full-length mirror with her mum beside her and both with their hands over their eyes as instructed.

'No peeking. Give me a minute to lay the bottom out properly for the full effect,' Olivia said.

Bella's heart was hammering at her ribs and her mouth was dry. What if she hated the wedding dress Olivia had designed for her? What if it looked wrong? It was one thing loving something on paper but actually seeing it real life was a whole different thing. Her hands shook and she inhaled a long, deep, calming breath.

'Are you okay, Bells? You're shaking like a leaf,' her mum said, gripping her hand.

'Your mum's right. Anyone would think you're scared you won't like the dress,' Olivia said with a giggle.

Bella cringed. Olivia knew her so well. 'No, don't be daft. I know I'll love it.' She was very much aware of how unconvincing she sounded.

Olivia sighed. 'Okay, I want to assure you I've taken all the new measurements into account, and it looks stunning, if I do say so myself. You're so beautiful though, Bells, you'd look incredible in a black sack.'

Bella swallowed. 'That's not what you've dressed

me in, though, is it?' She laughed nervously, verging on the hysterical. 'I feel like one of those women on that show *Say Yes to the Dress* where their mother has chosen something for them to try on and it's hideous.'

Her mum cleared her throat. 'Excuse me, I have impeccable taste, thank you very much.'

'I know that, Mum, I didn't mean you specifically. But I've seen that *Don't Tell the Bride* too where the tasteless fiancé has chosen a dress and when they open their eyes in front of the mirror it's fluorescent green with glow sticks dangling from the hemline. Or has fairy wings attached to the back. N-not that I think your designs are hideous, Liv, I'm not saying your designs are anything *like* that... I... I'm just nervous, that's all. I want to love it no matter what. But I just—' Bella was relieved to hear Olivia and her mum giggling.

Olivia interrupted. 'Good grief, Bells, you've built this up into something akin to a dentist visit, and it's supposed to be fun.'

Guilt niggled at Bella. 'You're right, you're right. I'm sorry. I just want this to be perfect. I've never been so uptight about an item of clothing.'

Olivia squeezed her arm. 'I promise you there's no fluorescent green or fairy wings, and not a glow stick in sight. You can both open your eyes and see for yourselves.'

Bella allowed her eyelids to flutter open and slowly she raked her gaze from the floor upwards. She turned to her mum, who had tears in her eyes.

'Oh, Bella,' was all her mum managed to say.

Bella covered her mouth with her hands as her stomach lurched. She was head to toe in ivory lace over a fitted satin shift. Pearls were scattered around the neckline and diamantes twinkled all over the bodice. The dress had long lace sleeves and a fitted waist that showed off her new figure beautifully and there was just enough of a train to make her feel like a princess without it being a trip hazard. She didn't quite look like herself. Or at least not the self she had always been used to seeing in her reflection. This self was the woman she had always dreamed of being. It was all a little overwhelming.

'Well?' her mum said, a wide smile on her face in spite of the tears. 'All I can say is your dad will burst with pride when he sees you. He's already excited to walk you down the aisle, Bella, but when he sees you... I bet he cries. I just know he will.'

When Bella didn't speak, Olivia covered her mouth with her hands, mirroring her stance, and mumbled, 'Oh God, you do hate it, don't you?' Before Bella could reply, Olivia held her hands up. 'Okay, let's not panic. The wedding is in four months... *ish*... so I can redesign. I'll make it a priority. I'm so sorry, Bells. You were supposed to love it. I'm so, *so* sorry.'

'Oh no, don't say that, Olivia, it's beautiful,' Bella's mum said and turned to glare at her daughter. 'Bella?' Her eyes were filled with panic and her tone filled with annoyance.

'No, no, it's fine. It has to be perfect,' Olivia said. 'I can start on a redesign right away.'

Bella turned to see tears in her friend's eyes and plonked a finger over her lips. 'Oy! Stop blethering, will you? The panic on both of your faces, seriously.' She shook her head. 'I was just taking it all in. But I love it! It's absolutely perfect. I've never felt more beautiful than I do in this bloody masterpiece. So, stop your fretting and hug me, both of you!'

Olivia stood there for what felt like an age, open-mouthed and wide-eyed. Then, as if someone had flicked her 'on' switch again, she leapt forward and threw her arms around Bella. Bella's mum quickly followed suit.

'Oh, thank goodness! I was heartbroken there for a wee second,' Olivia said. She pulled away and fixed her eyes on Bella again. 'Hang on, you're not just saying that, are you? Because if you are, you needn't try to make me feel better. I'd rather you got the dress you wanted, not one you hate. I don't want you to settle for second best.'

Bella shook her head and turned to face herself again. 'Liv, believe me, it's in no way second best, in fact, is there anything above first best because that's how I feel about this dress! It's the most perfect dress I've ever seen. And *I* get to wear it. *I* get to look this incredible for my wedding day. *Me!*'

'You're going to be the most stunning bride, sweetheart,' her mum said, blotting her eyes with a tissue. 'And as I said, just wait until your dad sees you.'

Olivia and Bella's mum flanked her on either side and smiled at her reflection in the gilt-framed mirror.

Olivia shook her head. 'Bells, you look this incredible all the time. You just don't see it. But Harris is going to be completely in awe when he sees you.'

'I can't believe I'm saying this, but I think you might be right. I just hope he recognises me,' Bella said, laughing. 'Maybe he'll think the wrong bride has turned up.' Then she turned to Olivia and took her hand. 'Thank you. I could never have found anything this perfect in a shop. I'm so sorry about all the stress and worry before. I'm honoured that you've gone to all this trouble for me.' Her eyes welled with tears again.

'She's right, Olivia. I think it's the most beautiful wedding gown I've ever seen,' Bella's mum said with a wavering voice.

Olivia's chin trembled. 'Oh, stop it, you'll have us all sobbing. And it was no trouble at all. You're one of my oldest and dearest friends, Bells. Think of it as my wedding gift to you.'

Bella chewed her lip. 'The expense though, Liv. You're already hosting the wedding. It's all too much. You're going to be completely out of pocket.'

Olivia placed a hand on both Bella's arms. 'Hey, you can stop that. Your designs for the reception area at the distillery are sublime and you won't let me pay you, so I think we are more than square. And anyway, it's my home so it's up to me what I do with it.' She put an arm around Bella's mum's shoulder. 'And your folks are contributing to the food and drink so it's all good. But I refuse to charge you for holding your wedding here when it's *my* business, Bells. Subject closed. End of. Finito! So, let's get the hem of this dress pinned, and tucked a little more in at the waist and then we can go for some lunch.'

Bella knew when to quit arguing with Olivia and

it appeared they had reached that point, so she stayed quiet for a while, storing the conversation in her memory to revisit at a later point.

8

Bella and Olivia waved goodbye to Bella's mum who had to get back home to continue with their clear-out. Her parents' house sale in Inverness was progressing and their offer had finally been accepted for Rowan Cottage at Dunan on Skye, so they had begun to downsize their possessions in readiness.

Bella and Olivia made their way around to the bistro-style café within the grounds of the castle where they were joined by new mum Skye. The café had been created from one of the old stable blocks that stood adjacent to the one that had been turned into holiday lets. In the café, each stall that was once home to a horse now had custom-built benches and oak plank tables. Horse brasses hung on the walls and framed black and white photos of horses that had been a part of the castle staff many years before. It was rustic and quirky through the day but at night-time, when the place was open as a bistro, the tables were covered in linen cloths and candles adorned the centres, creating a romantic and cosy ambience that Bella very much approved of, partly because she'd subtly had a hand in how they looked too.

The three friends placed their lunch orders for homemade quiche and salad and sat in their little private space drinking prosecco, except for Skye, who couldn't partake as she was still breastfeeding her four-month-old son. Today, Theo was at home having some daddy and son time, but every five minutes Skye received a WhatsApp message updating her on what facial expressions and noises their son had made.

'So, you love your dress then?' Skye asked. Bella had messaged her after the fitting and had gushed about how perfect it was.

Bella sighed dreamily. 'Oh, Skye, it's stunning. I won't want to take it off. I might just live in it like Miss Havisham from *Great Expectations*.'

'Only your fella won't be ditching you at the altar,' Skye replied.

'Oh, heck, I hope not.'

'On a scale of one to ten, how excited are you about the wedding?' Olivia asked.

Bella tapped her chin. 'About... a hundred and fifty.'

Skye and Olivia giggled along with her and Olivia added, 'Seriously, Bells, you will be the most stunning bride. What's Harris wearing? Please tell me he's going for a kilt.'

'I believe so. But he's keeping everything a secret. He says he's only going to discuss it with the men involved in the wedding so I'm leaving him to it. He'll be so cold in a kilt though!'

'He's a Scotsman, he's tough,' Skye said with a laugh. 'At least that's what most Scotsmen will say.'

Olivia took a sip of her drink. 'I can't believe you won't let us throw you a hen party.'

'Yeah, what's that about?' Skye asked, pouting.

'I just don't want to bother everyone with another event so close to Christmas. It's such a lot for people to be taking time out of the festive season for the wedding as it is.'

'So, let's have a hen do in October?' Skye said, as if it was the most obvious solution.

Bella smiled. 'I'll think about it.' She turned to Olivia and changed the subject again. 'Are you excited for the whisky launch and reception grand opening?'

Olivia nodded emphatically. 'I really am! Brodie and Uncle Innes are perhaps a little giddier than I am, but it will be great to be selling our own blend at last and to have somewhere stunning to sell it from, thanks to you, Bells. Once again, you've done a magnificent job.'

'Aye, well, the team that worked on it were fantastic. And I hear the gin has been going down a treat with people.'

Olivia smiled. 'Oh, it has. People seem to love it so much that we're planning on doing a couple of different lines of flavoured gin. But it doesn't feel like a proper distillery without our own brand of whisky, so we're all looking forward to seeing how it goes down. You're still coming over for the event, aren't you?'

It was Bella's turn to nod. 'Try and stop me.'

Skye huffed. 'I can't believe I won't be here.'

'Don't be daft, you're going on your first weekend way since Theo was born. Have fun and make the most of it,' Olivia said.

'Hmm, I'm not sure I'll be able to relax. We've never left him before,' Skye replied, chewing on her lip. 'Five months old feels too soon, what if he thinks we've abandoned him?'

'He'll be fine. Both sets of doting grandparents

will be on hand to cater to his every need. Just go and have fun,' Bella said, hoping to encourage her.

Olivia leaned in and whispered, 'And lots of sex, because those times are not easy to come by with a little one.' They all giggled like teenagers.

'Speaking of going away, what are you and Harris doing about a honeymoon?' Skye asked.

'We're delaying that for a while. I'm not sure how long for but Harris has got a lot on at work with there being a shortage of officers just now, and I have a few new clients in the pipeline so we can't really afford the time just now. We can go sometime in the future when things settle down a bit.'

'But if you don't go right after the wedding, you may never make the time to go,' Skye insisted.

Bella knew there was truth to Skye's words and the thought had crossed her mind too. 'We've promised each other that we'll make the time as soon as we can, don't worry.'

'Where would you want to go if you *were* going right after your wedding?' Skye asked.

Bella smiled. 'I've always wanted to go to Tuscany. There's something magical about the images you see online,' she said dreamily. 'I'd love to see Florence, and if we went in winter, I'd want to experience the Cavalcade of the Magi. I've seen videos online and it looks amazing. I'd love to stay in a pretty, romantic hotel overlooking a piazza, and having a trip to a vineyard would be amazing.'

'Now you're talking,' Olivia said. 'It's a shame you can't go sooner. But it will be wonderful when you do eventually get there. It's something to look forward to.'

Bella sighed, trying not to let her disappointment show. 'Aye, we'll get there at some point... hopefully.'

Olivia clearly thought it best to change the subject. 'Anyway, how is the hotel refurb going?'

'Really well. It's been a slow process compared to the distillery but it's getting there now. I'm trying to only go to the site if it's absolutely necessary, to be honest,' Bella replied.

'Oh no, does that mean the manager is still flirting with you?' Skye asked.

Bella took a sip of the sweet bubbles in her glass and placed it down. 'Not really, he seems to have got the message, finally,' she lied. 'But from the way he behaves it seems he's so used to getting what, and who, he wants. I mean, okay, he may sound like, and have the body of Matthew McConaughey, and I think that's why he was a little shocked when I turned him down. Like he was thinking, "But why would you pass me up?" but not all women fawn over men like that. I'm happy with Harris, thank you very much.'

Skye scoffed. 'Conceited pig. You'd think the diamond on your left hand would've been a massive giveaway that you weren't interested.'

The waitress arrived and placed plates of mouth-watering food on the table in front of each of them. The quiche was deep with a pastry base and crust that Bella knew from sight only would melt in her mouth.

Bella shook her head and shrugged. 'I honestly got the impression that my relationship status didn't matter to him. He's seen me talking with Harris on the phone and how loved up we are, and he still pursued me. It's almost like that makes the chase more amusing for him.'

Olivia reached out and squeezed her arm. 'Well, let's hope he's finally taken no for an answer.'

'Hmm, let's hope so because there's only so many times I can bump into him while he's shirtless and trouserless before I'll be talking to Harris, or his parents, about him anyway.'

Olivia and Skye paused with their forks en route to their mouths and shared a wide-eyed glance. 'He walks around shirtless *and* trouserless?' they both said in unison.

Bella felt her cheeks warming at the admission. 'It's only happened a couple of times but that's plenty. I mean, okay, he's ripped and looks like he's walked off the cover of *Men's Health*... I mean he actually *was* a model for catalogues, but it's inappropriate and I've told him so. He acted all innocent and made out like I'd caught him unawares, but the timing was too convenient for my liking.'

Olivia gasped and shook her head. 'What possible reason could he have for taking off his clothes around you?'

Bella almost wished she hadn't mentioned that bit now, she was trying to deal with it herself. 'Like I say, it's only been a couple of times.'

'The first time was too many!' Skye insisted.

Bella sighed. 'Yes... I know. The first time it happened I'd turned up for our first meeting and he'd been cutting down the ivy on the front of the building and he was all sweaty.' She shivered at the memory. 'But he knew I was coming and at what time, so he had plenty of opportunity to shower and dress before I arrived. He didn't apologise or anything. It's just not professional.'

'It's very sus,' Skye mumbled through a mouthful of food. 'He's clearly trying to seduce you.'

'Hmm,' Bella nodded in agreement. When she had swallowed, she continued, 'The second time he had been working out and he showed up in a pair of those tight boxers. And again, we'd made an appointment so it's not like me turning up was a surprise that caught him off guard. Not only was he half naked but he was late too.'

Olivia shook her head. 'He probably thinks you'll love seeing him in a state of undress. Especially seeing as he's a former model. Some women might but you're engaged. What an arrogant arse. Clearly loves himself.'

'Oh yes, and then some.'

'It's not good though, Bells,' Skye insisted. 'If he's really persistent, that's sexual harassment in the workplace and there are laws against that kind of thing.'

Bella felt her face heating. 'Anyway, enough about me, how's wee Freya, Liv? I can't believe she's only four months from being two. And Theo is four flipping months? Where has the time gone?'

Skye reached into her handbag. 'Here, look at his cheeky chubby little face.' She handed over her phone to Bella, of course the camera roll was full of candid snaps of the infant and his dad.

'He looks just like Ben,' Bella said with her hand over her heart. 'Such a cutie.'

'And my little twenty-month-old has quite the temper on her if she doesn't get her own way,' Olivia said. 'Not actually sure where she gets that from! Her favourite word is no.'

Bella laughed. 'Oh, heck, and that's before the terrible twos phase.' She turned to Skye. 'How's the feeding going?' Skye had struggled at first and had almost given up.

She rolled her eyes. 'Better now but he is such a greedy baby. I'm not sure my milk will be enough for him for much longer. We're thinking of switching to formula. We've been discussing it with the health visitor. I felt like a failure when it was first brought up, especially after how much I struggled at the start, but now I know it's a fairly common thing and it's not my fault. Heather, the health visitor, is so lovely and has really put my mind at rest.'

'Hey, you've done amazingly. You made a whole human in your body, don't forget that,' Bella said with a warm smile.

'Do you think you'll try for a family, Bells?' Olivia asked.

Bella dabbed at her mouth with her napkin.

'We've chatted about it, and we both definitely want kids, but I think we're planning on waiting a year or so before we start trying. My interior design business is going really well, and I want to make sure I'm properly established before we add to the family. Bertie will do for now.' She laughed. 'He's a handful as it is.'

'I bet he's a lot less trouble than a stroppy toddler who throws a tantrum when you give her the wrong yoghurt,' Olivia said with a giggle.

'Or a baby who waits until you have his nappy off to pee all over you,' Skye added, laughing.

'No, he has more of a tendency to pee on the floor when he's excited or to run away with my socks,' Bella said, with a chuckle. 'And the other day I couldn't find my left trainer anywhere, I searched in every room and thought I was going mad until Harris found it behind a bush in the garden.' They all joined in her laughter. 'Anyway, I bet neither of you would change your families for the world.'

Olivia smiled. 'I certainly wouldn't. Freya's already got her own personality, that's for sure. And she takes after her grandad Dougie when it comes to her love of mud. She's not afraid to get dirty. He's already said he can't wait to get her out planting trees around the estate like me and Brodie used to.'

'It's funny, you know, I was so house proud and terrified of my lovely home being overrun with baby things but now he's here it doesn't bother me as much as I expected,' Skye said. 'In fact, it's quite nice to see rattles and teddy bears all over the place.'

Bella sighed and smiled. 'Look at us three, all grown-up.'

Skye laughed. 'I know! When did that happen?'

'When we were least expecting it, for sure,' Olivia added.

* * *

Back at Drumblair that evening, Bella decided to head out for a walk down to the loch while Olivia bathed Freya. It was a walk she used to love taking and had missed it since relocating to Skye. She wandered down the gravel path past the stable block apartments that she'd had the honour of completing the interior design on – the job that really helped her to create a name for herself – and on by the trees, inhaling the fresh fragrance of pine. For a moment, she stopped and closed her eyes, listening to the birdsong. She had stood on this very spot so many times she had lost count and still its beauty tugged at her heart. She reached the chapel and walked around the outside, running her hand along the rough dips and striations of the stonework. Soon she would be here again to marry the love of her life. She couldn't wait.

'Oh, hey, Bella. Liv said you were here. How are you?'

Bella turned to see Kerr MacBain walking towards her, closely followed by his four-legged best friend, a bearded collie called Sir Lancelot. Kerr looked good. Fresh faced, clean-shaven and well. 'Hi, Kerr. I'm good, thanks. How are things with you?'

He nodded and smiled. 'Yeah, great. You're looking fantastic,' he said but then held up his hand. 'Not that you didn't before.'

She tucked her hair behind her ear. 'Thanks, you too.' Sir Lancelot sidled over, wagging his tail shyly and Bella bent to greet the dog. 'Hello, fella, it's lovely to see you. My Bertie would love you, yes, he would.'

She felt a little shy around Kerr. He had been her childhood crush, and the first man who had really broken her heart. She could still remember how she felt about him back then, and was grateful that those feelings had subsided following their brief, albeit disastrous, relationship where she publicly witnessed his true colours and the level of cruelty he was capable of. Thank goodness he had finally seen the error of his ways.

'So, what brings you here? You live in Inverness now, don't you?' she asked as she continued to stroke Sir Lancelot.

'Aye,' he said, nodding. 'I do but me and Lancey just stopped in to say hi to you as we were passing on our way to pick my lad up from the nursery. He works there on weekends but I'm off today.' Kerr had taken over the Drumblair plant and tree nursery when he had returned from a stint living on the streets in Glasgow. From what Olivia had said, he'd found his true calling and was making a huge success out of the business.

Bella smiled and shook her head. 'Wow, Kerr, you're a dad. How mad is that?'

Kerr's teenage son had been a shocking discovery when his mother had started working at Drumblair under the guise of needing the job following a divorce, when in fact she was a former one-night stand, trying to sus out Kerr and his suitability to play an active role in his son's life. Kerr hadn't taken the news too well to begin with, understandably when she had waited so long to make it known he was a father; he had missed out on so much of his son's life, oblivious to his existence, but now he was, by all accounts, an incredible father to the son he never knew existed.

Kerr's smile widened and his eyes lit up. 'Aye,

crazy, eh? Will's a star though. I couldn't have asked for a better son. His mother's done a grand job.'

'I'm so glad things have worked out for you,' Bella said.

Kerr smiled but it was tinged with a little sadness. 'Thanks. You'll be next with kids, I bet. Not long 'til the big day, eh?'

Bella's heart skipped as it did every time she thought of her impending nuptials. 'Not long at all.'

'Liv tells me you're here to try on your wedding dress. I bet you look stunning.' Again his smile didn't quite reach his eyes.

'Well, I do love it so that's a start. Your sister is ridiculously talented. Are you still coming to the wedding?'

Kerr stepped closer. 'I wouldn't miss it for the world. You deserve all the happiness coming your way, Bella. Harris is a lucky bloke but I'm sure he knows that.'

Bella felt her face warming. 'Oh, I don't know about that. You'd have to ask him.'

Kerr chuckled. 'Nah, I know he knows. You're a very special person, Arabella Douglas. And I'm so happy for you.'

Bella's eyes began to sting. She had never really seen this genuine side of Kerr and it made her a little sad he hadn't been like this when they were together. He really had changed from the self-centred, cold-hearted cad of a man she once knew. 'Don't, you'll have me bawling my eyes out. It doesn't take much at the moment.' She laughed as she dabbed at her eyes. 'So, any chance of wedding bells on the horizon for you and Charlotte?'

Kerr huffed the air from his lungs and turned to look out across the loch. The sky was a mix of blue, purple and orange as the sun had begun its descent behind them, taking its warmth with it. 'Honestly, I don't know. I think I'm still waiting for the next thing to go wrong. You know, waiting for the other shoe to drop. Don't get me wrong, I'd love for us to be a proper family but I'm still not sure I'm ready for that level of commitment.'

'You don't trust her?' Bella asked.

He shrugged. 'I don't think it's her I don't trust. I... I think it's me.'

'But you're sober now, and you've stopped gambling, haven't you?'

He nodded, still not making eye contact. 'I am and yes, I have. I'm a completely new man.' He gave a laugh. 'I just... I look back on the person I used to be and how I treated people, and I suppose I...' He sighed. 'I don't think I deserve to be happy.'

She reached up and turned his face with her hand, so he looked directly at her. 'Kerr MacBain, that's ridiculous and I think deep down you know it is. You've made amends. People have forgiven you.'

He gazed deep into her eyes, his brow crumpled in what seemed to be regret. 'Have you forgiven me, Bella?'

She nodded and smiled. 'Absolutely. One hundred per cent.'

A wide smile spread across his face and his eyes became glassy. He pulled her into a hug. 'Thank you. I mean that from the bottom of my heart. Thank you, Bella. You've just given me hope. Of all the people I hurt, you're the one who has the most right to hate me. Knowing you don't means the world to me.' He released her from his embrace and cleared his throat. 'Bloody hell. And you think you get emotional easily,' he said with a laugh as he wiped at his eyes.

Bella swiped her own tears away. 'We're a great pair, aren't we?'

He nodded and cleared his throat. 'I know thinking about what could've been is never really helpful, looking back is hard especially when you have so many regrets, but... Well, you know.' She understood his unspoken words, but she'd moved on and was happy with Harris. Kerr knew that, too, and she guessed that's why he left things unsaid.

He held out his elbow. 'Come on, I'll walk you back up to the castle, eh?' Bella linked her arm through his and they set off, leaving the still water behind them.

9

August breezed into September, and it was only a month since she had visited but Bella was excited to be heading back to Drumblair Castle. Bella's mum and dad had finally relocated to Skye, to beautiful Rowan Cottage, and were loving being closer to Bella and Isla. They had even rescued a mongrel called Charlie, a cross between a Staffordshire Bull Terrier and a black Labrador. He was the sweetest, most sensitive dog regardless of his huge head and wide mouth. He was completely black apart from a white patch on his chest that almost looked like he was wearing a tuxedo.

The whitewashed cottage was surrounded by a sage-green painted fence, its entrance door in the centre of the front elevation was the same colour, and the borders of the front garden were full of colourful flowers and evergreen shrubs. A bench made of drift-wood sat under the living room window and was the perfect vantage point to take in the stunning views of the Skye countryside on the shores of Loch na Cairidh, and across to the Isle of Scalpay with its four inhabitants (unlike the other, more bustling island of the same name with its population of 350, which is situated below the Isle of Harris). It was the quin-tessential cottage and Bella's mum and dad were over-joyed with the place. Her dad had already made a start on decorating the interior of the three bed-roomed house to their style and Charlie had been helping Bella's mum with the gardening by digging holes in the flower beds. Both her parents had al-ready decided it was the best move they had ever made.

Before they set off for Drumblair, they dropped Bertie off with Caitlin and Archie and stopped in to check on Bella's brother, Callum, who had come home from Glasgow under the guise of *looking after their parents' house* while their mum and dad had gone away to Inverness for a few days to visit their old friends and neighbours. Bella knew that it really meant he was coming home to eat decent food, seeing as their mum had cooked a load of his favourite meals and left them in the fridge and freezer, and to spend time with Charlie, who he had grown very fond of to the point he was contemplating looking for work on Skye so he could be closer to his new canine friend. He had used the excuse that he was sick of eating pasta and that was all his new flat-mates could cook and that it seemed silly to put Charlie in kennels when he was able to take a few days off work.

With Bella's business going so well, and of course with Harris manning the police station in Glentorrin, they didn't get to visit Drumblair as much as they had done when they first relocated. But Bella had been overjoyed to be back working on designs at Drum-blair and it had been a real labour of love, just like the stable block apartments. She had done much of the work remotely, the mood board had been met with great positivity and the Zoom meetings had all gone well, so she had only visited in person a couple of times; once when the decorators had started, to ensure her plans were being adhered to, and then at the end to see the final result. But the main contractor had kept in regular contact, by video call, throughout the whole process so Bella could keep abreast of the progress while she was working on her other projects.

Seeing her design finally come together had been so incredibly fulfilling; she got to see her work through fresh eyes and those of other people too.

Being back was wonderful. The distillery looked incredible, if Bella did think so herself. Very modern and fresh with the light-coloured wood and use of old brass ships' lights sourced from a reclamation company on the west coast of Scotland. Bella was ridiculously proud of the ambience she had achieved in the reception area, which was bright yet chic, and so welcoming.

Olivia and her Uncle Innes had gushed over the way Bella had used the old fixtures she had sourced with the new design features.

'How you come up with these designs is beyond me, Bella,' Innes had said. 'I love the slim vertical panelling around the curved wall that leads into the working part of the distillery. I would never have thought of doing something like that. But then again, that's why you're the designer and I'm not.' He had chuckled. 'And I'm so impressed that you found light fittings that look like they were designed just for this space.' He'd shaken his head. 'I see awards in your future, young lady. Many awards.'

The Master Blender, Colm Cassidy, had been touched by the use of the old black and white photos of McIver's distillery in Inverness that she'd had framed and displayed on the walls. It had been the place he had worked before and was happy she had made sure to show how the two companies had been merged. And, of course, Olivia's husband Brodie had written a book about the setting up of Drumblair Castle Distillery, and the distilling process, to sell in the shop. He had been heavily involved in the project and had become quite the expert, keeping a photographic diary of the construction.

Bella had spent a lot of time researching the production of whisky too and had visited several other distilleries to witness firsthand how the spaces functioned. Of course, she had been encouraged by each distillery to sample their own drinks and had even become more accustomed to the smoky and spicy flavour of each of the individual amber liquids.

The juxtaposition of old and new had been her main priority when creating a design that would suit Drumblair's new venture, and an earthy colour palette had seemed most fitting. The use of copper and brass to mirror the whisky stills had also been incorporated and added a touch of warmth and depth to the design.

It had been an incredible feeling to see her design featured in the *Inverness Courier* and even more exciting when it had been picked up by *Whisky Monthly*, which was an international online magazine. It had been this that had led to her expanding client list and many more leads, including a rather large private residence – a mansion house on the northern coast of Skye. She had tried to keep her work as close to her home as possible and so far it seemed to be working.

If Bella was really honest with herself, she was relieved to have been able to take time out of the hotel project to attend the launch of the latest Drumblair Castle Distillery beverages. Carlton, her present-day, Texan boss, had begun taking a different approach in his pointless attempts at trying to woo her. Lately he had been bringing her fancy lunches and specially brewed coffee from her favourite coffee shop in Portree. She had tried being nice and she had tried being *not* so nice, she had even dropped an email to the owners, Carlton's parents, requesting that she might deal with them instead. When they enquired as to why, she had to be honest and explain that Carlton was behaving a little too familiar for her liking, but they brushed it off.

'Oh, honey, pay no mind to him,' Mrs Somers had said when she called to 'put Bella's mind at rest'. 'My boy is just a real character, and people can sometimes misunderstand his intentions. It's his sense of humour, but he's as harmless as they come, I swear. I wouldn't have let him near you if I thought otherwise, even if he is my flesh and blood. He loves an attractive woman; you should take it as a compliment. He's a model, you know. Women usually tend to fall at his feet, or in some cases they can even take advantage of his looks and his good heart,' were some of the things Bella was told. And, 'You know what boys can be like. It's just his way of letting you know he's attracted to you. Some people just don't know how to take him. He knows you're engaged; it's just a little harmless fun is all. But leave it with me and I'll talk to him. He doesn't realise that the Brits have a... erm... *different* sense of humour. Just don't be too hard on him, honey. He's going through a lot just now.'

Even though his mother's opinion and comments were a tad disturbing really, coming from another woman, after that call Bella was left thinking she might be taking things a little too seriously. And in spite of the niggle to the contrary that she couldn't seem to shake, she ended up feeling as if she was being ridiculous and overreacting. And she wondered what it was that he was going through, because it didn't show outwardly. She doubted that being an arrogant arse was a coping mechanism.

But the truth was, nothing she did to deter him was working and it was preying on her mind. The only thing she hadn't done was tell Harris anything other than he was American and a tad difficult at the start of the project, even though they had promised to keep no more secrets from one another. And that just added to her anxiety. She didn't want him to think she couldn't handle herself. She was no damsel in distress and wouldn't let herself be forced into getting a man to sort out her problems for her. So, being at Drumblair was a *very* welcome escape.

* * *

Since the distillery had been up and running, the shelves of the castle gift shop had been stocked with their signature gin but today was all about the launch of the new blended whisky that had been produced using single malt from McIver's casks and malts sourced from various places around Scotland. It had been named the 'Lady MacBain Blend' after Olivia's mother, and the bottle's label featured a stunning, specially commissioned painting of the very much missed late custodian of the castle with Drumblair in the background. This had been created by Reid Mac-Kinnon, Bella's artist friend from Skye whose paintings she had originally sourced for the apartment design she had completed at the castle.

Lady Olivia MacLeod took to the small, raised platform in front of the curved wall and the press photographers sprang into action. Bella caught sight of Brodie off to the side, with Freya in his arms, and Olivia's Uncle Innes standing beside him, both men looking on in adoration.

Olivia wore tailored trousers in the MacBain tartan and a soft, pale blue cashmere sweater. She looked every bit the lady she was, classy and sophisticated. 'Good afternoon, everyone. Welcome to Drumblair Castle Distillery on this very auspicious occasion. As most of you will no doubt be aware, a whisky must legally be allowed to mature for a minimum of three years in its oak cask for it to be classed as single malt, hence our delicious gin being for sale first. We're an impatient bunch here at Drumblair, however, and so something had to be done about this one small matter.' A rumble of chuckles travelled the room. 'So, we set about researching the possibility of a blended drink, and after months of trial and error, that I have to say were quite fun in their own right,' more low laughter, 'we are here and so excited for today's launch of our very first blend which is now bottled and ready for your delectation. So many people have been involved in bringing this wonderful drink to you but at the forefront, aside from the very important job of the tasters, I'm looking at you, Uncle Innes and Brodie,' another rumble of laughter swept through those gathered and Innes and Brodie doffed invisible caps as they joined in the chuckles, 'the main person we need to thank is Mr Colm Cassidy. Although born in Ireland, Colm was a long-serving fixture at McIver's in Inverness for many years. When Mr McIver decided to call time on his business, we took on the casks and the staff from the distillery, and we were so grateful that Colm accepted the position as Distillery Manager. But we were even more delighted that he agreed to be our new Master Blender and brought his many years of experience to the role to help create the smooth, earthy, warming drink we are launching today. And I have to say it's just the perfect thing for a chilly autumn day such as this.'

Bella's phone began to ring and vibrate in her handbag and many heads turned her way. Her cheeks heated as she mouthed her apologies and reached into her bag to fumble around until she was able to flick the sound-off switch on the side of the handset.

Olivia continued, 'I have fond memories of whisky being consumed here at Drumblair, at parties and clan gatherings, and it warms my heart to know that we are now producing a drink that was a firm favourite of my father, one which I know deep down would make him incredibly proud—'

After only a few seconds, Bella's phone rang again, and she huffed as she took it out of her bag and tiptoed to the back of the room as Olivia continued speaking. She glanced at the screen and concern gripped her insides. Dorothy Lyndhurst's name flashed up on the screen. Bella was down as next of kin for her granny seeing as she lived closer than her parents, so why would the manager of the residential complex where Granny Isla lived be calling her unless it was serious? A shiver of dread shuddered down her spine, and she immediately opened the door and stepped outside.

The autumn sunshine had appeared deceptively warm from the interior of the distillery and Bella regretted taking off her jacket and hanging it in the cloak room, as, stepping through the door, the chilled air hit her skin and made goosebumps appear. Although it could have been the physical manifestation of dread at answering the incoming call. Her biggest fear was of that one inevitable yet horrifying call, to say her granny had passed away. Although spritely for her age, Isla was in her late eighties and Dorothy didn't usually make a habit of calling Bella.

'Dorothy? Is everything okay? Is my granny okay?' She failed miserably in her attempt to not panic.

'Erm... I don't know how to say this, Bella, but... she's... she's *gone*?' The distinct question in Dorothy's voice was a bizarre addition. Either she was or she wasn't, surely?

Bella's stomach plummeted and she felt the colour rapidly drain from her face towards her feet as her heart tripped over itself. 'What? No!' she cried out, leaning on the wall to steady herself as she felt her surroundings spinning and the ground falling away from her feet. Her insides knotted and she thought for a moment she might throw up. 'She can't be. She was fine when we left the day before yesterday, and she was fine when I spoke to her yesterday morning.' Her voice wobbled and her eyes welled with tears that clouded her vision and made the sunlight seem unbearable. What would she do without her? This couldn't be happening. Not to Granny Isla. Not now.

'No, Bella, I mean... not *gone* gone but... just *gone*. I... I take it she's not with you then?'

Bella was sure she should probably feel somewhat relieved but the concept of Isla actually being *missing* bothered her almost as much as the thought that she had passed away. 'No, she's not *with* me. What are you saying, Dorothy?'

Dorothy cleared her throat. 'Erm... she went out with Maeve yesterday, perhaps just after you had spoken to her. I saw them as they were heading to catch the bus to Portree, like they do regularly, so I thought nothing of it, and I presumed she'd arrived home later, and that I'd simply missed her, but when I did my rounds this morning she wasn't there.'

Bella's shoulders relaxed. 'Oh, I see, they've probably gone out again today. She's an early riser. What's the weather like there? It's dry and bright here so perhaps she's making the most of the sunshine while it lasts. She's probably taken Beau for a wee walk.'

'I wondered that too but...' Dorothy fell silent.

Bella's heart rate picked up, tripping over itself again. 'But what, Dorothy?'

'The thing is, Beau is with her neighbour Flora. But Flora can't remember why she has the dog or where Isla said she was going.'

'I'm sorry, what? That can't be right. Flora must know something. And Granny takes Beau everywhere with her.'

Dorothy continued, 'I should also mention that I, erm, checked the CCTV earlier and they never actually returned home yesterday. Bless her, Isla wouldn't know this, but Flora has recently been diagnosed with the onset of dementia and can't remember much recent stuff, but ask her to sing the Welsh national anthem, *in Welsh*, and—'

'Wait, hang on a minute. *They*? So, you're saying Maeve is missing too?' Her stomach took a dive once again as she turned and peered through the glass of the door to where her handsome fiancé was standing with his back to her. The pale blue linen of his shirt stretched across his muscular back as he listened to Olivia without a care in the world. He would be so worried when he found out his mum was missing along with her granny. But they couldn't drive back because they'd been sampling the gin and had had wine with lunch.

'Oh, sorry, yes, I'm afraid so,' Dorothy almost whispered.

Bella's heart pounded so hard she could almost hear it. 'Oh God, Dorothy, why are you only finding out *now* that they're missing? They could've been lying in a ditch all bloody night in the cold.'

'Bella, I understand you're upset but with the greatest of respect I'd like to remind you that this is a residential complex, not a high-security prison. The residents are allowed to come and go as they please. We don't keep them locked down like inmates.'

Bella knew she was right but the anger she felt gripped her insides so tightly she couldn't seem to unravel them. 'I know that, I do, I'm sorry, Dorothy, but I'm really worried now. Ooh, have you asked Tam? Maybe he knows where they were going.'

Dorothy sighed. 'I'm afraid Tam went to stay with his daughter on the day you left for Inverness, so it's unlikely he would know anything. Oh... just hang on a second, the other line's ringing.'

'Dorothy, please don't put me on h—' The line fell silent. Bella growled and stamped her foot before dragging her hand back through her shoulder-length hair. She paced for a few moments and then stopped and peered in through the glass again, waving her hand at the middle-aged man who was standing be-side Harris to get his attention. The man waved back with a crumple of confusion to his expression. She huffed and gestured again but this time by pointing her index finger in a jabbing motion at Harris. The man seemed totally baffled by what she was asking, and he contorted his face as he shrugged his shoul-ders. Eventually, after more of Bella's aggressive ges-ticulations, his eyes widened in realisation, and he tapped Harris on the shoulder. The man said some-thing to Harris, and he finally turned around to look

in Bella's direction, so she beckoned hurriedly for
him to come outside.

He opened the glass door and stepped through
the small gap. 'What is it? What's wrong?'

Bella, shivering now, sighed, wondering how on
earth she could tell him. Blunt and direct was best,
she decided. He was a policeman. It's what he was
used to. 'We have two absconded octogenarians on
our hands, Harris.'

He chuckled. 'Eh? What are you on about?'

'My granny and your mum—'

The line clicked. 'Erm... Bella...' The hesitation in
Dorothy's voice wasn't lost on Bella. 'I'm so sorry to
tell you this but... Tam isn't at his daughter's after all.'

Bella closed her eyes and shook her head. This
couldn't be happening. She opened them and looked
into her fiancé's concerned gaze. 'Make that three.'

10

'Please call me and keep me updated, won't you?' Olivia said as she clung tightly to Bella. 'I really want to come with you, Bells. I can't stay here and—'

'Hey, of course you can stay here,' Bella said. 'You have the launch going on and important people here. You can't leave now, Liv, you've worked towards this day for so long.'

'But you and Isla are far more important to me than they are,' Olivia insisted, a crease of worry indented her forehead. 'You're family to me.'

Bella pulled back from the embrace and fixed her determined gaze on her best friend. 'Please, Olivia, stay here and enjoy your launch. You've worked so hard to get to this point and I won't spoil it. My granny wouldn't want that either. I promise I'll call you with any developments.'

Olivia nodded, albeit with evident reluctance. She sighed. 'Do you want me to contact your mum and dad?'

Bella shook her head. 'No, they're away for a few days and I'd rather not worry them until I know what's going on.'

'I really hope they're all okay.'

Bella nodded and forced a smile. 'They will be. They've maybe got lost and don't have a phone charger or something equally as simple and silly. And Tam can't be in the same place as Maeve and Granny Isla because he left a day earlier so I'm sure his family are dealing with his absence. One less thing to worry about at least.' She tried to believe her own words and hoped desperately that she was right, even though her knotted stomach protested vehemently.

Newly promoted Sergeant Mel Sherburn, one of Harris's former colleagues from the Inverness Police Station, was waiting in the driver's seat of a police car as Bella and Harris said goodbye to their hosts. Harris hugged Olivia and shook hands with Brodie and then he and Bella climbed into the waiting vehicle. Bella tried her best to keep her composure as they pulled away along the long driveway of Drumblair Castle, but her heart pounded, and her jaw clenched almost involuntarily. She twisted in her seat to watch the stone structure and her best friend receding into the distance. The cornflower-blue sky that formed a backdrop to the building brought back memories of happy times playing hide and seek in the castle grounds. The castle had always been special to Bella and working with Olivia to bring it to the public had been such a privilege. It was always a pleasure to visit and always so sad to leave but today was extra painful.

* * *

Earlier that morning, before the launch event, Bella had awoken in one of the beautiful castle suites with Harris beside her. They had made love in an antique four-poster bed and had eaten a leisurely breakfast delivered to their room by Cecily, Mirren the housekeeper's new assistant. After breakfast, they had been taking advantage of uncharacteristically warm autumn weather, walking down by the loch with Olivia and Brodie and had called in at the little chapel on the shore.

'Just think, Bells, you and Harris will be walking

down this very aisle in a few months' time,' Olivia had said, squeezing Bella's hand. 'Imagine this, there'll be fresh flowers all across this back wall. Even though you're having a winter wedding we'll make sure the air is filled with wonderful fragrance. And I thought fairy lights and candles too. The violinist will play you in, unless you want a particular Spotify playlist, we have enhanced Wi-Fi down here now, so we could do that if you've changed your mind, it's an easy amendment. All the pews will have flowers at the ends, and I've arranged some lovely framed photos of the two of you to go on the ledges in between the candles. Oh, and of course, there'll be a gorgeous Christmas tree from the nursery, I've already spoken to Kerr, and it's ordered as priority. What do you think?'

Bella had sighed in contentment as she imagined the beautiful chapel all decked out. 'Sounds amazing. And so romantic. I still can't believe it's happening. I'm getting married at Christmas, Liv!' Both women had squealed and jumped up and down on the spot like the giddy schoolgirls they had once been, Bella's heart had skipped, and her stomach had rolled over with excitement. Their respective partners had looked on, laughing and shaking their heads.

Once their silliness had subsided, Olivia had said, 'He foxed us all by *not* proposing on Valentine's Day last year as we'd all predicted, we'd all been wagering on it, but I love that he chose Christmas morning. So romantic.'

'Who, me?' Harris had said as he'd arrived beside them and slipped his arm around Bella's shoulders.

'You've done it now, mate,' Brodie had said with a chuckle. 'You've a reputation to uphold as Mr Romance.' He'd nudged Harris with his shoulder. 'Think of how you're going to have to *one-up* yourself every year.'

Harris had kissed Bella's head and said, 'Aye, well, there's worse jobs. Seriously though, thank you again for letting us have the wedding here. It'll be great.'

Olivia had beamed. 'It's our pleasure. You're like family to us and it's always been Bella's dream to get married here, so I'm excited to help that dream come true.' She'd turned to Bella. 'You're going to be the most stunning bride.'

'I second that,' Harris had said.

'And I'm so happy you've allowed me to design your dress. Harris, you're in for a real treat and that's all I'm saying.'

Olivia's designs were stunning, and Bella couldn't

quite believe her luck to have had her working on the most important outfit of her life so far. Bella had hugged her. 'Who else would I trust to do such a significant thing?'

* * *

How wonderful things had felt only hours earlier. But now she was facing the prospect of Granny Isla being injured or lost. How could she think about getting married without her maid of honour? And how could she be happy until she knew her granny's fate?

Back in the present, Bella turned to face the front of the car and cleared her throat, trying to shake off the sadness that had descended over her. 'Thank you so much for taking us back to Skye, Mel. I'm so sorry we've had to rope you into this,' Bella said to Sergeant Sherburn, who was in her civvies, and her long, wavy dark hair, usually tied in a neat chignon or bun, was today loose around her shoulders as she drove the police car. 'We really could've got a taxi. I hate that we've interrupted your day off.'

'Aw, *dun't* worry, love. It's fine. I won't hear of you getting a cab when I can take you. *Owt* for good mates,' she replied in her broad Yorkshire accent. 'And anyway, I'd rather this than have to arrest yer for driving over't limit.' She winked at her in the rearview mirror.

Bella smiled briefly. 'I just feel bad for taking advantage of the police car. It's not exactly ethical.' She cringed as she gripped the leather of the seat. It was her first time in the back of a squad car that she could recall, and she was surprised at how clean it smelled.

Mel shrugged. 'Well, technically it's a missing persons case, and Isla and Maeve both have links to Inverness. Honestly, it's *reyt*. Neil's got my car up on't ramp. Summat wrong wi't exhaust this time, or I'd have brought that old heap. I reckon it might be time to get shut of it.'

Harris chuckled. 'Hey, that's no way to talk about my best buddy. Getting rid of him's a bit harsh, don't you think?' He was evidently trying to alleviate the stress of the situation.

Neil, Mel's husband, was a close friend of Harris's and a mechanic who owned a vehicle repair shop in Inverness. He had, in fact, been responsible for saving Bella's prized Citroën, Fifi.

Mel laughed. 'As if I could even think *abart* it. He's something I *can't* get shut of.' She laughed. 'Anyway, have you tried to phone Isla again? Or Maeve?'

Bella sighed. 'Yes, I've rung both mobiles but they're going to voicemail. I've left half a dozen messages but no reply so far. I'm so worried. And I feel really bad about not telling my mum and dad what's going on. What if something awful's happened and I haven't made them aware?' Her chin trembled and she closed her eyes briefly as she tried to stop the threatening tears from escaping.

Harris reached around and rubbed her leg as it was all he could touch from his position in the front passenger seat. 'It's best not to worry them until we know the facts, Bells, sweetheart. My team on Skye are out looking, and they'll call me if they hear anything.'

Bella couldn't settle in spite of his attempts to ease her mind. She watched as the trees and their shedding leaves of russet and orange whizzed by her window at speed and once they reached a clearer patch of road, she stared off into the purple-hued mountains in the distance, their tops circled by fluffy crowns of white cloud, and tried not to imagine her granny and her best friends out there somewhere, injured or in difficulty. 'Dorothy rang around the hospitals and medical centres earlier but... nothing,' she said, thinking out loud.

Mel replied, 'That's summat though, eh? Better than finding them *in* there.' She was right... to a point. Because Bella still had visions of them in a ditch, or lost, or worse. Had they been kidnapped? Although who would kidnap two elderly women? That's if Tam's disappearance *wasn't* connected. Although did coincidences like this happen with old folks? She doubted it really. And the more she thought about it, the more worried she was that the three of them had come to harm. Perhaps all three of them were being held somewhere. What if someone mistakenly presumed they were wealthy? Although there had been no ransom demands like you saw on TV crime shows. Was there a sick and twisted serial killer out there targeting old folks? Had they been conned into getting into a car with strangers? But for what purpose? Had they been convinced to clear out their life savings accounts and then dumped somewhere? She clenched her jaw. *Oh, for Pete's sake, stop it, Bella, they're in their bloody eighties, none of them is five, nor stupid for that matter.* She clenched her jaw and rolled her eyes at her inner, chastising dialogue.

'We'll get to the bottom of this, Bells, I promise,' Harris said, contorting in his seat to turn to face her. 'They can't have gone far.' His eyes were kind and soft; regardless of the worry he must've been feeling, he was clearly trying his absolute best to ease hers. Under normal circumstances he was a calming presence to her. But on this occasion Bella's head was so full of dread and guilt that even his positivity was struggling to make it into her mind. She chewed at the skin around her thumb until it was sore and took out her mobile again. She hit dial on Granny Isla's number. But once again it went straight to voicemail.

'Do I speak now? What do I say again, hen? Oh... right. Hello, this is Hisla Mae Douglas.' Her granny's mock-posh accent was usually amusing but today it simply made tears well in Bella's eyes. *'One can't come to the telephone right now has hi ham terribly busy. But please do leave one a message and one will return your call hat one's hearliest convenience, thank you muchly.'* Bella remembered the day she tutored her granny on how to record that very message. It had taken several attempts, with many of them ending in giggles. Since that day it had lightened her heart every time she had heard it, that was until the events of today. Now it made her insides churn as she pictured her lovely granny's beautiful beaming smile, her face framed by her purple and silver hair. What she wouldn't give to hug her again. Bella's heart ached and she placed her hand on her chest and closed her eyes.

The beep sounded and once again Bella left the same message as before. 'Granny, it's me, *please* just call me back, okay? I'm so worried about you and Maeve. And apparently Tam is missing, too, so it would be good to know if he's with you or not. I've left a few messages now and it's scaring me that you're not calling me back. I understand if you wanted a wee break, Granny, but just let me know you're okay. Please?' Her voice and chin trembled simultaneously as she hit the end-call button and closed her eyes, allowing tears to silently spill over.

* * *

Eventually, at around 3 p.m., they crossed the Skye Bridge and arrived in the small village of Glentorrin. Bella saw that a crowd of their neighbours and friends were waiting in the car park of the police station, and this caused more tears to come. Harris must have messaged to say they would be home soon, and their friends had rallied.

Bella, Harris and Mel climbed out of the police car and Bella spotted wee Bertie, her one-year-old golden retriever, straining at his lead to get to her. Caitlin the baker, who had been looking after him while they were at Drumblair, let him go and Bella crouched down to greet him. He jumped up and licked her face while emitting high-pitched squeaks. She inhaled the scent of his fur and buried her face in his neck.

'I've missed you, boy,' she told him as more tears trickled down her face and he squirmed to lick them away. She glanced up then. All her friends from the village were there; Caitlin, of course, Jules, the owner of the Lifeboat House Museum, Jules's best friend and sister-in-law, Millie, Morag, the grocery shop owner and Ruby, the Hollywood actress turned dance teacher. Their husbands had nicknamed them the *Sozzled Six* on account of all their girls' nights including lots of prosecco, and the women hadn't argued.

Bella stood as Harris took Bertie's lead and she was enveloped in a group hug.

'We'll find her, Bells,' Jules said, fixing a stern, determined gaze on her.

Bella couldn't speak, instead she just nodded.

'Right, folks,' Harris's voice bellowed. 'We need someone to head up to Pabay with Bella and Mel to look around there and Broadford. But can anyone maybe come with me to go around Portree? Kenna, my secretary, has printed off some photos we can take to show around. I just need to go in and grab them from her.'

Mitch, Ruby's husband, said, 'Aye, me and Reid could go there, eh, Reid?'

Reid, Jules's husband, nodded. 'Absolutely. Archie can come too maybe?'

Caitlin's husband stepped forward. 'Of course. Anything I can do to help is good with me.'

'Caitlin, Jules and I can help at Pabay too,' Millie added.

'Me and Morag can tackle the transport companies,' Ruby added.

'The thing is, I'm just not sure I want to leave Bertie on his own,' Bella said.

Jules smiled. 'We can leave Bertie with Evin and Chewie at our house.' Jules and Reid's son, Evin, was a responsible boy and his Hungarian Vizsla Chewie, aptly named after the *Star Wars* character to whom he bore a striking resemblance, were regular visitors to play in the garden at Bella's house since the arrival of the puppy.

Once again, Bella was overwhelmed with emotion. 'Thank you all so, so much. We're so lucky to have such a wonderful community and great friends around us.'

Archie made his way over to Bella. 'I remember when my wee Sophie went missing for a while, if it hadn't been for this lot I don't know what I would've done.' Bella had heard from Caitlin the story of that terrible incident when Archie's young daughter had tried to run away and how the village had rallied around him too. 'But we look after our own, Bella,' he said. 'And you're one of us now.'

His wife Caitlin nudged him. 'That doesn't sound at all creepy and ominous, love.' A light rumble of laughter reverberated around the group and Bella allowed herself to join in for a moment.

11

Mel parked the police car outside the residential complex and the five women climbed out.

'I'll just go in and speak to Dorothy to see if there have been any developments,' Bella said.

Mel nodded and reached out to touch her arm. 'If you give us the spare keys, me and't lasses can go an' have look at her flat. See if there's owt that looks outta place.'

Bella reached into her bag and handed the spare set of keys over. 'Thanks, Mel. I'll meet you there shortly.'

'Come on, I'll go see Dorothy with you,' Jules said, linking arms with Bella.

As the other three women headed towards the

units, Bella and Jules stepped in through the double doors and headed straight for the reception desk where Dorothy sat speaking to someone on the phone. Her usually immaculately made-up face was pale and makeup free today, and worry was evident in the dark circles around her eyes.

'Thank you. Please call if you hear anything,' Dorothy said into the handset. 'Isla's granddaughter has just walked in, so I'd better go.' She hung up the phone and stood. 'Bella, how are you?'

'Not great, Dorothy, to be honest. Anything to report?'

Dorothy shook her head. 'Not as yet. I've called all the shops on the main street at Broadway but no one has seen them. I'm so sorry about this. It's never happened before.'

There was that sinking feeling in Bella's stomach again, like she had gone over a steep bump in the road and was on a rapid descent. 'And I've never known my granny to just go off without telling anyone. She knows how worried and cross I'd be. It's just not like her and that's why I'm so terrified. But for *three* of them to be missing... It seems so weird and very suspicious.'

Dorothy nodded and a crease formed between her eyebrows. 'I know. Tam's disappearance may not be connected as Maeve and Isla went out together the day after he left but even so... We've informed the police, but it seems Harris had already instigated a search, which is understandable, of course. But please let me know if I can do anything else to help.'

Bella nodded. 'Thanks. My police sergeant friend has gone around to her unit to have a look around and then we're heading out to chat to people and see if anyone knows anything, or might have seen anything.'

Dorothy nodded and her chin trembled. 'I feel so terrible about this, Bella. I hope they're all okay. I will *never* forgive myself if anything has happened. I'm already considering handing in my resignation.'

Bella stepped closer. 'No, Dorothy, please don't do that. This isn't your fault. Like you said, you don't run a prison camp. I'm sorry for my attitude on the phone, it was uncalled for. I've just been beside myself with worry, but I shouldn't have taken it out on you.'

Dorothy reached for a tissue from a flowery pink box on the desk and dabbed at her eyes. 'Well, thank you, but I still feel awful.'

Bella smiled. 'There's really no need, honestly. Look, I'll keep you posted with any developments, okay? And you do the same if you hear anything else.'

Dorothy's face contorted, guilt and anguish evident in her features as she nodded. Bella turned and left the reception area, stepping outside where the weather had taken a turn now, and dark clouds were rolling in from the direction of the sea. The grey vista matched her mood; the ominous clouds a visual representation of the turmoil she felt inside.

The two friends walked across to Isla's apartment where they met Mel in the living room. 'Does your granny keep a diary?' she asked.

'She has a pocket one that she keeps in her handbag with her appointments in but I'm guessing she has that with her,' Bella replied with a despondent sigh.

The little apartment was tidy and smelled of the usual pot pourri that was kept in a bowl on the coffee table. She smiled as she remembered Beau, her granny's beagle, finding out the hard way that it wasn't a bowl of crisps. These days you only have to lift the bowl, and he runs and hides as if he fears you'll try and feed it to him. Daft wee thing.

There was a knock on the door and Bella answered it to find Flora from next door standing there with Beau sitting patiently beside her.

As soon as he saw Bella, he began to jump around

and bark excitedly, so she crouched down and hugged him as he wiggled in her arms.

Flora let go of his lead. 'Hello, dearie. I saw that you were here and thought you might like to keep wee Beau. I think it's what your granny would've wanted.' She dabbed at her eyes with a pristine white cotton hanky.

Bella tried to remain calm and not burst into more tears, but she peered up at the neatly presented old lady and her voice came out strained and a little sharp. 'Thanks, Flora, but she's not dead. She's just... away.'

After a brief moment where her brow crumpled and her mouth pursed in evident confusion, Flora waved a dismissive hand. 'Oh, aye, of course, hen. I'm sure she'll be back home very soon... But if she *isnae*, maybe you should take wee Beau anyway. He's pining for Isla, bless his heart.'

'Have you any idea where they might have gone, Flora? Or anything that might be significant?' Bella asked eagerly, hoping that something might have come back to her.

Flora shook her head. 'My memory's not what it was and I'm afraid all I can remember is Isla coming to ask if I'd watch Beau while she went... somewhere. Och, I'm sorry, hen. I just *cannae* remember.'

Bella nodded. 'That's okay. Thanks anyway. But if you do remember anything, no matter how insignificant it may seem, please tell Dorothy, okay?'

'Aye, hen. I will do. I'd best be off anyway; I need to let Beau out.'

Unsure how to handle the situation, Bella stood and smiled. 'It's okay, Flora, I have Beau now, so I'll take him with me.'

Flora shook her head. 'Och, yes, of course, dearie. Silly me. Well, bye just now. I'll be thinking of you. I was so sad to hear about your granny's passing.' She placed a hand over her heart and sighed. 'She was a good friend to me.'

Bella smiled as sadness washed over her, but she chose not to correct Flora again. She decided it would only add to the poor woman's confusion. 'Thank you, bye just now.'

Flora raised her hand and turned to walk away towards her own unit.

* * *

During the search they informed Callum of what was going on, and in spite of his protests and requests to be picked up so he could help, Bella asked him to stay by the phone in case Isla made contact. He reluctantly agreed but made his sister promise to call if anything happened. Around a couple of hours later, the search groups reconvened at the Coxswain pub in Glentorrin after a fruitless afternoon. Harris and Bella walked Mel to her car and there was a real nip to the air which made Bella even more worried as the awful images of ditches and lost old ladies replayed in her mind. They both thanked Mel for what felt like the hundredth time.

'Dun't be daft. Like a said, *owt* for good mates. Keep us posted, yeah?'

Bella nodded and hugged her tightly. 'We will. Drive safe and message when you get back, so we know you're home.'

Harris hugged her next. 'Give my best mate a hug from me too, eh?'

'Aye, I will. See you later. And don't give up hope. She's out there somewhere. She's a feisty old bird is Isla.' Mel climbed into the police car and drove away.

Bella's heart had sunk so many times during the day that she felt it was, metaphorically speaking, in her shoes right now. It had been such a long day, and she was completely drained physically but mentally her mind would not shut up. Constant unwanted images barraged her frontal cortex like a horror movie she was being forced to watch on repeat. She had refused many offers of alcohol to 'calm her nerves', feeling it was better to keep her wits about her, just in case.

Reid and Jules appeared in front of her where she sat with Harris at a small table by the unlit fire. Beau and Bertie were curled up together at her feet.

'We have news,' Jules said.

Bella's head sprang up, almost causing whiplash in the process, such was her desperation. 'Really? What? Has someone found them?'

Jules cringed. 'Oh, sorry, lovely, not that kind of news.'

Reid said, 'No, it's just that I've been speaking to my brother, Kendric. He's a TV presenter on the mainland and he wants to come and interview you in the morning, a sort of TV appeal that will go out all over Scotland. He thinks that it could really help the search and if they're watching, it will spur them to get in touch.'

Bella's eyes widened. 'Oh... I see. But... hasn't he got other stories to be covering? I mean it's not really a national emergency, is it?' Her tone was genuinely questioning as she really feared that perhaps it *was* now an incident of general interest. After all, if someone was out there taking advantage of old people it needed to be highlighted and stopped.

Reid's eyebrows raised and he shook his head as he told them, 'No, he says this is an important local story to cover so we may as well take advantage of it. He'll come here with his crew, no need for you to go anywhere. He'll interview you at home or at the station early on, around nine, then it can go on TV at lunchtime if there's still no news. Whatever you feel comfortable with. I just need to call him back ASAP to confirm.'

Bella turned to Harris. 'What do you think? It's your mum too.'

Harris clenched his jaw and gripped her hand. 'I think we take all the help we can get. They may be spritely for their age and rather cocky but they're still vulnerable, Bells.'

She nodded but then widened her eyes as an awful thought sprang to mind. 'Shit, I'll have to tell my mum and dad first. I can't have them finding out on TV. They would never forgive me. I'll have a lot of explaining to do because they think I'm looking out for her over here. They're already going to be so upset that I'm doing such a crap job of that.' Bella let out a sob and covered her face with her free hand. 'They still may never forgive me.'

Harris pulled her close. 'Hey, stop that. Isla's her own person and your dad knows how bloody stubborn she can be. I know the same about my mum too. Let's go home and video call your folks, eh?'

Bella nodded and wiped her face on a hanky that Jules passed her. 'Please tell Kendric we'd be grateful for the help. And that nine in the morning would be good.'

Harris helped her to her feet and after hugs from their friends they made the short walk across the village to the bothy police station with Beau and Bertie trotting happily alongside them, blissfully unaware of what was going on.

* * *

'What do you mean *missing*?' Bella's dad asked, scratching at his chin where stubble was visible. Bella had watched as the colour had drained from his face and guilt racked her insides.

'She went out with Maeve yesterday and didn't come back. I'm so sorry, Dad. I'm supposed to be keeping an eye on her.' Tears traced damp trails down her face, and she didn't bother to wipe them away.

'Hey, love, come on, it's not your fault. You're not her keeper. I just can't think why she would've done such a thing. It's so out of character. Where were you when you found out?'

'We were over at the whisky blend launch at Drumblair when Dorothy rang. I didn't want to worry you sooner in case it was a false alarm but we're doing an appeal on TV tomorrow, so of course I had to call you.'

'An appeal? Bloody hell, it's that serious?' her mum asked, covering her heart with a hand.

Bella shrugged and she ripped at the tissue she held. 'I honestly don't know but it feels like it at the moment. I've tried calling her and Harris has tried calling Maeve. We're just so worried.'

'Right, we're coming back over. We'll be there around eleven tonight if that's okay with you?'

Harris pulled Bella into his side as she sobbed and kissed her head. 'Of course it's okay. Callum is waiting by the phone at your house just in case so we'll let him know you'll be home early. But please, take it steady, okay? Don't rush. We'll no doubt be up.'

Bella's dad nodded. 'Aye, lad, we will. Bella, darlin', try and get some rest, eh? You look exhausted.'

She couldn't reply verbally so nodded and forced a smile through her tears. Harris hit the end-call button and pulled Bella into his lap. 'Come on, sweetheart, you have to stop blaming yourself. They're adults who make their own decisions. You can't parent an eighty-seven-year-old.'

* * *

Later that night, Bella's mum and dad stopped in on their way home. They hugged and chatted briefly – her dad once again trying to reassure her that none of this was her fault – before they continued their journey, doubtful that they would sleep even though exhausted from a combination of worry, travel and heartache. Callum had been in regular contact but had heard nothing back at his parents' house and when Bella insisted he get some sleep he promised to try but again asked them to update him if anything changed, regardless of the hour. He was understandably upset but Bella thanked him for staying by the phone.

All Bella wanted was to sleep and wake up to find the whole thing had been a nightmare. But sleep was erratic and when it did come was filled with nightmares that woke her sweating and crying out.

She eventually gave up on sleep and instead lay there remembering some of the fun times she had spent with her purple-haired, young-at-heart grandmother. And there were many memories to think about.

One particular memory that stood out was the time they had been in the car and Lewis Capaldi had begun to play on the radio. Bella had been impressed that Isla knew who he was but what had made her giggle uncontrollably was that Isla thought the actor Peter Capaldi had adopted Lewis and had been quite disappointed when she had discovered they were not related. Now every time she heard Lewis Capaldi she couldn't help but smile.

12

Bella made her way downstairs at seven in the morning while Harris was still asleep. She put the kettle on and opened the back door to let Beau and Bertie out. A blast of cold air entered the room as the dogs exited, and she wrapped her cardigan tighter around herself. Once the water had boiled, she stood at the window with a mug of steaming coffee, watching as Bertie and Beau chased each other around the garden at speed, unaware that Bella felt like her life was falling apart. The dogs didn't care about the drop in temperature, their thick furry coats kept it at bay as they frolicked around, barking, their ears and tails flapping wildly and tongues lolling out.

The sky overhead was overcast and grey, in fact, it

hadn't really got light since the evening before. And although it was autumn anyway, Bella couldn't help feeling the sun was missing Isla too and instead of putting *his hat on*, as the old song said, he had pulled the duvet over his head and decided to stay put.

She put on the radio to distract herself but after 'All By Myself' by Eric Carmen, 'Ain't No Sunshine When She's Gone' by Bill Withers, and 'Nothing Compares 2 U' by Sinead O'Connor had been the Radio Highland DJ's particular choices, she turned it off with a huff. It was as if he was conspiring against her to make her cry again.

Eventually Harris joined her, his hair damp from showering, and slipped his arms around her waist, resting his chin on her shoulder as he held her tightly. 'They adore each other, those two mad dugs,' he said with a chuckle.

'They do. It's a good thing when you consider...' Bella closed her eyes firmly, willing the threatening tears away.

'Hey,' Harris said as he turned her around in his arms and removed the mug from her hand to place it on the countertop. He pulled her close. 'We're not thinking like that. Beau will be going home to your granny soon enough. I just know it.'

Bella clenched her jaw and opened her eyes.

Speaking through gritted teeth, she said, 'You can't know that though, Harris. None of us can. How can you be so certain that things will be fine? How can you stand there acting so calmly?'

For a moment, he almost let his mask slip and Bella watched the infinitesimal shake of his head as he fought himself and whatever emotions he was pushing down. 'Because we're getting married on Christmas Eve and I can't imagine that happening without them both being there, Bella.' His voice broke and he immediately cleared his throat. 'They *will* be home. I have to cling to that with every ounce of my being because the alternative isn't— I just can't go there.' He forced a smile. 'Now why don't you go and shower, eh? Kendric and the TV folks will be here soon.'

She nodded and tiptoed up to kiss him tenderly, cupping his face in her palms. 'I love you so very much.' She turned and headed for the stairs.

After showering and drinking copious amounts of coffee, they were all sitting in the lounge waiting. Bella had talked to her parents about them being a part of the interview, but they insisted she and Harris were the best people for that particular job. They decided to head up to see Dorothy at Pabay View to see if there had been any further developments, and perhaps to have a look around the area themselves. Not that they felt things had been missed, they insisted, but they needed to feel useful.

* * *

Just after Bella's mum and dad had left, there was a knock at the door. Harris answered it and Bella heard introductions being made. Kendric MacKinnon walked through into the living room and immediately filled the space with his imposing manner and larger-than-life personality. Although it wasn't ego fuelled as Bella had anticipated from seeing the man on TV. He wore a smart, tailored navy-blue suit and a starched white shirt with a lilac tie, the colour of Isla's hair in the photos they had sent him. Bella wondered if that had been deliberate. If so, it was a sweet gesture.

He walked over and held out his hand. 'Bella, how are you doing?' His eyes were filled with genuine concern.

She stood and took his hand. 'I'm... okay, I think.' She nodded as if trying to convince everyone, including herself.

'I'm so sorry you're going through this, but I can

assure you we'll do all we can to help. This here is Corrinne who will be operating the camera.' The tall, slim, short-haired brunette woman raised a hand and smiled. 'And this is Dom, my producer.' Unlike Kendric, the other two people were casually dressed and didn't speak. 'We won't take up too much of your time but be as honest with your emotions as you can. It's important that people see how this is affecting you. That way it's more likely to make an impact and keep people vigilant.'

Bella nodded and Harris slipped his arm around her shoulders. 'Where would you like to film?'

Kendric looked around the living room. 'This space is perfect. Good light, nice and homely, no distracting clutter. Why don't the two of you sit on that sofa and I'll sit in this armchair.'

Everyone took their places, and the producer held up a monitor to Bella's face then looked at the small LED screen. 'Looks good,' he said. The camera operator nodded and gave a thumbs up.

Kendric turned his attention to Bella and Harris. 'Now, I'll ask you some questions and you just answer as best you can, okay?'

Bella suddenly realised she hadn't been the best host, and as if snapping out of a daze, shook her head and stood. 'Oh, my word, I haven't even offered you a drink, or... or food. Can I get you anything at all?'

Kendric smiled warmly. 'We're all fine, thank you. Don't worry about anything else. Just sit and try to relax.' Bella did as instructed, and clung to Harris's hand. 'The photo that you emailed this morning, showing Maeve and Isla, will be shown on the screen as we talk, along with the phone number of the police station for people to call with information. That number will divert to you, Harris, as you requested.' Harris nodded and squeezed Bella's hand.

The producer silently counted down with his fingers and the camera was aimed at them. When the producer pointed at Kendric and nodded, he smiled into the lens. 'Good afternoon, everyone. I'm here in beautiful Glentorrin on the Isle of Skye today covering a very concerning case of a trio of missing octogenarians whose families are, as you can imagine, extremely concerned and want them home as soon as possible. Bella Douglas's grandmother, Isla, and Harris Donaldson's mother, Maeve, have been incommunicado for approximately two days now and we need your help to bring them home safely. A third person, a gentleman from the same residential complex, is also missing but it's not known if these cases are connected. We're about to show you a photo of the two females, which was taken only last week so shows a very good resemblance of the two friends.'

He turned to Bella and Harris. 'Could you tell us a little bit about Isla and Maeve?'

Bella nodded, her heart was pounding and thumping at quite an alarming pace. 'Isla is a gregarious lady with purple hair and a wicked sense of humour. Family is her first concern, always, and she's very dear to me,' Bella said as her chin trembled. 'It's not like her to not stay in touch, it's so out of character. I just want her home. Or even to know that she's safe.'

Kendric turned to Harris. 'And your mother, Harris?'

Harris was always calm in a crisis. He smiled. 'Mum is such a kind-hearted person. She'd do anything for anyone and will always help if she can. She has a heart of gold and she and Isla are the best of friends. As my fiancée said, this is very much out of character for the two of them and our concern is growing with every minute.'

Kendric nodded, his expression serious and his demeanour oozed professionalism. 'Are there any places they're known to frequent, where people can keep a look out?'

Bella was struggling to get her words out now, so Harris took the lead. 'Both Isla and Maeve enjoy visiting Portree. That's where they were understood to be going. They usually go for tea and cake and have various cafés they like to frequent. Maeve isn't quite as distinctive to look at as Isla with her purple hair,' he said with a smile, 'although she loves bright colours and often wears them. But Isla hasn't quite managed to convince her to have her hair dyed yet.'

Kendric smiled. 'They sound like real characters. Is there a message you'd like to put out there in case either of the ladies or the gentleman are watching?'

Bella nodded, 'Yes... yes, please.'

Kendric addressed the audience who would be watching at home. 'We're putting the telephone number of Glentorrin Police Station on the screen right now, everyone.' He turned back to Bella. 'Bella, go ahead and speak right into the lens there, take your time.'

Bella cleared her throat, wiped her eyes and straightened her spine before lifting her chin to look at the camera. 'Granny and Maeve, if you're seeing this, please could one of you get in touch? You can call the police station number and you'll be diverted to Harris's phone. We're so worried about you and we miss you both very much.' Her voice broke and her throat ached. She forced a smile. 'We just want you home again to make us laugh because life's no fun without you. And... and Beau misses you too. We have him here with us so he's safe. Please just get in touch as soon as you can. We can come and get you, wherever you are, and we're not upset with you or anything like that. Just worried.'

The camera was turned once again to focus on Kendric. 'There you go, viewers, Maeve Donaldson and Isla Douglas, both in their late eighties, missing for two days. Their family and friends are incredibly worried, as you can imagine. Please take a good look at the photo on the screen and keep a look out. Call the number shown with any information, no matter how small or insignificant you think it may be, it could just be that vital, missing piece of the puzzle. Back to the studio.'

'And clear,' the producer announced. 'That went well. Thank you both for your time and I wish you well,' the man said. Then he and the camera operator began to gather their equipment together.

Once they were done, the camera operator walked over to where they sat. 'I hope they're found safe and well, they sound like real characters.' She smiled and then turned to Kendric. 'We'll see you over at the Coxswain. We can have a bite to eat and then get back,' she said before she, and the producer, left the house.

Kendric stood and held out his hand and Bella and Harris shook it in turn. 'Thank you both. The piece will go on air during the lunchtime programme and hopefully you'll get some leads.' He rubbed his chin. 'Just a warning though, you may also get some idiots who think it's funny to call and give either false sightings or just to say stupid and pointless things. It's par for the course, I'm afraid. But I'll be in touch once it's aired. I'll be thinking of you both and praying for a positive outcome.'

'Thanks, Kendric. We really appreciate you doing this,' Harris said.

'It's no bother at all. Best of luck to you both. I'm hoping the lovely ladies are home very soon,' he said as he turned and walked to the door with Harris following behind. 'Bye just now.'

Harris and Bella stood at the front door and watched as Kendric walked away in the direction of the village centre.

Once the door was closed, Harris pulled Bella into his arms. 'This is all so surreal. I know you said we're not upset with them for their disappearing act, but I might have a few choice words to say when they are home after what they're putting us through.'

Bella clung to him and inhaled his familiar scent. He was her safe space and just being in his arms somehow made things feel a tiny bit better. 'No, it's okay, honestly. I just want them home safe.'

'Me too, sweetheart, me too. Come on, I'll put the kettle on.'

13

Harris and Bella sat on one sofa and her parents sat on the other. They were all staring at the TV in silence, watching the lunchtime show's chef making a rather tasty-looking chicken shawarma with flatbread and homemade tzatziki, as they waited for the outside report from Kendric MacKinnon to be announced. Because, in turn, that would hopefully lead to finding Isla and Maeve.

Bella chewed the skin around her thumbnail which had become sore due to this repeated action over the last couple of days. She watched as the chef plated up the food and pondered that if she didn't feel so nauseated she could fancy it. She watched the other presenters tucking into the dish, ooh-ing and ah-ing about how succulent the chicken was and how the spices in the marinade came through with every bite. She almost envied them for having an appetite because hers had vanished.

The next segment was a travel piece on Shieldaig in Wester Ross, Northwest Highlands. An instrumental version of Dougie MacLean's 'Caledonia' played as the camera panned over the pretty village that was home to around eighty-five residents, and was surrounded by the stunningly rugged scenery of the Torridon Hills. After the voiceover had talked about the Celtman triathlon that was held in the area annually, there was an interview with a man called Jim who owned and ran a coffee bothy on the main street that looked quite idyllic. He waxed lyrical about the beauty of the area but insisted that the best bit was its people. Bella made a mental note that they should visit one day.

The main row of white-painted houses in Shieldaig looked out over the water and towards a tiny island that was, according to the reporter, mostly inhabited by birds and Scots pine trees. The island reminded Bella of Pabay, the wee island off the coast close to where her granny and Maeve lived. Once again, she was plunged back into a state of worry.

Harris sighed. 'You know, I always thought my

first TV appearance would be me in the background, on your arm, while we walked a red carpet at an awards ceremony for your interior designs.'

Bella nudged him with her shoulder. 'It's a lovely thought but I don't think there are any such grand events for the likes of me.'

He frowned. 'Hey, you never know, that posh English bloke Laurence Llewelyn-Bowen must have walked a few red carpets in his time. I used to love watching *Changing Rooms*,' he mused.

'Aw, Bella, you used to love watching that with your granny. He was her favourite,' her dad said.

Bella was reminded of her granny's name for the flamboyant designer and smiled. 'Yes, she used to call him Lulu Lemon.'

Harris threw his head back and guffawed. 'Oh God, that's hilarious, isn't that a company that makes fancy leggings?' Bella nodded. 'They really did break the mould after Isla Douglas was made,' he said, shaking his head and grinning.

Bella's dad chuckled. 'You think that's funny. She used to switch off *Antiques Roadshow* that followed *Changing Rooms*, because one of the presenters on that show, apparently, *gives her the Bee Gees*.'

Bella's mum giggled. 'I remember the time she told me about her neighbour back in Inverness who she was looking after because they'd just had Cadillac surgery.'

'And then there was her old hairdresser who used his scissors in his right *and* his left hand because he was *amphibious*,' her dad added.

They all laughed, their memories of Isla lightening the tense mood as they forgot themselves for a brief moment until they were silenced by the announcement on the TV.

'And we now cross to Kendric MacKinnon who's on the Isle of Skye, covering a heartbreaking and worrying story. Over to you, Kendric...'

Suddenly there they were on television. It felt a little like an out-of-body experience – much like this whole situation had. Bella hated seeing herself on the screen. She looked pale and drawn with sunken eyes. And even though they say the camera adds ten pounds, it didn't on this occasion. Bella noticed the hollows of her cheeks and for the first time she understood why her granny had been so worried about her. Although she felt sure that she didn't look like that under normal circumstances, just these current ones. She shook her head to dislodge the thought and reminded herself it didn't matter what she looked like. It was Isla and Maeve that were the focus. And Tam too if he hadn't miraculously turned up at his daughter's. She would need to call Dorothy and ask.

When the photo of Maeve and Isla was shown, the two of them giggling like teenagers, a lump lodged itself in Bella's throat. She vividly remembered taking the snap of them when they were round for Sunday lunch a couple of weeks before. As Harris was cooking the roast in the kitchen, they had been sitting in the lounge clutching their glasses of sweet sherry as they told Bella all about a film one of the home helpers had told them was her favourite, and they had subsequently watched it out of interest.

'Och, it was a strange one, wasn't it, Isla? Not our usual watch. We like to watch *Bergerac*, don't we? He has a lovely car, Bella, and he's *vera* handsome.' Maeve patted her hair with her free hand as her cheeks tinged with pink. 'Isn't he, Isla?'

Isla's face was scrunched as if she was deep in thought. 'Aye, aye. Now what was it called again, Maeve? The film that young Chelsea told us about.' Maeve had opened her mouth to speak but Isla had evidently had a light bulb moment. 'Och, aye, that's it! *Mechanic Mike*! We thought, *ooh, that'll be nice* because we liked their songs when they used to play them on Radio Highland back in the day, didn't we, Maeve,' Isla had said. 'He had a lovely voice, that singer chappy. Although that one song of theirs made me *greet* whenever I heard it. I think he wrote it about his dad or something, talking about all the things he wished he'd told him afore he passed away. I could *greet* now just thinking about it. So sad it was. But anyway, it turned out it *wasnae* about them! The film, I mean.'

'Aye, it *wasnae* about them at all!' Maeve had added for emphasis.

'No, really?' Bella had said, feigning shock and trying to keep a straight face.

'No! It was about male dancers.' Isla had looked around conspiratorially and whispered, '*Strippers*, Bella. *Male* strippers. The ones that take their clothes off and everything.' *As opposed to the strippers who stay fully dressed?* Bella had thought, chewing the inside of her cheek. Isla had pursed her lips and folded her arms across her chest as if completely disgusted, which had lasted all of five seconds. She had, of course, seen *Fifty Shades of Grey*!

Then the two elderly women had howled with laughter as they had described the scantily clad Channing Tatum 'cavorting' on the screen in a thong.

'They don't look comfy, those things,' Maeve had added with a crumple of disdain to her mouth. 'Right up the crack o' yer *erse* they go! I mean, who wants that?'

Bella had almost lost the fight with the laughter threatening to burst forth and Isla went on to insist she had no idea why it was called *Mechanic Mike* because... 'The thing was, Bella, he never seemed to be mending cars. Not once was he under a bonnet. And he never had anything up on a ramp either.' There had been genuine surprise in her expression and Bella had to fight extra hard not to fall on the floor in hysterical giggles.

Maeve had added, 'Mind you, he *didnae* really need to mend cars, did he, Isla? Because it looked like he was quite well paid by all the lassies stuffing money into his knickers!'

It was when Bella had explained that the film was actually called *Magic Mike* and that there was no connection to the band Mike + The Mechanics, or mechanics at all for that matter, that the laughter kicked up a notch. Isla had ended up holding her stomach and making a high-pitched squeaking noise that could've called all the village dogs to their house if it had continued. Maeve's face had been a shade of purple Bella had never seen on a human, and at one point, she was concerned an oxygen tank might be required. She had snapped the photo to remember the looks on their faces and the sheer hilarity of the situation. Priceless.

Back in the present, the news segment ended, and Harris squeezed Bella's hand. 'Are you okay? You seemed to drift off there for a bit.'

Bella shook her head. 'Yes, sorry, I was just thinking about the day that photo was taken.'

Harris chuckled. 'Oh, yeah, Mike and his stripping mechanics.' The room fell silent for a few moments.

'You did really well, both of you,' Bella's mum said, her chin trembling.

A wave of what could only be described as deep, overwhelming grief washed over Bella. Her stomach knotted and her heart lurched. 'Where are they? This island isn't so big that they can have completely vanished. So, where the hell are they?' Tears spilled over and streamed down her face leaving hot trails, and her head pounded from all the crying and worry.

Her dad leapt to his feet and made his way across the room to where she sat. He crouched down before her and took her hand. 'We'll get to the bottom of it, sweetheart. I just know it. The calls will start to come in and this mystery will be solved.'

Bella hoped with every ounce of her being that he was right because this not knowing was torture.

* * *

For the next two hours, Harris's phone went crazy. As Kendric had warned, however, there were some ridiculous calls from time wasters and some from genuine people who really thought they were helping, even though they weren't.

'Women of that age shouldn't have purple hair, it's ridiculous, they should be ashamed of themselves,' one elderly woman had told them as they all listened, with bated breath, to the speaker on Harris's phone.

Harris huffed out forcefully. 'With all due respect, madam, do you actually have anything to say that's pertinent to the case?' The woman had immediately hung up. 'No, that's what I thought, you daft old bat.'

Another call came in. 'I saw them last week doing karaoke in Torremolinos! Me and the wife go there every year. The weather wasn't as good this time though so we might try Tenerife next year.'

'Aye, pal, you do that, and thanks.' What they clearly seemed to have missed when watching the piece by Kendric is that the two elderly women were home safe the previous week and had only been missing two days.

'People just don't listen,' Bella's dad had grumbled in frustration.

Another caller suggested, 'You should try ringing their mobile phones or tracing their car registration.'

Harris's nostrils had flared, and he had shaken his head. 'Aye, we'll do that, thank you,' he had replied politely when it was clear from the redness of his cheeks that he was having to will himself not to scream down the phone, 'Don't you think we've tried all those things, you walloper?'

'I saw them in Tesco in Stoke on Trent yesterday. They were buying cigs and a bottle of merlot.' Harris had rolled his eyes at this one and had replied, *Away an' boil yer heid!* Why on earth would they be in Stoke on Trent of all places when they're two eighty-plus-year-olds from Scotland? And neither of them has ever smoked actually.' He had ended the call with a bang of his index finger to the screen and glanced around at Bella and her parents, all watching him with wide eyes. 'Sorry,' he said, cringing. 'They're doing *ma* head in.'

The final one of countless calls that angered Bella – because every second they were blocking the line they were halting the chance of a person with *actual* leads getting through – was from two very young-sounding kids who were struggling to remain serious throughout their prank. The main one was putting on a silly and obviously fake deep voice. 'I've got them here in my flat in Aberdeen and I want three million pounds in an unmarked envelope to be left outside in the bin by McNulty's sweetshop...' Whispering could be heard in the background. 'Or... or a new PlaySta-tion... And... and you're a smelly fart.' This was fol-lowed by giggles.

'You do realise you're talking to the police, and we can trace your call, don't you, lads?' Harris had said through clenched teeth.

There was a pause and the quieter of the two could be heard saying, 'Hang up, Davey, you *bawbag!* They'll come for us, and we'll get *kilt* by yer ma!'

The more talkative one said, 'Shit, Craig, you *didnae* have to say ma name!' And then, 'Whatever, get stuffed, pig!'

The call had ended abruptly, and Harris had thrown his handset onto the sofa. 'For heaven's sake, what are their parents teaching them?' he asked no one in particular, as he ran his hands back through his hair. 'I've a bloody good mind to actually trace them and go have a few stern words with their parents.'

It was clear that Harris was getting angrier by the second and Bella was pacing up and down the room, followed by two dogs who wondered why on earth she wasn't going anywhere else.

'Come and sit down, love, you're going to wear a hole in the rug,' her mum said, holding out her hand.

Bella sat and huffed, feeling more than a little bit deflated. She had been so sure this would work.

Two hours passed and the calls had slowed down but no valuable leads had come through. Bella was slumped on the sofa with her elbows resting on her knees and her head in her hands. She didn't want to give up hope of finding them but the longer this went on the harder it was to stay positive. She got up and walked over to where her dad stood looking out at the back garden where Beau and Bertie were digging a hole in the flowerbed. She hadn't even got the energy to bang on the glass and yell at them to stop. She leaned her head against her dad's shoulder, and they watched the sky becoming darker as the sun began its descent.

Harris's phone rang again. 'Oh, it's a video call request,' he said. 'I don't recognise the number.'

Bella and her dad turned sharply and dashed over to him.

'Answer it!' Bella's mum said as she gripped his arm. He did so and the four of them stared at the screen in anticipation.

A face none of them recognised came into view and stared back at them.

'Hello? Who is this?' Harris asked with a terse tone.

'Oh, hi. Harris Donaldson?' The man was smartly dressed in a white shirt and tartan tie with a navy jacket over the top.

Bella thought immediately it was some journalist from a tabloid wanting to do a dramatic story and her stomach plummeted along with her heart.

'Yes, that's me. Now who are *you*?'

The man cleared his throat. 'I have your mother, and her friend.'

14

Harris glared at the screen on his phone; his knuckles turned white. 'What the hell do you mean you have my mother?' he growled through gritted teeth. 'If you so much as—'

'Whoa, wait! No! No! I don't mean I *have* them, have them.' The man on the screen widened his eyes in apparent alarm. 'I mean I have them *here*, with me. But not in a sinister, kidnappy kind of way.'

'In what way *do* you mean then?' Harris snapped.

The man glanced off to the side. 'Maeve, Isla? Come here! I think you'd better speak to Mr Donaldson.'

The phone was fumbled and suddenly they were

looking at the gravel for a moment, and then the sky, until a new face could be seen on the screen.

Bella's heart leapt as her granny beamed at them. 'Hey, my loves! It's Granny Isla,' she said loudly as if they couldn't see her.

Relief flooded Bella and her legs weakened so she clung to Harris. 'We can see that! Are you okay?' she asked. 'Where's Maeve?'

Isla gestured with her head and suddenly Maeve appeared on screen too. 'Hi, ma wee darlins,' she said, sounding a little tipsy.

'What the heck is going on, Mum?' Harris asked. 'We've been worried sick.'

Isla held up her hand and wiggled her fingers towards the camera where a new, gold addition was visible. 'We got married!' she announced with a wide smile.

Bella, her parents and Harris all shared questioning glances. The rest of them were stunned into silence but Bella snatched the phone from Harris and glared at her granny. 'I'm sorry, what? You and Maeve have got married?'

Isla laughed. 'Och, you wee dafty, I'm not a thespian. No, me and Tam have got wed! Maeve was my flower girl and witness.' Tam's face appeared beside Isla.

'Oh! So, Tam *is* there!' Bella said, turning to her parents.

'His daughter must be so worried,' Bella's mum said, with one hand on her face and the other over her heart.

'Hello, *bella* Bella dearie, I've made an honest woman out of your granny,' Tam said, smiling proudly.

Bella's nostrils flared. 'I'm sorry but that's debatable at this point because she totally lied about this!'

Bella's dad slumped onto the sofa. 'Oh God, she's finally lost the plot,' he said with a sigh. 'She's actually gone and lost the bloody plot.'

'I did not lie, Arabella,' Isla said tersely. 'I just didn't tell you what I was doing, that's all.'

'Granny, that's what you call a lie by omission. And it's still a lie. You have some serious explaining to do,' Bella snapped. 'Where the hell are you for starters?'

'We're in Gretna, of course.'

Bella gasped. '*What!* The Gretna that's a five-and-a-half-hour drive away?'

'Aye, the very same,' Isla said, brushing the comment off as if that was a normal, everyday journey for her. 'We're talking to you on Murray's phone! He's the hotel manager. He was the nice man you spoke to earlier. He saw you on the news and told us we should contact you. But I don't know why you were so worried.'

Bella shook her head, trying to understand what on earth was going on because she felt like she had somehow fallen into a parallel universe where things made even less sense than normal. 'Oh, no, nothing to worry about at all when three octogenarians suddenly disappear without a trace.' She realised the sarcasm was unnecessary but couldn't help herself. 'And... why aren't you using *your* phone? Or Maeve's for that matter?'

Isla rolled her eyes. 'Ah well, you see, Maeve dropped hers in the loo on the day we got here, and I told her to put it in a bag of rice, but we didn't have any and the kitchen was closed at that point. But she didn't want to put her hand in to get it *oot* the loo anyway. And I said, "Well, I'm not putting my hand in there, Maeve Donaldson. I know we're best friends, but I have to draw the line somewhere." So, we had to wait for the cleaner to come with rubber gloves, and then they only had couscous in the kitchen because the rice was for something on the menu, and I wasn't sure if that would work the same as rice. So, by that time I think the phone was totally up the swanny and we just didn't bother.'

Bella was exhausted just listening to the explanation. 'Okay, so that explains Maeve's phone but what about Tam's? Or yours?' She was none the wiser at this point.

'Tam *doesnae* have a mobile telephone because he thinks they're bad for your health. You do hear all sorts about radiators getting into your brain, so I can understand his concerns. I may be almost eighty but I'm no ready to pop my clogs yet.'

Bella shared a smirk with her dad, who she guessed was thinking the same thing: *actually, you're kidding no one, you're almost ninety!* Oblivious to what they were thinking, Isla continued, 'But I do like my phone to watch the tick tack videos on and that's what I told Tam. Love me, love my mobile phone. But anyway, it ran out of juice, my phone, not my brain, that is, I'm still totally compos mental in that department.'

You're half right, Bella thought. 'And the portable phone charger I bought you for occasions such as this?'

Isla's face tinged pink and she cleared her throat. 'Ah yes, well, I sort of discovered that it doesn't work if you don't actually charge it to begin with. And I forgot to pick up my other one that plugs into the wall socket thingy.'

'Oh, Granny. Why didn't you borrow one? Everyone has a mobile these days. It wouldn't have been hard to find one.'

She held up her finger. 'Now hold on a minute, I did think of that, and I asked but Murray has an Andrex phone, so, his didn't fit with mine being an Apple. And Sadie on reception has a... whatchamacallit... Motormouth or something. Anyway, I thought you'd be okay because I texted you so many times from Sadie's phone, bless her, she's a wee sweety, and you didn't reply. So, I thought you must be busy doing the hotel decorating.'

'Granny, what are you talking about? I haven't had a single message from you. And like Harris said, we've been worried sick.'

'Ooh, they must have got lost in the whatsname then because I definitely texted you on the WhatsUp.'

Bella had a million questions scrambling for dominance. 'Wait a second, how did you text me if your phone was out of battery? How did you know my number?'

'I got it off your interior designer website,' she said proudly. 'I was showing Murray and he's going to keep you in mind for their refurbishment here by the way, and we saved it into Sadie's phone. Maeve couldn't remember Harris's number and we didn't want to ring the police station in case there was an emergency, and we stopped someone getting through. But I definitely texted you on...' She proceeded to reel off the number. 'See I've even got it memorised now!' She looked very impressed with herself.

Okay, that explains at least one thing, Bella thought. With a sigh, and hating to burst her bubble, she said, 'You got the last two numbers switched, Granny. There's no wonder I didn't reply. You've been texting some random person.'

Isla laughed. 'Really? Well, that's a bit daft of me, isn't it? And they never replied to tell me so. I'm *vera* sorry about that, hen. Anyway, I'd better go because we've a table booked for our wedding supper. I think I might have the salmon, it sounds delish.'

'Hang on, Mum!' Bella's dad called from his place on the sofa. 'You've still got plenty of explaining to do. Bella has Beau here because we didn't know where you were. She went on national TV trying to locate you! Your granddaughter has been on the verge of a bloody breakdown. The whole of Drumblair, Glentorrin and Pabay have been beside themselves with worry. And you were off getting *married*?'

Isla's smile disappeared. 'I'm sorry, loves. I didn't mean to worry you. It's just that we didn't want to wait any longer with us both being over seventy.' *And then some*, Bella thought, *what's with the pretending to be younger than she is all of a sudden?* 'And we didn't want to take the attention away from your wedding at Christmas, Arabella dearie. So, we thought we'd run away and do it. We weren't bothered about the big do and all that. That's for you young folks. And it's romantic, don't you think? Running away to get married?' she asked hopefully. 'We've been planning it for a while, and it was really hard keeping it from you all.' Her chin began to tremble. 'I just didn't want to spoil your wedding when you're so much more important to me, hen. I'm so excited to be your maid of honour and didn't want anything to overshadow your special day. I thought we were doing the right thing.'

Bella's heart softened and her eyes welled with tears. She hated to see her granny upset. 'Please don't cry, Granny. You could've told us and we could've made it special for you. We had no idea you were even considering getting married.'

Isla's chin continued to wobble and a wrinkly, liver-spotted hand wiped the tears away from her face with a tartan hanky. Isla smiled warmly at the owner of the hand who was now standing just out of sight. 'Thanks, Tam, love.'

Bella's stomach knotted with guilt. Had they all

just completely ruined her special day? 'Look, Granny, you go and enjoy your wedding supper, and we'll see you when you come home. Although, when might that be?'

Isla sniffed. 'Tomorrow, hen. Rab's Cabs was fully booked so Flora's nephew from Portree brought us and is picking us up to bring us home. Didn't Flora tell you when you collected my Beau?'

So, clearly Isla knew as much about Flora's dementia as Flora herself did. 'No, Granny, I'm afraid she didn't.'

'Ugh, well, I don't know why. She could've saved you all this upset. Anyway, we'll see you tomorrow, okay?'

Bella was exhausted. Drained of anger and tears, she simply nodded. 'See you tomorrow. Love you. And congratulations, *Mrs Guthrie.*'

A bright smile replaced the sadness in Isla's expression. 'Thank you. And I love you, Arabella dearie, so very much. And all of my wonderful family.' The sincerity in her granny's expression almost broke Bella again.

The call ended and Bella handed Harris his phone. He took it and stood there, staring blankly at it as if answers would spring forth from the blank screen. 'Did that just happen?' he eventually asked.

'Apparently so,' Bella's dad said, his eyebrows raised in disbelief. 'My eighty-seven-year-old mother has just eloped.'

Bella's mum said, 'I'm just so relieved they're all okay.'

'Me too.' Bella's mobile rang and Dorothy's name flashed up on the screen. 'Hi, Dorothy—'

Before she could utter another word, Dorothy blurted, 'I know where they are! Flora unknowingly held the secret all along!'

'Evidently so,' Bella replied. 'We've just been speaking to them.'

Dorothy's sigh of relief was loud and heavy. 'Ah, okay. It seems forgetfulness runs in the family. Flora's nephew, Davey, drove them to Gretna and was supposed to tell me the plans so I could tell Tam's daughter that he was delaying his trip by a week. But Davey completely forgot because when he arrived home he discovered his cat had escaped. It's a house cat and apparently doesn't go out at all so he was really worried and spent the whole of that day and night searching and then yesterday and this morning too. The cat was located in a neighbour's shed safe and well. But then he suddenly remembered he was supposed to pass the message on to me, so he rang me after he had seen you on the lunchtime show.'

'But that was hours ago, Dorothy.'

'Yes, I said the same. Turns out he was watching it on catch-up because he likes the recipes section, apparently, and had missed it while he was out looking for Mr Dibbs.'

'Okay. All's well that ends well, I suppose,' Bella said.

'Yes. I'm so relieved. You must be too. And now you have something to celebrate as well,' Dorothy said, her voice much brighter than when they had last spoken.

The call ended and Bella turned to the others. 'I wonder how quickly we can pull together a surprise party?'

* * *

'I can't believe we're about to celebrate Granny's wedding,' Bella said as she tied a knot in the pearlescent white balloon she had just finished blowing up. The main communal lounge area of the Pabay View residential home was a light and airy, if a little bland and functional, space and Dorothy was helping them move the furniture around to create a small area for dancing and create a better ambience.

'Although we'll hopefully not be needing any ambulances this time,' her mum said as she and Bella's dad carried a table to the corner where the wedding cake would be placed.

Bella shivered as she remembered the incident to which her mum was referring. It had been a tea dance Isla had attended at the day centre she used to visit back in Inverness. During the dance, Isla had fallen and bumped her head, knocking herself unconscious, but the worst part was she had broken her hip too. It had been a scary time and had been the catalyst for her relocation to Skye.

Bella snorted. 'I know, I thought that too. What is it about my granny and scaring us half to death? Anyone would think she was doing it on purpose.'

'Never a dull moment with Isla Douglas,' her dad said with a laugh.

'Isla Guthrie now, Dad!' Bella said.

'Oh, aye, Isla Guthrie. That's going to take some getting used to.'

Her mum placed a pristine white cloth over the table. 'It was so kind of your friend Caitlin to make a cake at such short notice.'

Bella smiled. 'She's a star. And it will no doubt be lovely, even though I insisted she not go to too much trouble with so little time.'

'Right, that's all the invites posted through the

doors of all the residents,' Jules said as she appeared
with her stepson, Evin, from the doorway that led to
the internal units. Evin had designed the invites on
his iPad, and they were really sweet – he was clearly
taking after his dad in the artistic talent department –
and Dorothy had printed them off in her office.

'What can we do now?' Evin asked, clapping his
hands and rubbing them together.

'You can help me blow up some more balloons,
please, if you don't mind,' Bella said as a loud pop
echoed around the room and Bertie yelped before
scooting under a table to hide. 'Especially seeing as
my daft pup keeps bursting them.'

15

Morag arrived at Pabay View carrying a box of wine bottles she had collected from the cash and carry she used for the shop. 'Jules, can you go and grab another box from Kenneth at the van, please?' she asked, a little out of breath.

'Sure!' Jules said as she skipped off in the direction of the exit.

'Thanks so much for picking that up, Morag, I really appreciate it.'

'Oh, it's no bother, hen. Can't have a celebration without a wee bit of fizz. What time are they getting back, Bella?' Morag asked as she placed the box down on a table.

'Around half five, I think.' Bella turned to look at the clock and her heart skipped.

Morag nodded. 'That gives us an hour and a half to finish off. Do you think we'll manage it?' She winced as she too stared at the clock on the wall as if doing so might make it turn back a wee bit.

Bella nodded confidently. 'I'm sure we will. Pizzas are ordered for half six, so that's the food sorted.'

'What will Isla think about having pizza for her wedding feast?' Evin asked as he strung three balloons together with some white curling ribbon. 'It's not really an old person's food, is it?'

Morag gasped. 'Hey, young man, us *oldies* love a stuffed crust, you know. And a garlic dip.'

Evin laughed. 'Sorry, Morag, I keep forgetting how cool you guys are.'

'Aye, well, we're very cool. I mean Isla has purple hair, so what's cooler than that?' Morag said, grinning. 'And Giovanni's pizzas are worthy of any wedding feast. My mouth's watering just thinking about his *quattro formaggi*.'

'Steady on, Morag, that sounds a bit like a euphemism,' Bella said, giggling.

'Maybe it was,' Morag whispered with a wink.

'Anyway, to answer your question, Evin, my granny is a bit of a pizza aficionado since she visited

Italy with my grandad a long time ago. She stayed in Florence and said it's the best pizza she's ever tasted. It's still one of her favourite meals so I'm pretty sure she'll be happy about it. And she did go and get married without telling anyone, which didn't leave us a lot of choice really.'

'Well, I for one, am not complaining,' Evin said. 'I love pizza too.'

Harris had roped in the members of the Glentorrin Four to come and play a set for the celebrations and he had gone to collect his gear and make sure his fiddle was in tune.

In the meantime, before only their second 'proper' gig, the other band members were busy with other party preparations. Reid was at his studio rustling up a banner to hang above the makeshift stage area, Archie was out collecting flowers for the table centres and Dex and his partner Millie were putting together a Spotify playlist for when the band weren't playing.

Even former Hollywood star Ruby and her husband Mitch were getting involved. They had volunteered to put together a quiz for everyone to take part in later in the evening – quizzes, crosswords and Sudoku were Tam's favourite things. He and Isla avidly watched game shows on a daily basis, a firm favourite being *The Chase* because, 'That Bradley Walsh is so funny and quite cheeky too,' Bella's granny had told her.

Tam's love of quizzes had been a lifelong passion, and he had even appeared on a TV show called *Countdown* back in the 1980s, winning his particular episode. He had a framed photo of himself with the presenters Richard Whiteley and Carol Vorderman on his living-room wall. Isla loved to tell people about Tam's claim to fame and whenever she did Tam would feign shyness with an, 'Och, no, it was a long time ago, I'd almost forgotten about it,' but Bella was sure that he loved it really; her being so proud of him.

'Did you manage to get hold of Tam's daughter, Dorothy?' Bella asked as the Pabay manager walked in from the direction of her office.

Dorothy sighed. 'I did. She can't make it at such short notice, which is understandable, I suppose. She didn't sound too pleased either. Poor Tam's going to have some serious explaining to do and I get the feeling his family won't be as understanding as Isla's.'

'I wonder where they're going to live now,' Bella was pondering out loud.

'I think Tam's unit is slightly bigger,' Dorothy said. 'But Isla's very house proud so I'm not sure she'll want to give up her own space. Especially with the lovely garden she has for Beau. Tam's outside space is smaller.'

'Maybe they'll just carry on as they are now,' Bella's dad said. 'They live next door to each other so it's not like they really have a need to move.'

'You're right,' Dorothy mused, and added, 'They spend most days together already at one or the other's home. And they eat most meals together.'

'Hmm, I just don't know if they'll want to live apart. It's not romantic, and Granny's nothing if not romantic.' Bella knew her granny probably better than anyone else these days and she had a feeling Tam would be the one relocating, even if it was only a few yards; Isla could be stubborn as they all knew very well.

* * *

Caitlin arrived with the cake. 'It's not as fancy as some of my wedding cakes but hopefully they'll still like it,' she said as she placed the box down on the table.

'Don't be daft, I just appreciate you making it at such short notice, so please don't worry. Your cakes are always lovely.' Bella opened the lid of the tall white box and gasped. Inside was a double-layered cylindrical cake, the top section slightly smaller than the bottom, and covered in a glass-smooth lilac frosting. Purple handmade icing flowers had been placed in a spiral from the top to the bottom and additional ones had been laid around the base along with icing sugar leaves. It was simple but artistic at the same time. 'Oh, Caitlin, it's stunning. I know they're going to love it.'

Caitlin stood with her hands clutched under her chin and on hearing Bella's words she huffed out her breath. 'Phew! I'm so glad you like it. It's quite basic, really.'

Bella put her arm around Caitlin's shoulder and kissed the side of her head. 'No, honestly, it's absolutely perfect. Thank you so much.'

'You're very welcome, honey.' She glanced around the room. 'This place is looking fabulous. Hardly recognisable. I'd better go get my glad rags on.'

Once the balloons were all blown up, 'congratulations' bunting had been strung around the room, confetti had been sprinkled on every available surface, and flowers had been placed in the centre of each table, Bella stood at the edge of the room with her mum and dad to assess what they had achieved in only a few hours. She was feeling quite excited now the panic had subsided.

Her dad put his arm around her shoulder. 'I have

to say, Arabella, for a usually functional space you've worked miracles on this place. It rivals those posh venues that people pay thousands of pounds for.' He shook his head. 'Seriously, your talents know no bounds, darlin'. I hope you know how proud of you your mum and I are.'

'Your dad's right, my lovely. It really does look wonderful,' her mum said, kissing her cheek.

Reid arrived with the finished banner and Harris returned from a quick detour via the police station and together they put the banner up over the makeshift stage area. He had painted Tam and Isla holding hands and smiling at each other right in the centre and had surrounded them with a variety of thistles and other purple flowers; Isla's favourite, and seeing it brought a lump of emotion to Bella's throat.

'Oh, Reid, it's absolutely gorgeous. Thank you so much. You've really captured them both.'

'The idea is that when the party is over, they can frame the centre part as a memento of their day. In fact, I can do that for them when they're ready. My wedding gift to them.'

'They'll absolutely love it. It'll make the occasion so special for them.' She hugged Reid.

'You're welcome. I'm an old romantic myself,' he said, blushing and rubbing bashfully at the back of his neck where a flush of embarrassment was creeping.

'I can vouch for that,' Jules said as she walked over and linked arms with her husband. 'The banner really does add a lovely finishing touch to a beautifully decorated room. Well done, Bella.'

'No, thank you all. I couldn't have pulled this off by myself.'

Olivia and Brodie had sent a huge bouquet of flowers which were placed on the table that had been set aside for the bride and groom and now all they needed was said happy couple to arrive.

The other members of the Glentorrin Four arrived and set up their instruments and a small PA system in readiness and little by little the other residents of Pabay View arrived in the lounge; each one had made an effort to look like they were attending an actual wedding, which made Bella's heart swell. She quickly headed to her granny's apartment to change and returned a short time later to find the place buzzing with chatter, and an air of excitement hummed around the room.

Evin was on watch at the window and at just after half past five he called, 'Everyone! They're here!' as he watched the car pulling into the car park.

'Has everyone got a glass of fizz?' Bella shouted

and a mumble of affirmation could be heard. Dorothy was waiting for them at the entrance to the building under the guise that she wanted to *have a word with them about their antics*. Dorothy could be quite stern when she wanted to be.

* * *

Instead of shouting 'surprise', which Bella didn't want to risk with the newlywed couple being well into their eighties, the Glentorrin Four played the opening bars to the 'Wedding March' and everyone applauded.

Isla and Tam were suitably stunned. Isla stood with one hand over her mouth and the other clutching Tam's arm. Tam was open-mouthed and shaking his head and Maeve joined in with the applause as soon as she realised what was going on. Isla was dressed in her favourite lilac and purple kaftan, and her hair was tied neatly in a chignon. She looked lovely and so very Isla-ish. Tam was sporting his usual bowtie, but this one was perfectly matched to the colour Isla was wearing. Bella had to force herself to stay rooted to the spot and not run and scoop her granny into her arms out of relief. But she would be giving her a stern telling-off later, that one thing was certain, she had decided. Instead, she watched as Beau did the very thing she had wanted to do. The little beagle ran towards his owner, his whole body wagging and his deep bark echoing loudly above everything else. Bella was sure he was telling Isla off for leaving him. Isla bent to hug her canine best friend and her eyes welled with tears as the dog licked at her face and couldn't get quite close enough to her.

Once the applause died down, one of the residents shouted, 'Speech!' and everyone laughed.

'Well, this is a lovely surprise,' Tam said as he glanced around, taking in the decorated surroundings. His eyes sparkled with emotion and for a moment he looked like he might shed a few tears. He composed himself, however, and said, 'You know, people often think that when you get to our time of life you should be on the shelf, in the background, seen and not heard and all that rubbish, but this lady here,' he took Isla's hand, 'has taught me that us oldies should do no such thing. That regardless of how long we have left on this earth we should make the most of every second. Just because we're closer to the end than the start doesn't mean that our remaining life isn't worth living. If anything, it's worth making every second count even more. And I'm so grateful that she moved here to Skye because she has given my life so much purpose. And she does make me laugh.' He shook his head as he turned to look lovingly at her. 'Sometimes it happens when she's trying to be serious, which I know annoys her.' He chuckled. 'But every day for the rest of my life I have time with my Isla to look forward to and I couldn't ask for anything more... well, apart from maybe even more time with her, but I'll take what I'm given, and I'll be eternally grateful.'

Bella dabbed at her eyes with a hanky that Dorothy had thrust into her hand. She glanced at Dorothy, who was already blubbing. And when she checked the rest of the room, she realised there was hardly anyone that hadn't been moved by Tam's words, even her dad and Harris were sniffling and swiping moisture away from their eyes. Applause and whistles travelled the room.

Isla waved her hand in the air and the applause subsided. 'I really can't follow that, but I just want to say firstly that I'm sorry we scared you all half to death by interloping.' Bella giggled at her choice of word.

Tam touched her arm. 'I think you mean eloping, dearie.'

Isla nodded. 'Aye, that's what I said.' Tam smiled

and shook his head and Isla continued, 'And secondly that we're so grateful that you've all gone to so much trouble. But can I just check, will there be food because I rang Giovanni's on the way home and they couldn't do us a pizza until nine tonight because they're doing a massive order for someone?'

Everyone laughed and Isla scrunched her brow in confusion.

Harris took his place at the microphone. 'Okay, everyone, please take your seats for a moment and we'll get this party started!'

Everyone did as he requested, and Dorothy and Bella went around to make sure all the guests had a drink in their hand. Bella showed Tam, Isla and Maeve to their 'top table' and once everyone was settled Harris spoke again. 'Now I know maybe it's not traditional for the entertainment to make a speech, but I just want to say a few words.' He cleared his throat. 'I'm sure you'll all agree that seeing how happy Isla and Tam are together gives us all hope. Tam mentioned earlier about finding love in later life but from what I've witnessed it's that love that's given them a whole new *lease* of life. And how special is that? They're both incredibly lucky to have found this kind of love twice and I want to wish them happiness for their future. May it be long and filled with laughter and love. Please raise your glasses, everyone, Tam and Isla!'

The rest of the room shouted in unison, 'Tam and Isla.'

'Now, don't worry, Isla, Giovanni's big job is actually *your* wedding reception, so you'll be getting fed soon enough.' Isla's eyes lit up and she clapped as everyone laughed. 'But in the meantime, we thought we'd play you some tunes. If you feel like dancing then go ahead, we've cleared a space. This first one is a nice gentle one to ease you into things. I'll be leading the vocals on this one, "Wild Mountain Thyme".'

Dex began the introduction on his guitar and within one verse of Harris singing, the rest of the people in the room had joined in with the beautiful old song and before long Bella was a swathe of swaying old folk. Tears streamed down her face but this time they were tears of happiness and ultimately relief. Her dad put his arm around her and gave her a squeeze and a kiss to her head. She wiped at her face and smiled as the voices in the room sang of blooming heather.

16

The wine was flowing, and the makeshift dancefloor was full for the whole night. Old people could certainly dance, regardless of what the media would have you believe about their energy levels. When the band were having a break, Dex connected his phone to the PA and played the party playlist he'd put together on Spotify which encouraged the dancing to continue. Lots of Abba, Frank Sinatra and Tom Jones; not artists you would ever normally associate with someone like Dex, who used to travel with rock bands for a living.

Caitlin's cake went down a treat, deliciously moist with a hint of Parma Violets about it, and it even spurred Dorothy on to arrange for Caitlin to make a monthly delivery of cupcakes for the residents' afternoon tea and quiz. Mitch was a hit as the quiz host and garnered quite the fan club with the ladies of Pabay View.

Evin had been charged with the job of wedding reception photographer, taking photos with Bella's digital camera, and he was having great fun taking the more candid shots. Someone had found a box of party hats and silly novelty spectacles left over from Christmas and groups of the residents were queuing up to have their photos taken wearing them, it was hilarious and so unexpected, and Bella loved that everyone was having such a good time at the last-minute party.

Bella's plan was to put an album together of the images to give to her granny and her new husband, and she couldn't wait to see the results. Jules had said Evin had inherited his dad's creative eye and had taken some lovely photos in and around Glentorrin that were going to be put on display in the village hall with some being made into postcards to be sold in the Lifeboat House Museum.

Bella sat with Granny Isla and Tam, soaking up the atmosphere and watching everyone dancing and having fun when Jules and Reid came over to chat.

'I hope it's okay but we let Kendric know that

you're home safe and he was overjoyed to hear about your wedding,' Reid said.

'Oooh, I watch him on the TV. *Vera* handsome young man,' Isla said and then turned to Tam. 'But you're my one and only, my dear, so no need to worry about me running away with him.' She giggled like a lovestruck teenager and Tam's face lit up. It was so clear how much they adored each other. Bella hoped she and Harris were the same at their age.

'The thing is, Isla, Kendric would like to come and interview you and Tam as a follow-up to the story he did on your... well... disappearance,' Jules said with a shrug, clearly trying to be as diplomatic as possible.

'You mean we'll be on the TV?' Isla asked, a surprising look of horror in her wide eyes.

'Oh, go on, Granny, I think people would like to know you're okay. The response to you being missing was so huge that I think it's only fair.'

'She's right, dearie,' Tam said. 'It's the least we can do after worrying everyone so much. It's easy being on TV.' He looked to Reid and Jules and added, 'I was on *Countdown*, you know, so I've experience of the cameras.'

Bella smiled to herself. It was the first time she had heard Tam offer the information willingly.

'Yes, I heard all about that. Well done, you,' Jules said with a tap to his arm. 'So what do you say, Isla?'

Isla paused for a moment and then grinned. 'Oh, go on then. I don't want to let my groupers down.' She winked at Bella, who laughed out loud.

All in all, the evening was just as Bella had hoped, and it went some way to making up for the fact that she hadn't been able to attend her granny's actual wedding.

* * *

The party went on until almost midnight when the die-hard guests finally gave up and left, all of them thanking Bella and Dorothy for an incredibly fun night as they passed them on their way out. They had danced and sang along to old traditional Scottish songs, but Harris had also inserted a song or two into the Glentorrin Four's set from Granny Isla's favourite musicians, including, of course, Tom Jones – 'What's New Pussycat' had been a crowd pleaser with everyone joining in at the chorus – Lewis Capaldi and her other, more recently discovered modern favourite. Bella couldn't help laughing when she remembered the first time she had talked with her granny about *that* particular performer...

They had been sitting at the kitchen table in Isla's little Pabay View unit, drinking tea and listing to the radio. Chris DeBurgh, another of Isla's golden oldie favourites, was singing about a 'Lady in Red'.

'This tea is lovely,' Isla had said. 'Very fruity.'

'It's a loose tea. Very posh. It's called Berry Burst infusion,' Bella had informed her.

Isla had gasped. 'Ooh, you know what they say about loose tea, don't you?'

Bella had frowned. 'No? What's that then?'

'Loose tea sinks ships,' Isla had said, pursing her lips and nodding seriously as if she had just imparted some terrifying fact.

Bella had almost snorted the berry drink up her nose. 'That would be *lips*, Granny.'

'Loose tea sinks lips? That doesn't make any sense. Lips don't float. Although some of these celebrities who have their bottom fat injected into their lips could use them as floating devices right enough.'

Bella had laughed. 'Loose lips sink ships, Granny, that's the saying. Tea has nothing to do with it.'

Isla had scowled. 'That makes no sense either.' She shook her head, and as 'Lady in Red' ended, she changed the subject. 'Don't you think that's a lovely song? He had big fluffy eyebrows if I remember right, like little caterpillars on his face.' Bella almost choked on her drink again, but Isla carried on regardless, 'That reminds me, there's a song I like that I've heard on Radio Highland, and I wondered if you like it too. You might have heard it. Although the strange thing is I've also seen the singer on daytime TV, and I must admit I was shocked when I saw him because he has a strange name really, when he looks like such a normal chap. He's a nice-looking boy, very smiley eyes and normal-sized eyebrows. But his stage name just doesn't make a lot of sense. Although I know lots of people don't use their own names these days, I mean look at Elton John and Cliff Richard. Ooh and Englebert Dumpertruck.' Bella gave up trying to drink her tea, lest she might need the Heimlich manoeuvre.

'Aye, to see him he's the kind of man you'd expect to see happily walking down the street in normal clothes, not like some Halloween reject as his name suggests. Because it makes him sound like he plays that awful metallic music. Well, if you can call it music. It's just noise to me. It'd give me a headache, that's for sure,' Isla had said with a shake of her head. 'Although what do I know? Kids these days love that drum and bass stuff too which is horrendous in my opinion. You get lads driving by you with that rubbish playing so loud it's a wonder their heads don't fall off with the vibration. Give me a nice bit of Tom Jones any day. Now *he* could sing. He had the moves too.'

Fearing that Isla might never get to the point, Bella had intervened. 'Which singer are you talking about then, Granny? And what's this song you like so much?'

Isla placed down her cup and clasped her hands like a newsreader. 'Get this, his name is *Head Shearer*. Strange, eh? He sings some lovely songs and even with a name like that his voice is really nice too. Not all growly and hoarse like you'd expect, like those metallic singers. And he's got a full head of hair, too, so he doesn't shear his own head.' She scowled and curled her lip. 'It's just not a name you'd put together with such romantic words.' Then as if a light bulb had flicked on, her eyebrows shot up and she said, 'Although! Maybe he works on a sheep farm on the days he's not out singing. Maybe he *is* the Head Shearer, the boss of all the other sheep shearers! That'd make more sense. Why didn't I think of that before? I'm such a wee dafty. Although why he'd use that as his stage name I've no idea. It's no Ziggy Stardust, is it?' She had chuckled and shaken her head before picking up and sipping her tea again.

Bella had crumpled her brow and fought the threatening giggle. 'I'm sorry, *who*?'

Isla had shrugged. 'See. I told you; it's not a good name. I wonder if his management have thought about getting him to change it before he gets too famous. If he changes it now before he's too well known, it won't matter.'

Bella had pursed her lips and chewed the inside of her cheek. 'What song does this *Head Shearer* sing that you like so much? You're not becoming a secret head banger, are you, Granny?' she'd teased, grinning. 'You've got the purple hair.'

'Och, no chance. I like my brain right where it is, thank you very much. Now, let me think, the one I really like is called "Thinking Out Loud", I think that's right. It's so sweet and the words are beautiful.' Bella couldn't hold back any longer. She'd burst into hysterical laughter and her eyes watered. Isla had raised her eyebrows. 'What? What's so funny? What did I say? I don't get it, Arabella.'

Holding her stomach, and once she had calmed herself down, Bella had managed to say, 'Granny, you really are hilarious. His name is *Ed Sheeran*, not *Head Shearer*. And he's already *very* famous! He's been around years and has won tons of awards.'

Isla had laughed too. 'Oh! Ed Sheeran! That's a

much better name! I'll no be writing to his manager then.' Seeing Isla laugh was one of Bella's favourite things in the world.

Of course, on the night of the wedding celebration Harris had sung 'Thinking Out Loud' and Isla and Tam had taken to the floor for a slow dance as everyone looked on with hands on hearts and tilted heads, oblivious to the story behind the song choice.

The word, 'Awww,' had been uttered at least a hundred times that evening, most occurrences of which had been during that one dance. They both had the biggest smiles, and it was clear they adored each other.

* * *

Towards the end of the night, Dorothy had insisted that the cleaning and tidying would be dealt with the following morning and told Bella to get the minibus taxi ordered to take her and the others back to Glentorrin. Harris dealt with the call while Bella walked down to Isla's home with her and Tam.

Isla linked her arm through Bella's as they walked. 'I'm so sorry, Arabella. I really did think I'd messaged the right number. I would never upset you or make you worry on purpose. I hope you know that.'

'Of course I know that, Granny. I just wish you'd felt able to tell me your plans. I would've loved to have been there to see you get married.'

They came to a stop at Isla's front door and Tam turned to them. 'I'll go and take wee Beau in. He'll be wanting his bed.'

Bella knew he was giving them some space, and she appreciated it. Once the front door was closed, she said, 'I am happy for you, Granny. I hope *you* know *that*.'

Isla reached up and cupped her face in one wrinkly hand. 'Thank you, hen. That means the world to me. And I'm sorry I didn't tell you. I just didn't want to steal your thunder. We're only a couple of oldies but I suppose time was a factor. We're not getting any younger and our wedding wasn't as big a deal as yours will be.'

'You're wrong there. You're as old as you feel and of course your wedding is as big a deal.'

'Ooh, that rhymed.' Isla smiled up at her. 'Thank you for this evening. The music, the cake, the pizza, the Head Shearer song.' She laughed. 'It couldn't have been any more perfect if I'd planned it myself.'

'You're welcome. By the way, where are you going to live now you're married?'

Isla winked. 'Where do you think?'

Bella smiled. 'Erm...' She tapped her chin and glanced skyward. 'I'm thinking *your* place?'

Isla smiled back and narrowed her eyes. 'Ah, you know me so well.' She opened her front door, went inside and turned around to face Bella. 'I love you very much, my dear, precious Arabella.'

'I love you too, Granny. Sweet dreams.' She turned and wandered back to the main building with a smile on her face. All was definitely forgiven.

* * *

Back at home that night, as they were getting ready for bed, Bella checked her phone to find several messages from Carlton Somers.

> We need to meet as soon as possible. I have some ideas for a games room. I think we could convert the old laundry building behind the gym. I need your input.

And then,

Perhaps we can meet and discuss
things over lunch this coming
week. Let me know when you're
free. I promise to wear a shirt
(winky face).

And then,

Obviously the shirt is optional
though (another winky face).

And then,

Let me know if you'll be wearing a
shirt and I'll take it from there.
Wouldn't want to be overdressed
(third winky face).

And then,

Are you ignoring me? I'm guessing
you are. I was only joking about the
shirt thing.

And finally,

I understand it's the weekend, Bella, but I would appreciate an answer as soon as possible because I'm heading back to the States soon for a few days. I have a thing to attend to. A situation if you will.

She wondered what kind of situation would require him to fly all the way back to the US that couldn't be dealt with over video call. Although it would be a relief to have a small reprieve from his flirting.

Harris had already climbed into bed and turned off his lamp, but she caught him watching her in her periphery with a crumple of concern to his brow as she frowned at her phone. 'Is everything okay, sweetheart? You look annoyed.'

She switched her phone off and put it on the bedside table, screen down, to doubly ensure Carlton couldn't bother her again and spoil what had been such a lovely night. And then turned off her own lamp. 'It's nothing.' She snuggled up in Harris's arms, the emotion of the last few days had caught up with her and drained her of every ounce of energy she had previously possessed. She'd clearly been running on adrenaline since her granny had gone missing and it was only now beginning to subside.

Harris put his arm over her body and pulled her in tighter, so her back was pressed against his front. He kissed her head. 'Okay. I know you'll tell me when you're ready.'

Remembering their talk about Alba, suddenly she was wide awake. She turned in his arms to face him in the darkness. 'Okay, I know we said no secrets.'

She felt him nod. 'We did. And I've seen that expression a few times now when you've been reading messages. I'm guessing it's a work thing and I have to say I've been a bit concerned. I didn't want to pry but I'm here if I can help.'

She closed her eyes for a moment, inhaled a deep breath and opened them again. She could make out his silhouette where the moonlight was shining in through a crack in the curtains and casting a white outline to his face. 'It is a work thing. A *male* work thing.'

Harris reached behind himself and flicked on the lamp. He sat up, the crease between his brows had deepened. 'I'm listening.'

She pulled herself upright and sighed. 'His name is Carlton Somers and he's the owner's son.'

'Oh, aye, he's the guy who was in the local news

for rescuing the old place. Isn't he an ex-model or something? I read about him in an online article. Saw the photo too. Good-looking bloke. You're not going to tell me you're running away with him, are you?'

Bella scoffed. 'Quite the opposite. I'm more likely to run away *from* him.'

'Okay, now I'm intrigued. Tough customer?'

She nodded. 'Not in the way you might think.'

'You'll have to tell me now. I won't sleep wondering about it.' He was teasing her; the glint in his eyes gave him away.

'Okay... The thing is, he's asked me out and told me, in no uncertain terms, that he won't give up until I say yes. I've told him I'm engaged and not in the slightest bit interested but he's being persistent. He's walked around shirtless in front of me a couple of times as if he's trying to show me what I'm missing out on.' She rolled her eyes. 'I even tried speaking to his parents, but they shrugged it off as nothing in an almost *boys will be boys* way which I found disturbing. He sometimes makes me feel uncomfortable, that's all.'

Harris's frown deepened. 'What the hell? Who does he think he is? Just because he's a model doesn't give him the right to make you feel like that, Bella. I've a good mind to—'

'I can handle it, Harris, so please don't worry. So long as you know I'm not flirting back.' She gazed into his eyes, hoping he could read the truth there.

Harris took her hand and shook his head. 'Bella, that thought hasn't even crossed my mind. I'm just angry that you feel like that because of some bawbag who doesn't respect you. But of course I trust you, Bella. I have no reason not to.' She watched his jaw tensing and waited, knowing he had more to say. 'The shirt thing is a bit pathetic though. He clearly doesn't know you at all if he thinks abs and pecs are going to turn your head. Look, you know I'm not one of these caveman types, these "Get your hands off my woman" types, and I don't claim to own you, and rightly never would, but if this guy is bothering you as much as he seems to be I'm prepared to go and speak to him. It's not right that he's harassing you when you've made your feelings clear.' The anger he felt was evident in the way his hand tightened around hers, not painful or aggressive, just protective. 'I've handled prats like this before, so I know his type. I'm not at all happy about this, Bella. You shouldn't have been suffering in silence, sweetheart.'

'I know, it's just... he's sort of my boss, and I don't want to jeopardise this design. I'm loving working on the hotel and bringing it back to life. But he said he's going to try and keep me there as long as possible and he'll keep finding things for me to do, that's what that string of messages was about,' she said, pointing to her now sleeping phone. 'Which is sort of a compliment if he's that happy with my work but... if it's not my work he's interested in it's a bit creepy.'

'Too right it's creepy. He's abusing his position to sexually harass you, Bells. That says an awful lot about who he is. By the sounds of it he's a spoiled mummy's boy who's not used to hearing the word *no*.' He spoke through clenched teeth, clearly holding back the venom he would've liked to have spat.

'You're right. But I'll handle it. Thank you for offering, I just don't want to be one of those damsels in distress. Because I'm not really in distress. I'm just irritated. And I can look after myself.'

He smiled. 'Oh, I know you can. I remember the Kerr situation and how you whacked him after he'd been a shit. But the offer's there. I could even go in my official capacity if that helps.'

Bella waved a dismissive hand. 'Oh, no, really, there's no need. It'll be fine. I'll just be professional and aloof. He'll get the message eventually.'

Harris leaned forward and kissed her tenderly. 'The trouble is you're too beautiful,' he stated matter-of-factly. 'Maybe you need to go in wearing an awful dingy outfit with spinach in your teeth and unwashed hair.'

She laughed. 'Erm, yuck. No thanks.'

He pulled her down on top of him and kissed her neck, making her squeal as ticklish shivers travelled her spine.

He gave a silly growl. 'What do you mean yuck? I'd still fancy you. Ooh, it'd be lovely. I can imagine it now. Spinach and maybe a poppy seed or two.'

She whacked his chest. 'Eeew! You're revolting,' she told him, laughing uncontrollably as she squirmed.

'Aye, but that says something about you, when you think about it; you agreed to marry me!'

'And I can't wait,' Bella said, kissing him tenderly.

He reached up and tucked her hair behind her ear, the anger fully subsided now. 'I feel the same. I think I'm boring everyone when I'm out on my rounds. It's all I can talk about.'

'Really? That's so sweet.'

'You're the most important subject I can think of,' he replied with a shrug as if it should be completely obvious. 'And I can't wait to share my name with you.'

'I'll be so proud to be Mrs Arabella Donaldson.' She sighed.

'Not half as proud as I'll be to introduce you as my wife,' he said.

'Ugh, listen to us. We're sickening, aren't we?' Bella laughed. 'It's a good job no one can hear us.'

'I don't care if they can. I'd shout it from the rooftops given half a chance.'

'God, I love you, Harris,' she said as he enveloped her in his arms.

17

How can it be October 2025 already? Bella thought as she got ready for work. The countdown was on to Christmas Eve and her wedding and even though she knew she shouldn't wish the time away she couldn't help it. She often found herself daydreaming about walking down the aisle towards Harris and seeing his reaction to her in the amazing dress Olivia had designed.

Whoever was in charge of the weather had been efficient, that's for sure; the temperature had plummeted overnight, and rain had set in. It was a miserable day that matched her solemn mood at having to return to Iolair-Mhara, knowing full well that Carlton would be there.

After a thoroughly enjoyable weekend, all Bella wanted to do was roll over and pull the duvet over her head; anything to avoid the innuendos and being undressed by the American's eyes. But instead, she showered, dressed in a smart trouser suit over a loose top, applied minimal makeup and stared at her reflection. She hated that she was having to second guess everything she was going to wear in case it encouraged Carlton. In reality she should've been able to wear whatever the hell she liked but she knew that he would scrutinise her whole outfit and try to read hidden come-ons that didn't exist. So, the more plainly dressed she was, the better.

With reluctance, she arrived at the hotel determined to deal with the Carlton situation once and for all. She felt so much better now that Harris knew what had been going on and it had spurred her on to make sure the arrogant arse knew she was engaged to the most wonderful man and had no intentions of that changing.

The hotel was surprisingly, and eerily, quiet when she arrived, which confused her somewhat. The crew were supposed to be in with a team kitting out the catering kitchen and another dealing with her snagging list for the lounge, while another started on the first-floor bedrooms. She wandered around the place to see if anyone had bothered to turn up for work but was met with silence and sparse, dark rooms with the restored original shutters closed.

She wandered up the stairs to check the bedrooms which were now devoid of the awful fitted Formica furniture and instead had bare plaster walls in readiness for the next phase of her designs. There were still a few tools scattered around that the construction crew had left behind but, frustratingly, no one was there to operate them.

Thankfully, when eradicating the seventies from the place, they had uncovered many of the old Victorian building's original features; the ceiling roses and cornices hidden above suspended ceilings and the shutters and balustrades that had been boarded in were Bella's favourites so far.

There was a lot to still be done and for the first time she wondered if she had bitten off more than she could chew. Although nothing would get done without the workers here to do it, so she took out her phone, chuntering to herself, and was just about to make the call when a hand landed firmly on her shoulder, causing her to squeal and lash out as she turned to face her assailant.

Carlton laughed, holding onto her arms. 'Whoa there, Bella! What's got you all riled up?' He stood there in dark jeans and a tight white T-shirt that clung to his biceps and pectoral muscles. *At least he's wearing clothes on this occasion.* A crease appeared between his brows, but the smile remained in place. 'You look like you've seen a ghost, but I thought they'd all left with the seventies crap.'

She yanked her arms from his grasp. 'Carlton! You can't sneak up on people like that, you almost gave me a heart attack,' she snapped, placing her hand over the pounding in her chest.

He held out his hands, palms up, and shook his head. 'Hey, it's not my fault you're so highly strung. You need to relax a little bit. Maybe I can help you with that.'

Here we go again. 'I'm not here to relax, I'm here to work. Speaking of which, where are the building and decorating crews?'

He shrugged. 'Oh, I gave them the day off. Thought we needed a little alone time.' He smirked, licking his lips suggestively. 'To talk about my new ideas for the games room, obviously.' His mouth curled up into that irritating half-smile he seemed to save especially for her.

Realising this meant she was here alone with him sent a shiver of unease down her back. 'You had no right to do that without consulting me. There's plenty for them to be getting on with. A list of jobs I gave them, in fact, to work on towards the finished design your parents are paying me to deliver. I need them here to get on with it, otherwise the schedule falls behind, and I'm sure you don't want that.'

'You're so damned serious.' He pulled his lower lip between his teeth and released it slowly while looking her up and down. 'But you're sexy as all hell when you're annoyed. I like 'em feisty.' He winked and her stomach roiled. 'And I have to say I love that shirt. It clings in all the right places.'

Bella had chosen the shirt because it didn't cling at all, so it was clear he was goading her and his comments were becoming more frequent and intense. She clenched her jaw, refusing to react outwardly to his comments, and reached for her phone. 'It's okay, I'll call and get them to come in as soon as possible. The day's not lost yet.'

He shoved his hands into his pockets and shrugged his shoulders. 'No point. They're working on another job now in the south of the island. They'll be back tomorrow, as *I* requested; after all, it is *my* hotel. Now, I thought we'd start our discussions downstairs in the dining room. In fact, you're right on time because the food I ordered for us was delivered about five minutes ago. Follow me.' He turned to walk towards the staircase that led down to the foyer, but Bella stayed completely still. He stopped and turned around to face her, grinning. 'Oh, come on now. I'm not gonna bite you. Unless you want me to, of course. I'd certainly enjoy that.' He flicked his eyebrows upwards.

Bella had had enough. He may have borne a striking resemblance to a younger Matthew Mc-Conaughey, but it made no difference to her, she still wasn't about to jump into bed with him. 'Right, that's it. You need to stop this, right now.' She jabbed a finger in the direction of the ground for emphasis.

His smile disappeared and he feigned innocence. 'Stop what? I don't know what you're talking about, Bella.' He held out his hands as if to show he was unarmed.

Her nostrils flared and she folded her arms across her chest. 'The innuendos, the flirting, the ridiculous attempts at seduction. It's highly inappropriate. I've told you I'm engaged and absolutely *not* interested. Read the room and know when you're wasting your time.'

He took a few steps towards her again. 'Did y'all leave your sense of humour locked in one of your fiancé's jail cells back home?'

Her heart pounded at her ribs as she glared at

him. 'This is nothing to do with having a sense of humour, Carlton. It has *everything* to do with being
pissed off at being sexually harassed when I'm simply
trying to do the job your parents employed me to do.'

He held up both hands in a halting motion and
scowled. 'Now hang on there just a damn minute,
Bella. I'm not *sexually harassing* you, and I don't know
why you'd say that. Jeez, what is wrong with you
women? I take offence. I'm not some kind of per-
verted deviant, for Chrissake. Where I'm from we call
it a bit of harmless fun. A little bit of flirting to pass
the time is all.'

Through gritted teeth, she said, 'Well, where *I'm*
from it's called sexual harassment, and it makes
women feel objectified and extremely uncomfortable.
Now please, let's be professional, otherwise I'll be
pulling out of the contract, and you'll have lots of explaining to do to your parents.'

He smiled snidely. 'If you do that, they'll just call
our lawyers and you'll be in a whole mess of trouble,'
he said, then chuckled. 'You're so overdramatic, you
know that? Now I'm starving, let's go eat.'

Once again, she remained on the spot, and he
laughed. 'It's lunch, for heaven's sakes. I'm not gonna
poison ya. I'll take a bite of everything first to prove it
if you like.' When she still didn't move, he sighed, and

his smile disappeared. 'Okay, I get it. You're British, uptight and not interested in having fun at work—'

'*I take offence at that!* Being British has nothing to do with it, Carlton. It's simply that it's *not* fun.' Her jaw ached from being clenched so hard and her heart was racing, partly due to anger and partly due to anxiety.

He held up his hands in a surrendering gesture. 'Okay, okay, you're engaged and not interested. Message received loud and clear. From now on I'll be the perfect gentleman. But you have seen what you're missing out on.' He held his arms out as if to make it clearer. 'There's not many women who'd pass up a night with this face and body.'

Good grief, love yourself much? 'Believe it or not, good things don't always come in pretty packaging. You've only got to look at Ted Bundy.'

He raised his eyebrows. 'You did *not* just compare me to a deranged serial killer.'

Perhaps that was a step too far, Bella, he hasn't tried to murder you... yet. 'All I'm saying is that looks aren't everything.'

'Your cop not a looker then?'

She scowled. 'That's not what I'm saying at all. And I'm not having this conversation with you any longer.'

'Look, can we please go eat and discuss my ideas already? I wasn't kidding, I've been lifting some serious weights this mornin' and it's made me damn hungry.' He flexed his biceps and grinned.

He really doesn't know when to give up.

Bella reluctantly followed Carlton down the stairs, and through the foyer, past paint pots, ladders and all manner of construction detritus, to the dining room and there, in the centre of the vast space, was a single table with a white cloth, two chairs, candles, a bottle of white wine and a variety of dishes laid out. It looked like something Harris would prepare for her at home on a romantic occasion. It was presumptuous, and once again, inappropriate.

'Come on before it gets completely cold.'

A delicious aroma of spices reached Bella's nose, and her stomach betrayed her with a growl. 'I'm not actually hungry,' she lied, pulling out a chair and sitting down.

'Suit yourself. Mind if I eat?'

'Go ahead.'

'Okay, so...' He began to spoon Greek salad complete with the crumbliest feta cheese onto his plate along with what appeared to be lamb koftas. Then he spooned tzatziki onto the plate and licked his thumb and finger. The food looked and smelled rather delicious, but Bella wasn't going to give him the satisfaction of admitting that. 'The games room...' he said through a mouthful of food as he opened the bottle of white wine and poured some into each of the two glasses that were on the table.

'I'm driving,' she told him, shaking her head when he offered her one of the glasses.

'Oh, come on, one won't hurt.'

'I don't drink and drive in *any* amount. Not only am I not stupid and value my life, but the police on Skye have a zero-tolerance policy when it comes to drink driving, and I should know because I'm marrying one of them. Now what about these plans?'

For the next thirty minutes, Carlton talked enthusiastically about his idea for a games room at the rear of the hotel in the old laundry building as he polished off the whole bottle of wine, rather too quickly in Bella's opinion. But he didn't want just *any* games room, he wanted a casino-style place for residents to be able to play the tables and have 'a little fun', something he seemed obsessed with, and Bella wondered how on earth he was going to make a go of the serious part of the business, which he never seemed to mention or acknowledge.

To Bella his ideas seemed a little crass and the antithesis of the whole vibe she had created for the beautiful old place. 'You do realise you'll need per-missions from the relevant authorities to have gam-bling on the premises, don't you? And what have your parents said about this? It's their hotel, after all, and it doesn't really seem to fit in with the overall ethos of the place,' Bella said, unsure as to whether such a place was needed or, what's more, *wanted* in a peace-ful, rural location such as this that would exude ro-mance once finished.

His jaw clenched under his skin. 'Of course I've spoken to them. I have carte blanche to do what I want with the old laundry,' he informed her tersely. 'I'm in charge.' He had the attitude of a spoiled tod-dler. 'It's *my* hotel.'

Bella's phone vibrated and she picked it up to see a message from Harris.

> Hey beautiful. How is it going? Are you ok? Has he got the message?

She hit reply.

> All good. I think it's finally sunk in for him. Love you.

She put her phone back in her bag and put her bag on the floor.

'Who was that?' Carlton asked, nodding to her phone. 'The ball and chain? Checking that you haven't had a better offer?'

'He knows that wouldn't happen. There is no better offer out there.'

Carlton sucked air through his teeth. 'Okay, okay. I get it. You're marrying Mr Perfect. Jeez. What is it you Scots say? *That's me telt*?' His attempt at her accent was terrible.

'Aye, that's about right.'

He ran his hands back through his hair and rested them atop his head. 'I give up already. I never have to work this hard to get a woman into bed.'

'I've told you right from the start that it won't be happening, Carlton, *ever*.' She hoped he was being truthful, about the giving up part anyway.

'Okay... okay. Look, while you're here can we go on up and check out the presidential suite? I have some ideas for that too.'

The room to which he was referring took up a third of the top floor and was actually known to her and the team as the *Bridal* Suite and the design had already been agreed, in fact it was the first of the upstairs rooms that was to be worked on in readiness for the photographs for the new website. Bella had fig-ured it would have the biggest appeal considering the stunning views and dual-aspect windows, perfect for a wedding night.

She narrowed her eyes. 'You're wanting to change the design? It's the one you seemed happiest with when you saw it initially. It's the one the team were due to start on today, in fact.' She couldn't help the twinge of annoyance that knotted her stomach.

'Oh, I'm happy with it. I just want to go over the wallpaper samples again. I think I found one I pre-ferred to the one you originally suggested.'

He was clearly trying to assert his dominance. The paper had already been delivered but it was fairly neutral, so could be utilised elsewhere, if neces-sary, she just hoped that didn't have to be the case because in her mind it was perfect.

She lifted her chin and forced a smile. 'I see, okay, well, the samples are through in the foyer on the old reception desk so we can just go look there.'

He stood. 'No, they're up in the suite. I took them up when I went up there earlier before you got here, so I could hold them against the wall to see which worked best with the natural light that comes into that room. It won't take a minute.' *So, you're a designer now, are you?* was what she wanted to say.

Something felt off. Her stomach was knotted, and her heart rate had picked up. But he was her boss, and she possibly was overreacting. Although her Granny Isla had always told her to listen to her gut – if something felt off it probably was. Nervously, she followed him back through to the foyer, partly dreading what could happen to her alone in this place in the middle of nowhere and it would be her word against his, and partly dreading which paper he was going to ask her to order. Some of the samples were quite bright and didn't at all gel with the calming, romantic aesthetic she had gone for on her mood board. The previously agreed and signed off mood board.

'You can leave your bag. We're just looking at paper.'

Not on your nelly, pal, she thought as she slung her bag across her body and followed him, *I'm keeping my phone to hand*. He paused at the single elevator in the foyer. A rickety old thing that had been installed in the seventies and that Bella wouldn't trust with a tray of food, never mind a human being.

'I'll be taking the stairs,' she informed him. 'The lift hasn't been serviced yet and it'll definitely need work, or even to be condemned and removed. That's why the hazard tape was on it.'

'Oh, that? Yeah, I took that off.' His words were slurring a little now. 'I've been using the elevator all week and it's been fine. My legs are tired from my workout, so I don't feel like stomping up three flights again. Come on. Live a little.' The door opened and he stepped inside. 'Bella?'

She stepped forward but hesitated. *Wait, why the hell am I actually considering this? Wasn't I just comparing him to Ted Bundy? And wasn't I just telling him this lift is a death trap?*

She shook her head. 'Nah. I'll meet you up there.' She turned to walk away but he reached out and grabbed her hand, laughing as he yanked her inside and into his arms.

As the door closed, he pushed her against the fake wood-panelled wall and pressed his mouth to hers.

She shoved at his chest and reached up to scratch his face, then swiftly kneed him in the crotch as she screamed, 'Get off me!'

He stepped back and dropped to his knees, holding his groin. 'Ow! What the hell was that for?' He coughed, his voice was strained and his face red.

The lift was moving now, and she yelled at him, 'You arrogant shithead! How *dare* you—'

He clambered to his feet. 'Oh, come on, I've only done what you wanted me to do.'

'I didn't want any such thing, Carlton. I haven't exactly been subtle about things. I told you in no uncertain terms that I'm not interested!' There was a loud clunk, and the lift halted with a judder, shunting her towards him once more.

He grabbed for her again and held her tightly. 'You don't need to carry on playing hard to get, Bella. Harris isn't here; it's just us, so give in to it. I've seen how you look at me.' He laughed, reminding her of a movie villain.

She flailed, kicking his shin. 'Let go of me!' she squealed.

He continued to laugh but released her. 'Ow! Take it easy. I'm only messin' around. I just wanted a little kiss, that's all. Don't tell me you haven't thought about it.'

Bella's chest heaved as she glared at him, wide-eyed. 'My God, you're so conceited. No. I have *not* thought about kissing you. What part of *no* do you not get? You do know that was assault, don't you?'

He rubbed at his cheek where visible red lines had formed. 'Says the woman who tried to scratch my eyes out and then kicked me in the nuts.'

'In self-defence!' she yelled.

He held out his arms. 'Why would you need to defend yourself against me? I'm not gonna hurt you. It was just a kiss.'

'It was an unwanted advance, Carlton, and that is absolutely not okay!' He didn't speak, instead he stood there with a smug smirk on his face that she was desperate to slap away. She tried to take deep breaths to calm herself. 'I honestly can't believe your behaviour. In this day and age too. You've heard of the "me too" movement, I presume? Do you even realise how serious this is? My fiancé is—'

He rolled his eyes and huffed. '*An officer of the law,* yeah, yeah,' he mocked in a childish tone. 'I'm no criminal so that's your word against mine. Jeez, you sound just like Helena.'

'Yeah, well, I know who he'll agree with, because I'm not the conceited arse forcing himself on someone!' Her chest heaved, partly in fear and partly in anger. *How dare he?* Realising he had mentioned, potentially, another of his prey, she scowled. 'Hang on, who's Helena?'

His smile disappeared and he appeared shocked. 'What?' He clearly hadn't meant to say her name out loud.

'You said I sound *just like Helena.* Who is Helena?'

He sighed like an errant teenager. 'Ugh, the

makeup artist that accused me of sexual harassment back in the States. The reason I'm no longer modelling and why I've been exiled here to this shithole, and the reason I have to go home next week for a meeting with my folks' lawyers to sign the settlement,' he barked. 'You're just like her. Can't take a damn joke and let your eyes say one thing while your mouth says another.'

She backed herself to the wall of the lift, knowing full well that her eyes and her mouth had definitely been on the same page all along. 'Can you not read body language? Because mine was telling you to eff off from the start.'

He tilted his head. 'Yeah, yeah, whatever you say. But we both know the truth.'

A thought dawned on her. 'I don't suppose I should be shocked that I'm not your first victim.'

He curled his lip. '*Victim*? Seriously?' He laughed without any shred of humour. 'My God, you're all the damn same. And the Oscar for overreacting goes to...' he said into an imaginary microphone. 'Well, don't expect any money, because Helena's getting it all. My folks are having to pay her off. Bitch threatened to go to the police just because I slapped her ass when she bent over in a tight skirt to supposedly pick somethin' up.' He made inverted commas in the air. 'As if it wasn't a damned invitation.'

Guessing that that particular action couldn't have been the only thing to cause his parents to send him away, Bella widened her eyes. 'I can assure you it won't have been a bloody invitation. You can't do things like that! What else did you do to her? I'm not surprised she threatened to report you.' She curled her lip. 'Your parents must be so proud.'

Ignoring her, Carlton stared at the door, his eyes now wide and filled with what looked like fear. 'Why isn't that door opening?' he said suddenly, jabbing a finger towards the exit. 'We stopped so the doors should've opened. Why haven't they opened?'

Bella scoffed with incredulity. 'Because we're stuck between floors, you absolute walloper,' she exclaimed what she had presumed was blatantly obvious. 'What did you think that loud crunching noise was?'

His eyes flitted from her to the door and back again. 'What? We can't be stuck. That's the dumbest thing I ever heard. It's been working fine.' This time his laughter verged on maniacal as he took two steps over to the panel and banged his finger on each button in turn. 'We can't be stuck.'

Bella held out her arms and let them flop to her

sides in exasperation. 'I did warn you that it needed servicing... or condemning.'

'No. No. It can't be stuck,' he repeated. He then bashed at the door with his fists and shouted, 'Help!'

Bella almost jumped out of her skin as she flung herself back against the wood panelling, heart racing and chest heaving. 'Bloody hell, Carlton, there's no need for that. You terrified me.'

'Hello, anybody!' His voice was high-pitched and sounded wrong coming from his body. 'We need some help in here!' Only a short time ago he had been flexing his muscles, trying to be the big man, and now he was squealing like a wounded animal.

The pounding, combined with his screeches, echoed around the 4ft-by-4ft container and Bella covered her ears. 'Well, you just carry on doing that, it's bound to help,' she shouted, her tone dripping with sarcasm.

He turned to her; the colour had drained from his usually tanned face, leaving him rather grey and pallid. 'No, no, I can't be in here, Bella. I can't. I can't breathe.' He pulled at the neck of his T-shirt, but it wasn't even tight.

She shook her head. 'It's fine. I'll call someone.' She reached into her bag. 'Shit, where's my phone?'

She frantically rummaged around the contents, but her phone wasn't there.

Carlton gripped his hair with his hands. 'It's on the floor under the table in the dining room.'

Slowly Bella lifted her chin and glared at him. 'What?'

'It fell out of your bag, and I slid it away with my foot.'

Bella crumpled her face in disgust. 'Why the hell did you do that?' And then she felt the colour drain from her own face. 'What were you planning to do to me when we got upstairs?'

He chewed on his thumb. 'Nothing. Nothing at all. I was just messing around. I was annoyed when your fiancé messaged so I slid it away so he couldn't bother you for a while. We were getting on fine until he messaged you.'

'You really are quite delusional, aren't you?' A voice in her head was screaming at her to be nicer, seeing as she was in such a vulnerable position, but anger was getting the better of her fear. 'Were you planning on telling me where my phone was?'

He was staring at the door, wide-eyed, and he was visibly shaking. 'I... I thought I could pretend to help you look for it later, and you'd think I was sweet when I found it.'

She clenched her jaw and hissed, 'I can assure you that I will *never* think you're sweet, you absolute idiot.' *Steady on, Bella, too far, you can't escape, remember.*

'Wait a minute. You can call someone on your iPad,' he said, pointing at her bag.

'It's not SIM enabled, so no, I can't. I suggest *you* call someone because I don't want to spend a second longer than I have to trapped in here with *you.*'

He slid down the wood-panelled wall until his bottom hit the floor. 'I would call someone— I really would— if I had my phone.'

'What? Where's *your* phone?' Bella asked as anger turned her cheeks hot.

'I left it in my room. I didn't want any distractions today.' He stared at the floor for a few silent moments but then Bella watched as his shoulders began to move up and down rapidly. He began rocking back and forth and when he eventually lifted his chin his eyes had welled with tears, and he stared pleadingly up at her as his breathing became more and more erratic. 'I can't be in here, Bella, we have to get out. We— have— to. I'm— I'm really— badly— claust— claustrophobic.'

18

Bella stared down at Carlton where he sat crumpled in a ball on the floor of the lift. 'Oh, good grief, I really have heard it all now. All your other attempts have failed so now you're trying to garner sympathy by pretending to be claustrophobic as a way to try and get me into bed. You really are pathetic. Haven't you ever been told no? Is that it? You're so used to getting your own way that you'll go to extremes the first time it happens?' Meanwhile, Carlton continued to rock back and forth.

He's a really good actor though, I'll give him credit for that, she thought. *If I didn't know what he was up to I could really be fooled. He looks genuinely scared. Someone, get this man a Tony award.*

He slowly shook his head and tears spilled over from his eyes. 'You— have to— believe me— B-Bella. It's not— I'm not— I'm not lying— I can't be here— I can't breathe.'

She sneered. 'What were you saying earlier about Oscars? I think this performance is definitely worthy.' She folded her arms across her chest. 'And you're not fooling me, by the way. It won't work, just so you know.'

He rubbed his hands over his face. 'Please, Bella... I'm not lying... I need to get out.' Then out of the blue he lurched to his feet and screamed, 'Heeeeeelp! Anybody!' while hammering his fists on the door again.

'Carlton, you're wasting your time. No one's out there to hear you. You sent them home, remember?'

Ignoring her, he continued to yell, 'Pleeeeease! Anybody!' His voice sounded hoarse now. As if he had exhausted himself, he dropped to the floor once more and curled up again in the corner of the lift.

Realising he might actually be telling the truth after all, because surely no one could fake fear this convincingly, Bella crouched down in front of him. 'But you said you'd been using the lift all week, so how *can* you be claustrophobic? Claustrophobic people don't use lifts. Everyone knows that.'

He closed his eyes. 'I lied.' He swallowed hard.

'About using the lift, I mean. I've sent it up... and down a few times. Empty though... Mainly when I've... run up the stairs... to try and beat it. Just for fun. But I hadn't actually been *in* it... until today.' He seemed to be on the verge of hyperventilating again.

Bella flopped to the floor to join him. 'Why the hell did you pull me into it and hit the button if you feel that way? What on earth were you thinking?'

He shook his head; his breathing still coming in fits and starts. 'It was bravado, I guess. I wanted— to impress you. I wanted to— seem brave when you were scared— about using the old elevator. It was— it was stupid.'

Bella tilted her head and curled her lip. 'You think?'

He lifted his chin and stared at her. 'What are we gonna do, Bella? How will we get out?'

Seeing him so vulnerable, even after what he'd said and done, filled her with pity. She fixed a determined gaze on him. 'First of all, you need to calm your breathing, or you'll hyperventilate. So, follow me. In, two, three, four, five, hold it... out, two, three, four, five...' She made gestures up and down with her hands in rhythm with her words. Keeping his eyes focused on hers, he began to copy her. 'That's it... In, two, three, four, five, hold it... out, two, three, four, five. That's better. Keep doing that.' She breathed with him for a couple of minutes until he seemed to calm down a little.

'Someone will come, you know. It's not like we're going to be stuck forever, or die in here,' she told him, in the hopes it would put his mind at rest. *Although maybe mentioning death wasn't the best idea*, she thought, cringing inwardly.

'But how will anyone know to even look for us? The construction guys won't be back until tomorrow. Neither of us have our phones. How will we get out? No one knows we're even here, Bella. Not a single person will know we're stuck in this goddamn box. It's like a coffin.' He tugged at strands of his hair with fisted hands. 'Oh, jeez. I can't do this. I really can't, Bella. I'm not kidding, I can't be here. What if we run out of oxygen?' He spread his arms out, clawing at the walls as his breathing rate increased again.

Bella reached out and put a hand on his arm. 'Hey, let's go back to the steady breathing, shall we?' She was more concerned about the fact that she hadn't eaten and might need the loo at some point. *Now* she regretted refusing that delicious-smelling food as her stomach made its protestations.

After a few more minutes, she managed to calm

Carlton down again. His breathing was more even, and his eyes were back to their normal size.

'You asked who'll know we're here. Well, Harris knows I'm here, and when I don't come home or answer my phone, he'll get worried and come up to find me.'

'He will? How long will that take? When will he be here? Will it be soon?' He sounded like a scared little boy.

'Try and stay calm, Carlton. He may be a while because he's working, but he'll come. And there are air vents if you look up there.' She pointed to the ceiling. 'But Harris will see that I'm not home and he'll call me. When I don't answer he'll guess something is wrong. I know he will, okay?'

Carlton nodded, chewing on his fingers. 'Okay, yeah. He'll be here. He'll know something's wrong.' He repeated her words parrot fashion as if trying to convince himself. 'He'll definitely be here. It won't be too long.'

Bella forced a smile. 'That's right. Now in the meantime why don't we chat to pass the time?'

Carlton lifted his T-shirt and for a bizarre moment Bella thought he was going to undress and suggest another way to pass the time, but instead he lifted the hem up to his face and wiped the tears away. 'What do you want to talk about?' he asked, sniffing.

'Why don't you tell me about your modelling career? How did you get into that?'

He huffed. 'Where do I start?' He shrugged, thankfully seeming much calmer now. 'I was always a good-looking kid.' He looked at her. 'I'm not being conceited this time. It's what I was always told. *Oh, aren't you a handsome boy? Look at that beautiful face,*' he said in a high-pitched tone that clearly mocked the people who'd said it about him. 'Modelling seemed an obvious choice, so my mom got me an agent when I was pretty young, and it went from there. It's all I was good for really.'

So now he's self-deprecating? 'What do you mean by that?'

He picked at a thread on the outer seam of his jeans. 'I wasn't as bright as my sister and brother. They got the brains. Sindy went to Harvard and Nate Junior went to Stanford. I went to community college. Not because I was dumb but because I was lazy. Basically, I knew my face would be my key to money and success so there was no need for me to try at education. I know that was dumb when I look back now but at the time it felt like an easy choice. But I can't complain. It's opened plenty of doors. Not literally, of course.' He chuckled.

'See, you're making jokes now. That's good.' She smiled and patted his arm as she relaxed a little.

'Look, I'm sorry about earlier. I was a total ass,' he said. A line had formed between his brows, and there was sincerity in his eyes.

Bella nodded. 'Yes, you were.'

'I guess you were right, I'm so used to women wanting me that I just expect it to be the case with everyone I want for myself. That they'll just want me too.' Although he did sound a little conceited, she understood what he was saying. 'And before you say anything I know that makes me sound like an egotistical dick. But... it's true. Women have always kinda fallen at my feet, so to speak.'

'Wow, sucks to be you,' Bella teased.

'Although not literally, I might add. I've never drugged anyone or anything as dumb as that.'

'Good to know.'

'And I swear I wasn't going to do anything to you when were upstairs. I'm not that kind of guy. I may be an asshole but I'm not a criminal.' When she didn't answer he continued. 'So, you're getting married at Christmas, huh?'

She nodded. 'I am.'

'What you got planned? For the wedding, I mean. Where are you tying the knot?'

'We're heading over to Inverness. My friend is Lady Olivia MacLeod, and she owns Drumblair Castle.'

'No shit? You're getting married at a real-life castle?'

He sounded like a child and Bella couldn't help smiling. 'We are, yes. At the chapel in the grounds anyway. Then we're having the wedding breakfast in the castle's picture gallery, surrounded by Olivia's ancestral portraits.'

'Wow, sounds grand. And I bet the place will be all decked out for Christmas, too, huh?'

'It sure will. They have a plant and tree nursery in the grounds, so their trees are out of this world. Their fragrance is so fresh; the epitome of Christmas. They always have the most stunningly decorated Scots pines and these huge garlands of holly and ivy over every mantel. I've been going to the castle since I was a kid so getting married there will be very special.'

'So, this Lady MacLeod, does she do lots of state visits and stuff? Is she related to royalty?'

'Not as such, no. She's a fashion designer in her daily life and has her own line. In fact, she used to design for Nina Picarro in New York.'

His eyes widened. 'You're kidding me right now. You said her name is Olivia?' Bella nodded and he shook his head, smiling. 'Not Olivia MacBain?'

Bella narrowed her eyes. 'Yes, that's right.'

He slapped his thigh and let out a laugh. 'I knew her! I was in the New York office, years ago now, and Nina introduced me to her. She was working on a fashion show I was in, and she did my fittings. Great gal. Beautiful but kinda quiet. Huh, small world.'

'She's designed my wedding dress,' Bella said, feeling a lot more relaxed now.

'Really? Then you're definitely gonna look hot. I mean... sorry... I mean you'll look beautiful in her design.'

She let his comment slide. 'I hope so.'

'So, what are your bridesmaids wearing? What colour did you go for?' She scrunched her brow, surprised by his questions so he pointed at himself and responded with, 'Model, remember? I've done a few wedding catalogue shoots.' He shrugged.

'Fair point. They're wearing a deep, rich green colour and their dresses are long with floaty sleeves. They have shawls too in Donaldson tartan.'

He nodded. 'Makes sense with the temperatures in Scotland. I like green. Good choice.' He fell silent for a moment but then said, 'I bet you're excited, huh?'

'Very. It's going to be the wedding I always dreamed of having. And I'm truly marrying the most incredible man.'

Carlton nodded. 'He's a lucky guy. It's clear he adores you from the size of the rock.' He nodded at her hand. 'But why wouldn't he?' He gave a small smile.

He fell silent for a while so, to keep the distraction going, she asked, 'So have you ever been in love?'

He clenched his jaw and nodded slowly. 'I have. Well, I think I have. It was pretty one-sided and it didn't work out, but there's no surprise there, huh?' There was a distinct look of sadness in his eyes.

'I'm sorry to hear that.'

He shrugged. 'Thanks.'

'Who was she?' Bella asked, both from intrigue and to keep him talking.

'She was a model too. Jet-black hair and eyes that almost matched. She was tall, had these long tan legs, nice natural lips. Francine was her name. She was beautiful... on the outside at least. We did a few shoots together for Sears and Bloomingdales, and I fell... *hard*. We went on a few dates, kissed... slept to-gether. I thought she felt the same way until a famous rock star came along, who was old enough to be her dad by the way, and the chick... sorry, the *lady*... was off like a taffeta gown after prom, see,' he said, mimicking a forties New York reporter, jabbing his thumb over his shoulder.

Bella gave a light laugh. 'Delightful analogy.'

He closed his eyes briefly. 'Sorry. I really need to work on myself, huh?'

She nodded. 'Indeed, you do.'

'She broke my heart.' His words were almost a whisper. The air was thick with melancholy and there was another period of silence. 'I swore I'd never fall in love again. That I'm not the kind of guy who has proper relationships. One-night stands are more my thing. Or that's what I keep telling myself. But the truth is, we all want to be loved.'

Bella was shocked by his candidness. She checked the time on her iPad. They had been stuck for almost two hours now. She was hungry, thirsty and wished she'd listened to her granny about carrying snacks with her. She wondered if Harris had tried to call, or if he'd messaged. Would he be concerned yet about the fact she hadn't replied, or would he just presume she was busy?

'So, how did you get into decorating?' Carlton asked out of the blue.

'I've always loved home improvement shows and when I was younger, I loved helping my mum and dad and granny to pick out colours and fabrics for their homes. Then, when I started earning my own money, I used to have a little flat that I worked really hard on before I lost it.'

'Why'd you lose it?' he asked. 'Or is that too private?'

'Lost my job. It was silly really, but I moved in with my granny after that.'

'Old people are great, huh?'

'My granny is a real character,' Bella said, smiling as she wondered if her granny might be worried too.

The light above their heads flickered and they both looked up. 'Oh, shit, no,' Carlton said as they were plunged into darkness. 'Oh God, this can't be happening.' He started flailing and grabbing at the walls again as if trying to find a gap he could crawl out of.

'Carlton,' she snapped loudly, hoping to get his attention. 'It's fine, just keep breathing how I showed you. Close your eyes and keep talking.'

'Can-can I sit a little closer to you?' he asked in a small wavering voice. If Bella hadn't known better, she'd have been forgiven for thinking this had all been a ploy. She slid herself closer to him and he grabbed for her hand and clung to it tightly. 'Is this okay? I just don't think I can handle this in the dark, Bella. It's like all my worst nightmares coming true. I feel like I've been buried alive.'

'Well, you haven't and you're going to be absolutely fine. Although, I'm not so sure about my fingers. Maybe loosen your grip, eh? You're cutting my circulation off.'

'Oh, sure, sorry.' He slackened his hold a little as requested. 'Please keep talking. I need something to distract me.' In the dark, Bella's hearing was heightened and the fear he was feeling was evident in both his strained voice and his shallow breaths.

'Slow your breathing down. We're fine. It won't be long before Harris comes. I know it.'

'You trust him implicitly, don't you?' He sounded a little calmer again and Bella felt like she was on a rollercoaster ride.

'I do. He's my safe place. My home.' She smiled as she pictured Harris's handsome face and the way his eyes crinkled when he laughed.

'I suppose it helps that he's a cop. All masculine and heroic.'

'It's not that. I admire those things about him but he's so considerate and compassionate. That's important to me. And he respects me.'

'Sounds exciting.'

Bella could hear the sarcasm in his tone. 'You can joke about things like respect, but love is so much more than sex, Carlton. I've known men who think they can just take what they want and treat women however they like. It's not attractive. At all. Regardless of the package it's offered in.'

'So, you're one of these women who doesn't go for looks, I take it?'

'Oh, don't get me wrong, I'm ridiculously attracted to Harris. In my eyes he's absolutely gorgeous. But it goes much deeper than that. Looks fade as we age but if the person you're with makes you laugh and feel good...'

'But what about excitement? Passion? Fun?'

'I think you have a skewed idea of what those things are. I have all of those things in abundance with Harris. But we have a solid foundation based on friendship and respect too.'

'I... I think you have me all wrong. I respect women.'

Bella huffed. 'I'm sorry but if you think it's acceptable for you to slap a woman's bottom just because she bends over in front of you then you really don't know much about respect at all, or what women want.'

'I didn't mean anything bad by it,' he insisted. 'It was a compliment when you think about it. And it was only done in fun.'

His comments annoyed her all over again. 'Fun for whom? Because I can assure you if a man slapped me on my behind, I wouldn't think it was fun. And I wouldn't take it as a compliment either. I'd feel degraded, humiliated and angry.'

She felt him move to face her. 'Humiliated? Really?'

Bella sighed. 'How can you not realise that? Women aren't objects for your entertainment, Carlton. Just because you usually get any woman you want doesn't mean you can take any woman when she's said no.'

'She'd flirted with me too. She was just playing hard to get.'

Bella yanked her hand free. 'No, Carlton. She wasn't. You can't make excuses like that. Next you'll be saying she was wearing a short or tight skirt on purpose, that she was asking for it. Women shouldn't have to explain themselves in detail to you. Nor should they have to consider what to wear to stop you from behaving like that. No doesn't mean *maybe if you slap my bottom I'll think about it*. No means no. She owed you nothing.'

Anger bubbled up from deep within her. 'Men don't seem to realise that women all over the world are faced with this kind of stuff on daily basis, and we're expected to deal with it quietly. Say nothing or else we'll be seen as – what did you call me? Overdramatic? – try being terrified of walking the streets at night in case some guy attacks you. Try having to watch what you wear in case a man can't control himself around you, because you'll be blamed if he can't. We're expected to have a sense of humour when men say things to us that make us uncomfortable. We're expected to accept the whole *boys will be boys* thing but it's shit, Carlton. It's hard. It can be terrifying being female. There are so many assumptions put on us and we're just expected to accept our lot in life. It's not fair. And it's not fun at all. Just imagine you had a daughter, and a man slapped her bottom without her consent. Would you laugh and think *oh, he was only doing it in fun*? What if she came home and told you her boss had been walking around half naked in front of her? In a work environment, shirtless and wearing only boxers. Would that just be him playing around? What if she told you a man she hardly knew had pulled her into a lift and pushed her up against a wall and forced himself on her?'

'But it was only a kiss, I—'

'No, Carlton! An unwanted kiss is *assault*. An unwanted slap to the behind is *assault*. Pinning someone down without consent is assault. How was I to know you weren't about to do something worse? We're here alone. I was afraid.'

'You were *afraid*? Of me?' He sounded genuinely surprised.

'Yes. I was afraid of what you might do next. You hid my phone, so I had no way to contact anyone if I'd wanted to. That's not something a normal person does. I've already told you I'm engaged on numerous occasions, and that I'm not interested. You had absolutely no right to do *any* of what you've done today, or before today for that matter.' Her eyes welled with angry tears, and she wanted nothing more than to be at home with Harris, in the arms of a man who knew how to treat people and would never force himself on anyone.

She heard Carlton swallow, but he didn't speak for a few moments. Eventually he reached out and took her hand again. 'I'm sorry, Bella. I'm a jackass. I hate that you were afraid of me. I really like you and I hate that you see me as this monster.' His voice trembled as he spoke and he fell silent again for a while until he eventually said, 'You're right, too, if I had a daughter and she'd been in any of those situations I'd wanna go and beat the guy to a pulp.'

'Exactly.'

'Do you think you can forgive me?'

'Right now, I'm not sure. Because if I'm going to continue working on this project, I need to feel safe, so I need you to please think before you say inappropriate things to me in future. And I need you to wear clothes.'

'I... I will. And I won't say anything... or do anything wrong to you again. I really am sorry. Please don't pull out of the job. You're the right person for it. I know how passionate you are about this place and your ideas are amazing. And I swear I'll even stay out of your way if you'd rather. Although I'm kinda hoping we can maybe get past this eventually. I promise I'll be better. And I really am sorry, Bella.'

'Thank you.' She didn't say she accepted his apology because at that precise moment she didn't know whether he was being genuine or just feeling scared due to the situation they were in. She wanted to further request that he stop belittling her and her qualifications but decided against mentioning that particular thing at that moment. Although she wouldn't hold back if he said anything like it again.

They sat in silence for what felt like hours and

Bella was fighting sleep. But in the distance, they heard a voice.

Bella sat bolt upright. 'Did you hear that?'

Carlton squeezed her hand and then scrambled to his feet. 'I did. I did! Hey! We're in the elevator! We're stuck!' He banged on the door, making Bella cringe at the piercing volume of the sound that felt like pins in her ears.

'Bella?' The voice got louder. 'Bella?'

'Harris!' Bella shouted, smiling with relief. 'Harris! Carlton and I are stuck in the lift!'

'Bella! Are you okay?' Harris shouted. His voice was closer now. 'Are you hurt? Do you need an ambulance?'

'No! We're fine. Just cold and sitting in the dark.'

'I'm going to go call the Fire Brigade. They'll be able to get you out. Sit tight.'

'Okay, thank you!' And then to Carlton she said, 'I told you he'd come.'

'I'm so glad you were right because I couldn't have been in here all night. I'd have gone crazy.'

'He never lets me down,' she replied, matter-of-factly.

After a few moments, Carlton spoke again. 'Look, thanks for helping me earlier. You didn't have to do that after how I've behaved toward you, so I want you to know I really appreciate it. You have a very calming way about you. And that's not me trying to flirt. I'm just stating a fact. And I hope it's okay to say this but... Harris is a very lucky guy, although I'm sure he knows that.'

Bella didn't respond.

* * *

A short time later they heard the wailing siren of a fire engine, and following that, more voices. Before they knew it the door was being pried open, and a torch was being shone down on them.

'Are you both okay? Any injuries?' a man's voice Bella didn't recognise asked. 'Any need of medical attention?'

'No, thank you, we're both fine. Just ready to get out of here.'

19

Harris hugged Bella close to him. 'Are you sure you're okay?' he asked, kissing her head. They had been out of the lift for around five minutes and had made their way back down to the hotel foyer from where the lift had been stuck. She was shivering and he had draped his jacket around her shoulders. Carlton had gone straight to the room he'd been sleeping in on the second floor to retrieve a bottle of Jack Daniel's. He walked back into the foyer swigging from it, no doubt to counteract the panic he had been feeling when they were trapped.

Bella nodded. 'I'm absolutely fine. I'm glad to be out of there but I'm unharmed, don't worry.'

'Has he been okay with you?' Harris whispered as he gave a sideways glance to Carlton.

She debated for a moment whether to say anything but remembered their agreement to keep no secrets from each other. 'We had words. I'll tell you more when we get home. Speaking of which, can we go? I'm starving and still cold.'

Carlton was now talking to the fire crew and nodding as the main firefighter, ironically female, pointed at the lift. Bella couldn't make out everything that was being said but the words *dangerous* and *condemned* stood out. Carlton was clearly taking it all in, thankfully.

Eventually he walked over to where Harris and Bella stood. He glanced sheepishly at Harris. 'Thanks again for coming to our rescue, Inspector Donaldson. It's been quite an unpleasant experience. I'm just glad Bella was with me because I'm not sure I would've survived on my own. I'm sure she's told you that I cried like a baby in there.'

Harris crumpled his brow and shook his head. 'She didn't, actually. Are you hurt? Do you need an ambulance after all, Mr Somers?'

Carlton's face turned pink as he turned to Bella. 'You didn't? Ah... okay. No, no thanks, I'm good. No physical injuries. And thanks, Bella. I imagined you'd probably have enjoyed filling him in on that little juicy snippet. But I appreciate your discretion, even if I've blown my own cover.' He smiled.

Bella was a little hurt that he would presume such a thing of her when she had given him no reason to. 'I'm not a mean person, Carlton. I don't take delight in people's phobias.'

Harris's brow crumpled. 'Phobias? What phobias?'

Carlton explained, his face colouring a new shade of pink. 'I... erm... I'm claustrophobic. Always have been. I was terrified in there. And then the lights went out and made it a hundred times worse.'

Harris's frown remained in place. 'So why use the lift? Claustrophobic people don't use lifts. Everyone knows that.'

Bella couldn't help smiling at the fact he had repeated her exact words.

Carlton rubbed the back of his neck, clearly embarrassed. 'Yeah... I just... I'm an idiot. What else can I say? I'm guessing Bella will explain.' He turned to Bella. 'And once again, I'm truly sorry, Bella. I completely understand if you want to rethink working on this place. Although I sincerely hope you don't. I doubt anyone else could do as good a job.'

Harris's nostrils flared and his cheeks flamed too

but for very different reasons. He pointed his index finger in Carlton's face and spoke through gritted teeth. 'Okay, why are you apologising to Bella? What exactly happened in there with you two? Is there something I should know?' He turned to Bella and gestured at Carlton. 'Should I be arresting him?'

Bella placed a hand on his chest. 'It's fine, Harris. It's been dealt with. Let's just go home, eh?'

Harris nodded but glared at Carlton then nodded towards the bottle he was clutching. 'Don't drink too much of that stuff. It doesn't mix well with the aftereffects of shock, and don't even think of driving anywhere because I wouldn't hesitate to arrest you and throw you in jail.'

Carlton glanced down at the bottle then saluted with his empty hand. 'Duly noted, Inspector. I'll be staying put and ordering a pizza.'

'Goodnight, Carlton. Take it easy,' Bella said.

He nodded. 'Thanks again... for everything.'

* * *

Once they arrived home, Harris lit the log burner in the lounge and made spaghetti carbonara, then they sat at the dining table eating as Bella explained the goings on of the day, leaving nothing out, in the name of transparency and their no-secrets agreement. Watching Harris's reactions wasn't easy for Bella. Once again, the colour of his face spoke volumes on how he was feeling.

Harris clenched his jaw and shook his head. 'The arrogant shit. Who the hell does he think he is, kissing you like that when you've told him countless times you're not interested? I know I said I'm not a caveman type, Bella, but I'm raging. If you'd told me this when we were back there I would've punched him and sod the consequences.'

Bella sighed. 'That's exactly why I didn't. He's not worth losing your career over. And I can stick up for myself, remember.'

He reached out and took her hand. 'Aye, I know you can, darlin'. But... just thinking about what his intentions were makes me...' His jaw ticked under his skin again and his lips curled up tightly for a moment. 'And the fact that he made sure you didn't have your phone... What kind of man is he?'

'Not a great one. And nothing happened so you don't need to think about it any more. Okay?'

'But something *did* happen, Bella. He forced himself on you and trapped you in a broken lift. That's assault and false imprisonment right there. I should arrest him. I should go back there and—' He made to stand up.

'No! Please don't do that. It's fine, honestly. He's realised his mistakes. I don't want to take things any further.'

He sat again. 'But what about the design job? You're not going to carry on there, are you?'

Bella chewed thoughtfully for a moment, relishing the flavour of the creamy pasta sauce. 'I think I have to. For the sake of the building. I've put so much work into the project and it's going to be wonderful when it's done. I genuinely don't think I'll get any more trouble from Carlton. I really think I made him see that his behaviour wasn't acceptable.'

'In my opinion, he's never going to be able to make a go of that place, you know. He's far too immature. I bet you he doesn't last a month when the place is open. He's a model not a businessman. I doubt he's ever run a place like that, or anything remotely similar, and it seems to me like he has no interest in the business side of things.' He had a point.

'I've thought the same things too. But thankfully I don't have to be there to watch him fail. Once my designs are fully implemented and completed, I can move on and never look back.'

'Will you inform his parents about what happened?'

Bella hadn't quite made her mind up about that. 'I feel like I should, seeing as I tried to tell them what he was like before, and evidently this isn't his first rodeo. Maybe if they had acted this wouldn't have happened, who knows. But I don't want to come across as a trouble causer. I'm not sure I want that reputation. It won't be helpful going forward.'

Harris heaved a deep sigh. 'You're not a trouble causer. He's a predator. It's his reputation that should be ruined, not yours. If he ever does anything that you find the slightest bit unnerving, or if he makes you the tiniest bit uncomfortable again, you need to tell me. I'll arrest him like a shot.'

Bella squeezed his hand. 'If it happens, I promise I'll tell you. But I don't think it will.'

* * *

A week later, Bella returned to Iolair-Mhara to check on the progress the teams had been making. She hadn't yet spoken to Mrs or Mr Somers about their son and wondered how things would be with Carlton seeing as she hadn't heard from him since the lift incident either.

She walked into the foyer and was happy to hear the sound of a sander and in the distance, somewhere in the building a man was singing out of tune to an ELO track on the radio; never had 'Mr Blue Sky' sounded more like stormy weather, metaphorically speaking.

Bella glanced over at the lift which had been bolted shut and the control panel removed, rendering it completely unusable, and a shiver made the hairs on her arms stand up.

She had pushed for the pace to be picked up and the painting and decorating company had sent extra bodies to ensure the work would be completed in a timely manner. She loved the building but no longer loved what it represented for her and wanted it to be over sooner rather than later.

'You must be Bella,' a voice said, making her jump. She turned to see a tall man aged around thirty-five with short blond hair. He looked like an older, slightly less handsome version of Carlton. He was wearing jeans and a checked shirt tucked in. He held out his hand. 'Nate Somers Junior, pleased to make your acquaintance.'

She shook his hand. 'Oh, nice to meet you too. Where's Carlton?' she asked, glancing behind him, expecting to see his younger brother.

Nate Junior rested his fingertips on his hips and sucked air in through his teeth. 'My little brother is back home learning how to respect women,' he said. 'I must apologise on behalf of my parents for what happened. They refuse to acknowledge what he can be like. Well, until now, that is. Unlike them, I'm very much aware that he's a dumbass and an embarrassment. Pardon my language. I was horrified when I heard what he'd done.' He shook his head. 'You'd have been well within your rights to press charges.'

Bella wondered how on earth he knew about what had happened when she hadn't told anyone but Harris. And surely *he* wouldn't have gone behind her back? 'Erm... Sorry, but how do you—'

'Know about what happened?' Bella nodded. 'He finally did something right and told Mom and Dad before you could. Figured it would sound better coming from him.'

'Was he honest about it all?'

Nate Junior raised his eyebrows and huffed the air from his lungs. 'Oh, yeah. We got the elevator situation, the comments, the suggestive way he dressed... or undressed around you. The whole nine yards. He's gone into therapy.'

Bella was surprised he had come clean so willingly and hadn't hidden anything. 'Ah. I see.'

'Yeah, I can't say I was either surprised or impressed. He's a spoiled brat who thinks his looks will just get him everywhere and get him out of trouble too. But I think maybe he's learned his lesson now. Only time will tell.'

'Won't he be coming back here at all?' Bella felt a small niggle of guilt but quickly brushed it aside, remembering how he had behaved and that none of it had been her fault. A very important thing for her to keep in mind.

'I think my folks are hoping to send him back once he's been punished thoroughly. The thing I didn't expect is that he actually wants to come back. Says he's grown very fond of the place, and of Skye in general. Says he found a certain amount of peace here that he's never felt before. That is until he acted like an asshole. He's currently working for free for my dad doing property maintenance, which Dad says will be good practice for if he does return to manage this place.' He glanced around the foyer. 'I'm guessing you know about the situation with Helena Katsaros. She was a makeup artist he worked with on his last modelling job.'

Bella nodded. 'He did mention something about that, yes.'

'Yeah, she ended his modelling career, and rightly

so in my opinion. Jackass. Oh, pardon my language. No one would hire him after what he did to her came out. He doesn't seem to get that people talk. Anyway, I'm here to oversee things for a while, although looking at your work I don't think there'll be much for me to do. Which I'm happy about because that means I can get back home to my wife and son, and my own job.' He smiled and Bella wondered how on earth two brothers could be so diametrically opposed in character.

'I mean, we're cracking on well,' Bella said, also glancing around. 'The rooms are coming together great, so I'm fine with you going back to the States and I can just keep in touch via video if that helps? I wouldn't want to keep you from your family.'

Nate Junior smiled and shook his head. 'Your accent is pretty awesome. I think I could listen to you reading a long grocery list and not get bored.' He cringed and rubbed a hand over his face. 'Jeez, that sounded like something my baby brother would say. My apologies. I can assure you I'm not flirting. I adore my wife, Deandra. And thank you. I think it's very clear I can trust you to do a great job without me peering over your shoulder. I'm staying at a hotel in Portree tonight,' Bella was surprised that he pronounced it correctly, 'and tomorrow, but I think I'll book my return flights. With today's technology there's no real reason for me to be here. I came on my parents' request to make sure you were okay after... And it's not like I know anything about interior design. I mean, I know what I like but it's nowhere near as tasteful as this place. That's why my wife won't let me near a colour chart or a Home Depot.' He laughed. 'Well, I'll let you *crack on* a little more. I think I might go souvenir shopping for my son, DJ. He's into castles and I'm sure I'll find something he'll like.'

Bella smiled. 'That sounds like a lovely idea. Have fun.'

'Thanks. And again, I'm so sorry about what my brother put you through. My parents don't always see what he's like with him being the baby of the family. But I mean, he's thirty years old so there comes a point he has to be treated like an adult and realise his actions have to have consequences, know what I mean? Good to meet you, Bella. So long.' He saluted her and then walked away in the direction of the stairs; Bella presumed to collect his jacket.

Nate Somers Junior seemed like a nice man and clearly knew his brother well. Bella felt a rush of relief flood her veins knowing that she had been believed and vindicated.

20

Granny Isla and Tam were interviewed by Kendric
MacKinnon during the last week in November and
the show aired as part of a special St Andrew's Day
celebration. He had made the journey to Skye to visit
them at their home – formerly Isla's home – with the
same crew that had accompanied him the last time,
and had made such a fuss of them, bringing them a
hamper of goodies including a bottle of champagne
as a belated congratulations on their wedding.

When the show was aired, the family had gathered at Pabay View to watch it in the TV lounge with
the other residents, who applauded enthusiastically
when their segment arrived on screen. Isla and Tam
had a sort of celebrity status now. Isla had worn the

obligatory lilac kaftan dress, only this time she wore a deep purple polo neck underneath due to the cold, and Tam had, of course, gone for a matching bowtie, and the pair had beamed with pride as Kendric asked them questions about their surprising long journey to get married at Gretna.

When asked if they had any regrets about the situation, Isla replied, 'When you get to our age you've got to grab life with two hands and make the most of every second. *You're a lang time deid*, as my father used to say. So, I have no regrets about marrying my Tam.' She patted her husband's hand. 'My only regret is that we interloped so that our families couldn't be there.'

Tam leaned towards her and whispered, 'I think you mean *eloped*, dearie.'

Without breaking her smile, or her focus on Kendric, Isla replied, 'Aye, hen, that's what a said.'

* * *

The month of Bella and Harris's wedding arrived in a glittering, frosty package, and the temperature dropped significantly with it. And, while Bella was wondering why on earth they chose the get married in December instead of, say, *June*, she was getting more excited, and nervous, by the day about the up-coming Christmas Eve nuptials. Their Christmas tree arrived on the fifth of the month, via courier from Drumblair nursery this year due to time constraints, and because Harris was off work on that day Bella took the day off too and they had spent a good couple of hours decorating it.

Of course, there was a brief interlude when the mistletoe was hung; Harris was irresistible, after all. He had tugged her beneath the doorframe where he had pinned the very realistic-looking but faux bunch of the plant (on account of Bertie chewing anything that had the audacity to fall to the floor), the stems of which were wrapped in burgundy ribbon, and had slipped his hands into her hair. Without speaking he had gazed into her eyes and smoothed his thumbs lightly over her cheeks before lowering his mouth to hers and kissing her. Her legs had weakened, and she wondered how he always managed to affect her that way. Shivers travelled her spine as she reciprocated the passion he was showing her, and her hands gripped the strands of his hair as the heat between them built.

Teasingly, he abruptly stopped his ministrations and placed a kiss on her nose. 'Hold that thought, Miss Douglas.'

Her eyes fluttered open. 'What thought?' she asked, smiling knowingly.

He chuckled. 'You know very well what thought, you saucy minx,' he said in his best imitation of Hugh Grant's voice. 'Come on, let's get this tree finished.'

Bella had the urge to protest but they couldn't very well leave the tree half done, could they? Especially when there were boxes of decorations on the floor and Bertie had already run away with the angel for the top. Bella and Harris had chased him around the garden for twenty minutes until teamwork and a well-executed pincer manoeuvre had rendered the dog trapped for a *very* brief moment. The joy in his eyes as they were chasing him had been lovely to see. He had clearly enjoyed the game.

Their decorations were a combination of things they had chosen together and things they had each bought when alone. It was an eclectic mix, but the tree told their own unique story. Amongst the traditional baubles in red, green, gold and tartan there was a glass teddy bear policeman that Bella had bought for Harris online as a stocking filler the previous Christmas. And a rather silly Harry Styles bust ornament on which the singer was wearing a sparkly black vest top. Harris had bought it from the Self-ridges website the same year, stating with a laugh,

'You make me listen to his music so I'm making you put him on the Christmas tree.' She wasn't sure how the two things were comparable but was more than happy to acquiesce, even if his CD had once almost decapitated her when she'd hit a pothole and Fifi had subsequently broken down. And speaking of Fifi, one of Bella's favourite ornaments was a little red Citroën 2CV that Harris had found for her on their first Christmas together. She adored her little car, so this was a very special item that she would always treasure. Now, they bought at least one special decoration each year, it had become a tradition.

All in all, it was a fun tree that neither of them took too seriously these days. Gone were the days when it had to be perfect and in keeping with the ambience of the room. Quite the opposite of what Bella had envisioned having, and had always insisted on when living alone or with Granny Isla. And it was certainly a talking point when friends came to visit.

* * *

Once the decorating was done, they sat, snuggled up on the sofa in the glow of the log burner and the coloured twinkly lights, admiring their handiwork. Bella laid her head in Harris's lap and The Darkness sang about 'Christmas Time' with bells in the background, the lyrics never failing to make Bella chuckle. The fresh, sweet smell of the pine tree, and the warming fragrance of cinnamon from the sticks hung upon it, infiltrated her senses and Bella sighed in contentment. She loved this time of year. She always had.

Bertie was lying on the rug before the fire, as always, on his back, legs in the air and tongue lolling out the side of his mouth. His favourite bunny toy was right next to his head, looking a little worse for wear after a year of being dragged and tossed around the garden. He'd had it since he was adopted, and it was the only toy he hadn't completely chewed up and destroyed.

The new Santa toy that Harris had picked up for him lay under the coffee table, virtually untouched. It had been hilarious seeing Bertie's reaction to it when Harris brought it home the day before. He had sniffed it, pawed at it and then proceeded to get down on his front paws and bark at it. But if either she or Harris tried to put it near him he ran off and hid behind the sofa.

'Have you spoken to Isla today?' Harris asked.

'I have, she was in the middle of supervising Tam while he put some pictures up in the lounge. They now have the one of them with Kendric MacKinnon to go with the one of Tam with Carol Vorderman and Richard Whiteley from *Countdown*.'

Harris chuckled. 'I wonder who they'll get to meet next.' He shook his head. 'It'll be strange not going to your granny's at Pabay for Christmas lunch this year.'

'It will but it'll be lovely to spend it at Drumblair Castle. The place is even more stunning when it's the festive season. The tree they get for the foyer reminds me of the one at the Rockefeller Centre. Although not *quite* as big. And the castle is usually decked out in tartan bows and red, gold and green.'

'So that's where your fascination comes from, is it?' Harris said.

'I think it probably is, yes. And Mirren bakes the best Christmas cake. You can smell it for days when she's been baking. Cinnamon and all spice wafts through the air, making your mouth water. I just hope it snows because it's like an old Christmas card scene when it does.'

'Aye, I've seen the place in the snow. It's beautiful, right enough.'

'Olivia is insistent that we all have lunch together in the dining hall on Christmas Day this year. It's a good thing the table is huge but I'm not sure how Mirren will cope with cooking dinner for so many people. She's apparently turned down any offers of help so she must be happy to do it.'

'Ah, Mirren's a star; she'll be in her element. Looking after people is her calling in life.' He fell silent for a moment and Bella looked up to see him chewing his lip.

'What's wrong?' she asked. 'I know that face.'

He lowered his eyes to meet hers again. 'Be honest with me. Are you disappointed at not getting to go on honeymoon right away?' he asked as he stroked her hair.

Bella shrugged. 'Not really. Yes, it would have been nice to go but we'll do it in a couple of years when we can properly make the time. That way we have a while to save up and plan better for cover at the police station.' She reached up and touched his face. 'The most important thing as far as I'm concerned is that I'm marrying you.'

'Aye, same here,' he replied with a smile that made his eyes crinkle at the corners.

His phone pinged and Bella sat up. 'Ugh, it's not a work thing, is it? You're supposed to be off today.'

Harris picked up the handset and looked at the screen. A crease formed between his brows. 'No... it's... it's an email from an address I don't know. *B M* at...' He shook his head, avidly concentrating on the screen.

'Probably a scam. Just ignore it,' Bella said. She glanced at her watch to see it was two o'clock and stood from the sofa. 'I reckon it must be five o'clock somewhere so I'll pour us some sherry, shall I? You can't *not* drink sherry today of all days. Will you join me, seeing as it's a special occasion?' She walked over and grabbed the bottle off the top of the bookcase.

'What occasion is that?' he asked, a little distracted.

'Tree decorating day, *obviously*.' She picked up a couple of glasses from the dresser. 'I think if you look it up in your police manuals you'll find it's the law to drink sherry on tree day,' she said with a giggle.

Harris leaned forward. 'This email... It's from Alba's husband.' He lifted his chin. His mouth was downturned, and his eyes filled with sadness.

Bella was a little confused. 'Why is *he* emailing you?'

He swallowed and whispered, 'She... she passed away.'

Bella placed the bottle and glasses down again and walked over to sit beside him. 'Oh, Harris. I'm so sorry.'

He shook his head. 'I can't believe it. I... I didn't

think it would happen so soon. I mean, yes, she said she wasn't sure how long she had left but...' Bella tried to put her arms around him, but he stood quickly and placed his phone on the table as if he couldn't bear to touch it any more. 'Sorry but... it's a lot to process... she was *my* age... I... I just need to be alone for a bit,' he said and left the room.

Bella watched his retreating form and felt powerless to help. She could see the email had been left open on the screen of his phone and picked it up.

Hello Harris,

My name is Bryn Morgan. You were friends with my wife, Alba. I understand you were close, and she told me to contact you in the event of her passing, so I'm afraid this is the main reason for my email. I'm sorry to inform you that she died five days ago, peacefully and in her sleep, with me and her mum by her side. It's been a very difficult time these past few months. Seeing a loved one suffering so much is not something I would wish on anyone, and it almost makes falling in love something I wish I had avoided, because I'm not sure what I will do now she is no longer here. My life revolved around her you see. And now I'm left with nothing but memories.

She left a padded envelope for you and asked that it be sent on to you when she passed away. I have no clue what's in it and so, I'm writing to ask for your postal address in order that I can carry out her wishes.

I'm aware she told you that I had abandoned her after her terminal diagnosis, I have now seen the emails between you both, but I'd like you to know that it wasn't the truth. So far from it, in fact. I never left her side and never would have. It was the illness talking. She was very confused in her final months, you see, and was struggling to understand what reality was, often hallucinating due to the medication, and lashing out in fear and anger, which of course I don't blame her for. She fought hard to keep her life.

She always spoke very highly of you and the love you had once shared, and while some men would be jealous of the high esteem in which she held you, I simply see you as a very important part of her past that, in a way, led her to me. Please know that I adored my wife and miss her terribly.

Alba told me you are soon to be married yourself. My sincere congratulations. My advice to you is hold onto your loved ones, Harris, and make every single moment count because it can all be snatched away so cruelly when you least expect it, and the memories you have are all you are left with to cling to, to keep a connection.

I will await your reply.

Regards,

Bryn

Bella stood to follow Harris, she needed to hold him and tell him she was there for him. But as she approached the kitchen door, she heard his motorbike revving outside and then the sound of it pulling off the forecourt of the police station as he drove away.

* * *

A little while later, Bella was still awaiting his return and concern was niggling at her all over again. She didn't want to make this about her, but his reaction had spooked her once more. Should she be worried? Was he rethinking marrying her now because he was scared that if he ever found himself in the same situation as Bryn it would hurt too much? Had he decided that it was too big a risk? Had Bryn's words been the final *coup de grâce* that had taken away her chance at happiness? Harris had told her when he first found out about Alba's illness that he was scared of losing her. How could she make him see that she had no intention of leaving him? Not by choice, anyway. And that their love was absolutely worth the risk.

She needed a distraction and decided to take Bertie for a walk. The air was frigid and there was already a layer of frost covering the cars and causing the ground to twinkle. The village was looking pretty festive already. A huge tree had been placed on the green by the village hall complete with white lights and hollow aluminium baubles in gold and silver, and lights had been strewn around the inlet of water that Glentorrin arced around. The water beneath was quite calm apart from a light ripple on the surface and Bella shivered as she remembered Jules telling her the story of when she jumped in to save Chewie, who had fallen into the water, all before the railings had been installed. *She was very brave,* Bella thought.

Flickering coloured lights adorned the windows of Morag and Caitlin's shops and a small tree with lights sat in a pot outside the Lifeboat House Museum, too, and somewhere in the distance she could hear Nat King Cole singing 'The Christmas Song'. She inhaled lungfuls of the icy sea air and breathed out a cloud of fog as she watched a seagull picking at some pastry that had no doubt been dropped by someone leaving the bakery. As she stood there taking in the festive scene before her, and as if she had manifested her by simply thinking, Jules appeared from the direction of the lane that led to her house. She wore a red coat and a bobble hat that was pulled down to cover her ears. Chewie trotted happily beside her, glancing up every so often as if to say thank you for his walk. Jules waved and made her way over.

When they reached the railings, Chewie immediately jumped down on his front two legs with his bottom in the air and gave a playful growl, as Bertie bounced around him excitedly, yipping his joy at seeing his friend.

'Hey! How are you doing? The countdown's on! Not long now, eh? Are you excited or terrified?' Jules asked, grinning.

'Oh, you know... A bit of both.' She was very much aware of how deflated she sounded.

'Is everything okay? You look a little down.'

Bella sighed. 'I'll be fine. I won't bore you with my woes.'

Jules tilted her head. 'Don't be daft. What are friends for? Come and have a seat for a while.' She nodded to the bench situated by the railings of the inlet. 'I've got time to spare.'

They sat on the bench and as Bertie and Chewie jumped on, and chewed at, each other, Bella explained the situation she found herself in.

'Oh, honey. I'm so sorry for Harris. But the thing is life is full of loves and losses. You can't avoid it unless you live in a cave all by yourself and speak to no one, but what kind of life would that be? Harris adores you and he would be so miserable without you, and I'm pretty sure he knows that. I think this reaction will just be the shock of losing someone he once loved.'

'I'm sure you're right. I'm just worried, because as we get closer to the wedding I think I'm waiting for something to go wrong. I have in the back of my mind that he'll be thinking about backing out because of what he read in that email.'

'I'm sure he isn't thinking that at all. We've all seen how he looks at you, Bells.' She paused for a moment and then continued, 'I look back at my marriage to

Laurie and ask myself if I'd known he was going to die would I have done anything to avoid falling for him and the truth is – no, I wouldn't. Because loving him made me who I am today. Losing him was horrendous, of course, and I was determined not to fall in love again because the pain was so bad, but then I met Reid, and I couldn't help myself. Yes, it crossed my mind that I could lose him in the same way I lost Laurie, but there's also the chance we'll have a long happy life together and that made me want to be with him even more. To make every second count and to make as many wonderful memories as possible, taking every day as it comes. Just give Harris time, honey. It's a lot to process and it does sort of make you question a lot of things when someone your age dies. He'll come home and everything will be fine. I somehow just *know* it.'

Bella smiled, grateful for her friendship and for sharing the experience of her own loss. 'Thanks, Jules. I really appreciate that.'

Jules placed a hand on her arm. 'Anytime. I mean it. And if you need to talk again just drop me a message and we can go for a drink or something. You don't have to suffer in silence.'

Bella smiled. 'Likewise, if ever you need an ear or a shoulder.'

Jules stood and with a warm smile said, 'Thanks,

honey. I'd better get this dog walked before he eats Bertie.'

They both laughed as they glanced down at the dogs whose ears were now matted and slimy. 'I think someone needs a bath now,' Bella said, scrunching her nose.

* * *

A little while later, Bella was sitting at the kitchen table going through photos on her phone that she had snapped of them decorating the tree earlier, before the mood had drastically changed, when Granny Isla's face popped up requesting a WhatsApp video call.

'Hi, dearie. What are you up to today on your day off?' she asked.

'We've been decorating the Christmas tree, hang on and I'll show you.' She walked through to the lounge and turned the camera around.

'Ooh, that's *vera* pretty, hen. You'll have to watch Bertie doesn't try to eat the baubles like he does with everything else. Where's Harris? I thought he was off today too.'

Bella decided not to worry her. 'Oh, he's fine. He's just gone to Portree to pick up a parcel. I'm hoping he picks up a Chinese takeaway while he's there because I haven't a clue what we'll have for tea if not.' She forced a laugh.

'How are the wedding plans coming along, *bella* Bella?' Tam asked as he took a seat beside Isla.

'We're pretty much sorted now, Tam. Just waiting for the big day to arrive.' *If it actually does. Oh, stop it, Bella. You're such a pessimistic cow.*

Oblivious to her inner monologue, Tam continued, 'And is Harris excited about his nuptials?'

Isla whacked his arm. 'Tam! What sort of a question is that? You *cannae* ask about another man's nuptials out of the blue like that. It's *vera* personal.'

Tam frowned. 'Why not? It's his wedding too.'

As if Bella somehow wouldn't hear her, Isla whispered, 'Aye, but you can't ask about a thing like *that*. His nuptials are *his* business.'

Tam's brow furrowed. 'Aye and Bella's, too, so what's the issue?'

Isla glanced at the camera and through a forced smile where she barely moved her lips, and again as if Bella wouldn't hear, she said, *à la* ventriloquist's dummy, 'It's just a very private thing to ask a young lady about her betrothed, Tam. That's all I'm saying. It's inappropriate.'

Bella pursed her lips, holding in her laughter. 'Granny, exactly *what* do you think nuptials are?'

Isla patted her hair and pursed her lips. She raised her eyebrows and leaned forward, closer to the camera. 'Well, if *you* don't know maybe you shouldn't be marrying a man that's got them, hen,' she said in a theatrical whisper.

Tam turned to her and patted her arm. 'Isla dearie, nuptials is just another way of saying *wedding*.'

Isla's eyebrows raised, and then crumpled, then raised again as she simultaneously opened and closed her mouth like a goldfish. 'Aye... I know that,' she said.

But clearly she didn't.

21

Bella had no way of contacting Harris, seeing as he had left his phone behind, so all she could do was wait for his return. She glanced at the clock on the microwave just as it ticked over to 5 p.m. He had been gone such a long time, and she wasn't sure whether to be angry or worried. *He's an adult, and he's a police inspector, he's very sensible*, she told herself. *He doesn't speed, and he doesn't take silly chances. He'll be absolutely fine.* If only she was as convincing to herself as she could be to other people.

She fed Bertie and watched as he wolfed down his food as if it would be stolen at any second. Then she looked through the fridge and cupboards, figuring Harris would be hungry when he got back from wherever the heck he'd been, and she had no way of telling him to pick up a takeaway. She gathered potatoes, onions and some leftover roast beef and was standing at the cooker making a pan of stovies when she heard Harris's motorbike pull into the driveway.

'Finally,' she said to Bertie, who tilted his head and wagged his tail as if he completely understood every word.

Harris walked into the kitchen with his crash helmet under his arm. There was something innately sexy about a man in a leather biker jacket, but there was something even better about *her* man in a leather biker jacket.

'Hey, are you okay?' she asked, wiping her hands on a towel as he put his crash helmet on the table and walked towards her. 'You've been gone ages.'

He didn't speak. Instead, he pulled her into his arms and held her close, the familiar, earthy smell of the leather and the heat of his body making her relax a little.

He kissed the top of her head. 'I'm sorry, sweetheart. I shouldn't have gone off like that. And I shouldn't have left my phone behind. You've every right to be angry and upset with me.'

She pulled away and gazed up at him. 'I'm not angry or upset. I was just worried about you. You seemed so sad when you left, and I wanted to help but you rode away before I had a chance.'

He kissed her tenderly. 'I'm all good. And I have something I need to tell you. Come and sit down.' He took off his leather jacket and placed it on the countertop. She turned the stove down to a simmer and then allowed him to lead her to the table where they sat down facing each other. She wasn't sure whether to be worried or not, as his expressionless face gave nothing away.

He took a deep breath and released it. 'Okay... I don't want you to be mad at me but...'

Ah, so she should *maybe* be a little worried because no good conversation started with those words. 'But what?' Her heart skipped.

'I rode for a bit and then I ended up at the Quiraing viewpoint. It's a crisp day so the view was clear. And I was just alone with my thoughts and memories for a bit.' This wasn't an explanation so far and that concerned Bella further. What was he building up to say? 'The situation with Alba...' He shook his head and frowned. 'It's really made me think about everything, us... the wedding... the future.'

Her stomach lurched and for a moment she thought she might throw up. *He was going to say they maybe should delay, or maybe shouldn't get married at all, wasn't he?*

'And?' she asked, in almost mortal dread for the answer.

He pulled his lips between his teeth and nodded. 'Okay, so I've sort of done a thing.'

Her nostrils flared and her eyes began to sting. She covered her mouth with her hands as her heart tried to escape through her chest. 'You've cancelled the wedding,' she said. He stared at her blankly, or was he shocked that she had guessed? Either way, it confirmed her fear. 'Look, I know you're scared of losing me, Harris, I feel the exact same way about you, but this isn't the way to handle things. I under-stand your grief, of course I do, but—'

He shook his head. 'Why is it that your mind al-ways goes straight there, Bella? That *that's* always your immediate thought? That I'm going to call things off? What have I ever done to make you jump straight to that conclusion? Bella, sweetheart, I'm not Kerr. And I have no intentions of cancelling the wed-ding. You're stuck with me until death us do part, Bella Douglas, soon to be Donaldson.' He smiled.

Relief flooded her veins, and she relaxed a little more. 'I don't know... I suppose what you said about being scared of losing me and now Alba's gone, and what the email said... I just—' *Shit*. She clamped her mouth closed.

'You read it then.'

She nodded. 'I'm sorry, Harris, it was there, and I didn't know what was going on. I shouldn't have—'

He smiled. 'It's fine. I have nothing to hide from you. You can read all my emails. I don't mind at all.'

She shook her head. 'Then you disappeared, and I didn't know what to think. You have to realise that I'm scared of losing you, too, but I don't go running off without explanation.'

He nodded slowly. 'You are mad at me. And I totally understand. But the thing is, Bella, Alba's death felt like a call to action. I had to do something immediately, and, no disrespect, without you having a chance to talk me out of it.'

No wiser, Bella shrugged. 'Okay... But what was so urgent? What have you done?' *Oh God, has he gone and got a commemorative tattoo for another woman?*

He reached into his jacket and pulled out an envelope. He paused a moment, evidently trying to weigh up his decision and trying to pre-empt her reaction to it. He slid the envelope across the table to her. 'Open it.'

With shaking hands, she opened the envelope and pulled out several folded pieces of A4 paper. She flattened them out and stared at the information before her. She couldn't quite believe her eyes. Was this really happening? Had he really done this?

She peered at the paper and then at Harris. 'What have you done?'

A wide smile spread across his face. 'Hear me out, Bella. I know how much you've wanted to visit Tuscany. And Alba's death has made me realise that we shouldn't be putting off making special memories at all. We should be grabbing each opportunity for happiness that we can, with *both* hands. And it would make me so happy to take you to Tuscany for our honeymoon. So... we're going,' he stated matter-of-factly. 'We fly on 29 December and we're there for ten days. It's all booked. I've spoken to Olivia and okayed it for us to stay at the castle until we fly, and she said absolutely no problem. I was going to leave it as a surprise for the wedding day but I'm so bloody excited I had to tell you straightaway. There's no way I could've held onto it. We'll be there in time to see the Cavalcade of the Three Wise Men in Florence on the 6th, something I know you've always wanted to see. We're going to visit a vineyard and have a wine tasting by a roaring fireplace. We're going to see the Duomo in Florence, the Uffizi Gallery, all open in January, we checked. The travel agent up in Portree was so helpful. We planned the whole trip. I know the weather won't be sunbathing temperatures, but you love winter, and I figured this was going to be amazing, regardless of the cold. And we'll have each other to keep us warm.'

Tears welled in Bella's eyes and spilled over. 'But... your savings, Harris. And what about the station?'

'All sorted. Bertie too. All dealt with. You have nothing to worry about.' He shrugged and pulled her into his lap. 'Bella, if I've taken anything from Alba's death, and the letter from Bryn, it's that I want to make you happy and to make every memory I possibly can with you. I don't want to put things off if we don't have to. What's the point of saving for a rainy day that may never come? You're my future and although no particular length of time is ever guaranteed, we can't sit around focusing on the end when we're only at our beginning.' She was utterly gobsmacked and sat in silence trying to take it all in. He sighed. 'Are you disappointed? Or angry with me for doing this without your agreement?'

She widened her eyes and wiped away her tears. 'Absolutely not! Harris, this is the loveliest, most special thing anyone has ever done for me. You're giving me my dream honeymoon. How could I possibly be disappointed?' She threw her arms around his neck and peppered his face with kisses. 'We're going to Tuscany!' she said as the excitement finally kicked in to replace the worry and anxiety that had plagued her for the last few hours. 'Tuscany!'

* * *

The group video call was scheduled on Zoom for the following day at 7 p.m. and Bella sat, her heart doing somersaults as she waited for everyone to join. One by one their friends and family logged in and Harris kissed her hand.

When everyone was present and had said hello to one another, Bella began. 'Thanks for logging on, everyone, and Granny, please tell Dorothy thanks from me for helping you and Tam with Zoom.'

'I thought it was a washing powder,' Isla said. 'I had no clue this thing existed. I'm only familiar with the WhatsUp.'

'Well, you're here now and that's all that matters. We just wanted to share our exciting news with you all.'

'Are you pregnant?' Ben asked, wide-eyed. 'Because I'm telling you now, I've forgotten what sleep is.'

'But it's definitely worth it,' Skye added, giving him a swift dig in the ribs.

'Oh, aye, it's so worth it,' Ben agreed.

Bella giggled. 'Sorry, no, no babies yet. But it's something we didn't think was going to happen.'

'Come on, Bella, my suspenders are killing me!' Isla said and everyone laughed.

'Erm, Mum, I think you mean the *suspense* is killing you,' Bella's dad said, cringing.

Isla winked at the camera. 'I know what I meant,' she said and at this point no one could hold a straight face.

'Harris has been very naughty,' Bella said.

'Maybe that's not a topic for video call?' Brodie said and another rumble of laughter travelled the ether.

'Come on, Bells, just say it, or you'll never get a word in with this lot,' Olivia said with a roll of her eyes.

The excitement had got too much, and Bella was ready to burst. 'Harris has booked for us to go to Tuscany for our honeymoon!' she blurted, almost in a squeal.

This was met with a cheer and applause. 'Oh, that's amazing, Bells! Well done, Harris.'

'Absolutely brilliant!'

'You'll love it!'

'I'm so jealous.'

The comments kept rolling in and Bella sat there beaming as Harris squeezed her hand.

'You have to go to the Uffizi,' Reid said. 'It's incredible. Seeing Botticelli's *The Birth of Venus* up close was an emotional experience for me.'

'And the pizza is divine in Italy,' Granny Isla added. 'None of this processed rubbish you get in supermarkets. Proper cheese and an authentic Italian base. Nothing like it. Giovanni's in Portree comes a close second, but it helps that he's a proper Italian.'

'We're going to a wine tasting by candlelight,' Bella said, swooning.

'Bloody 'ell, Harris, you've done it now. Us blokes are all gonna be compared to you, you romantic sod,' Neil said in his broad Yorkshire accent.

'Aye, that's one way to ruin all our street cred, pal,' Dex added in his Geordie twang. 'Not only are you a good-looking bloody hero who plays fiddle, but you book romantic holidays too. Jeez, what hope have we got?' He was grinning as he spoke.

'Take a leaf out of his book, boys!' Ruby said, nudging Mitch. 'You could all do with some lessons from Harris.'

'So, you're telling me a tent in midge season is no

longer classed as romantic?' Archie asked, feigning ignorance, and was swiftly whacked on the arm by Caitlin.

Everyone was laughing and Bella was ecstatically happy that they had all been so lovely about it.

When the call ended, Bella turned to Harris. 'Thank you again, Harris. I can't quite believe how lucky I am.'

He cupped her face in his hand and kissed her. 'It wasn't luck, sweetheart, it was fate. You and me? That's what you call meant to be.'

22

A package arrived for Harris from Bryn a few days later and he sat with it in front of him on the table for a while just staring at it.

'Are you going to open that?' Bella asked when she walked through from her office in the spare downstairs bedroom to make a cup of tea. She was working on a new design for a detached house in the north of Skye and was enjoying the task greatly.

'Aye, I will. I'm just working my way up to it.' He moved the padded envelope around on the table and then picked it up, turning it over in his hands and examining it.

Bella placed a hand on his shoulder. 'What are you afraid of?'

He shrugged. 'I'm not really sure. It was all so long ago now.'

'You've never really told me your story with Alba,' Bella said.

He frowned. 'I... I didn't think you'd want to know.'

Bella wasn't sure if it was because Alba had passed away, but she wondered about their relationship. 'Maybe it would help you to talk about her?'

He kept his eyes fixed on the parcel. 'Alba and I met at college and dated for a while, then we split up and I didn't see her for a couple of years. Then we met again at a police recruitment event when we were both twenty-one-ish. She was my first love, and I suppose my first and last heartbreak. There's nothing much to say really. She relocated to Glasgow for a promotion as you already know, and I didn't want to go. It wasn't particularly acrimonious. We tried to remain friends but... it just didn't work, as she was so busy, and I'd made a new life for myself in Inverness.' He held up the package. 'The thing is, I have no idea what's in this envelope... but there's one thing that I really hope is in there.'

Intrigued now, Bella sat. 'What is it?'

He placed the parcel down again. 'When I was sixteen, my mum gave me a St Christopher that had belonged to my grandad. She'd had it for a while but deemed me old enough on my sixteenth birthday because it was so sentimental. It was something he had worn every day and after it came to me, I wore it every day too. Never took it off from the day Mum gave me it. As you know he meant the world to me, so the St Christopher did too. He was a constant in my life. A father figure to me when my own dad let me down time after time. He cared for me in a way my own dad never could.

'But then one night, after me and Alba had been together around a year, she was asking me about the St Christopher, so I told her all about my grandad and how we used to go birdwatching, and how he loved me like I was his son. She was intrigued and couldn't take her eyes off the pendant. Said she'd never had anything from her grandparents. So, I took it off and fastened it around her neck. I think at the time I just meant for her to try it on but... she kept it. And I didn't have the heart to ask for it back because she loved it, and used to talk about how it meant so much to her because of how special it was to me. Then we split and... I never saw the necklace again. I know it was just a *thing* and that my memories of my grandad are what really matters but that necklace was something tangible, you know? Something I could hold and remember him wearing. I meant to ask for her to return it but... after we broke up there never seemed to be a good moment to ask. So... I never did. And now here is this parcel from her. If it contains the necklace, I'll be so happy, Bells. But if it's not there, and it's just a load of photos and cinema stubs that reminded her of me... it means that the St Christopher is probably lost forever.' He shrugged. 'It almost feels like it's better not to know.'

'But whatever *is* in there was important enough for her to keep it for you. That counts for something, doesn't it?' Bella said. 'And she's a significant part of your history, however it ended between you.'

He nodded. 'Aye... I suppose.'

Bella made to stand. 'I'll leave you to it.'

He reached up and grabbed her hand. 'Can you maybe stay a few minutes? Just until I've seen what's in it.'

She smiled and sat again. 'Of course I can.'

He paused and took a deep breath before ripping open the envelope. He pulled out a pile of photographs first. The Harris Bella saw in them was hardly recognisable with his youthful face and longer hair. Alba was pretty, with shoulder-length brown hair and smiling eyes, and it was clear from the way she looked at him in the pictures that she adored

Harris. He thumbed through the photos, pausing at each one to smile or give a chuckle and shake of his head.

'This one was when we went on a pub crawl dressed as old women,' he said with a laugh, holding up a photo in which he was wearing a head scarf and rollers along with a flowery dress and cardigan. 'Turned out it was an eighties night but one of the lads had got the wrong end of the stick and told us we'd all to dress like eighty-year-olds. So, we'd all gotten clothes from charity shops, and we must have looked a sight. We got a lot of attention, that's for sure. And my mate never lived his mistake down. But it was a fun night, but boy, did I pay the morning after. I don't think I've ever felt so ill. That night was one of the reasons I decided to stop drinking.' He shook his head. 'And this one... this was at our friends' wedding. They were a wee bit older than us and got married at the registry office in Edinburgh.' In this one Harris was dressed in a kilt, jacket and white ruffled shirt. He was clean-shaven and looked so young. He laughed. 'I felt so uncomfortable in that kilt. I was terrified it was going to fall down because it was too big, and I didn't have time to get it altered. The belt was too big, and I had to punch a new hole in it, but it still didn't fit right. And this one of me on my own was taken at Leith. My grandad was from there originally and I decided I wanted to go visit so Alba came with me. She snapped this when I was feeling all melancholic.' It was a lovely photo, in which he was sitting looking out across the water with the sunset-tinged sky behind him. *Worthy of a frame,* Bella thought. She would have to buy one and surprise him.

Hearing about the life Harris had before he met her was strange. And seeing photographs of him with his arm around another woman was a little hard to swallow but she had no reason to be jealous, she knew that really. He and Alba had split long before she met him. But there had definitely been a deep fondness between them, that much was evident.

Harris reached into the envelope and pulled out a batch of concert ticket stubs. 'Ah, this was before everything was done on your phone. You actually got to keep the stubs. I always wondered what had happened to these things.' One last reach into the envelope produced another envelope and inside that was a note and a little black velvet pouch. He held the pouch in his hand and read the note, and his chin began to tremble. The writing was scrawly and barely legible, but he read it aloud.

Dearest Harris,

I remember the night you gave this to me so vividly, even though I'm struggling to remember a lot of things now. Although I know that deep down you never meant for me to keep it because of what it meant to you. But for years I couldn't let it go because it was my one last link to you. And now I'm not going to be around to cling to it, it seems only right that I return it to its rightful owner. I'm so sorry I didn't send it back before. Keeping it was such a selfish thing for me to do.

I hope you can forgive me, and that you will wear it always from now and think of your lovely grandad every time you see it.

Love, Alba

Harris emptied the contents of the little black velvet pouch into his hand and burst into tears that racked his body as the silver chain glistened in his palm. He closed his fist around it and sobbed. Bella stood and wrapped her arms around him and held him as he was swallowed up by grief for his grandad, and for his first love.

Once his tears had subsided, Bella took the chain and fastened it around his neck. 'There, back where it belongs,' she said as she touched the small medallion and then tucked it down his shirt.

'How can I be so sad and so happy all at the same time?' he asked with a light laugh as he swiped the moisture from his face.

'It's completely understandable. Alba was your first love, and I can only imagine how hard it must be for you. And I know how much your grandad meant to you too.'

He reached up and pulled her close, resting his head on her middle. 'Thanks for being so incredible about this. You really have been so supportive and understanding.'

'Because I love you, Harris. And I always will.'

* * *

The Iolair-Mhara design was completely finished, and the Somers family were overjoyed with the place. Bella's wallpaper choice had remained for the Bridal Suite, much to her delight and relief, and the whole hotel had a luxurious, cosy feel about it. The laundry had been repurposed as a yoga studio rather than a miniature casino, after Carlton had been for therapy and discovered the calming, meditative practice. The Somerses were planning a grand opening and of

course Bella had been invited. It was to take place on
12 December, and after that Carlton would be rein-
stalled as the manager. Bella hadn't seen him since
the lift incident and the rest of the job had gone off
without a hitch.

Contact from Mrs Somers had been non-existent,
but Nate Junior said that it was because she was horrified and embarrassed about her youngest son's behaviour. Every so often Nate Junior would video call
Bella and she would show him around the hotel so he
could see the progress. She chatted with his wife, Deandra, too, and got to meet their son Dawson John, or
DJ for short. Dealing with them had certainly been a
more relaxed affair. Nate and his wife had flown over
to see the hotel when it was signed off by the contrac-
tors and they'd had nothing but praise for Bella. She
had kindly turned down the invitation to attend the
opening event, figuring she had done her bit and had
so much going on with the wedding. But Mr and Mrs
Somers had paid her extra money once the hotel was
signed off. At first it felt like they were buying her silence but after talking it through with Harris she had
accepted it more as payment for a job well done.

She was now onto the next design. The detached
property she was working on now would become a
dog-friendly holiday let for six when finished and

was situated on the shores of Loch Dunvegan, a sea loch on the north coast of the isle. The views were stunning, and you could often see dolphins playfully jumping and diving in the water from the front windows. The owners had asked for a simple and fresh design that would complement the views and the surroundings and be hardwearing to stand the number of guests they were hoping to receive. Bella had chosen a colour scheme of blues and greens with natural wood accents and the owners had been delighted. Each window had views that were like living paintings, changing with the weather and the seasons, so artwork had been commissioned from Reid MacKinnon again to fit the landscapes in which the house sat.

Now that the Iolair-Mhara was done, Bella could relax and focus a little more on the wedding.

23

Bella sat on her suitcase. She was rather keen in packing so early but was determined not to forget anything, so the sooner everything was sorted the better. They were flying from Inverness to Gatwick on 29 December, and then from there to Florence, so they wouldn't be returning home in between the wedding and honeymoon, meaning she had to sort her clothes out for both trips. She had gone through her entire wardrobe and pulled out everything that she deemed suitable for their stay in Inverness, and then their ten-day honeymoon. It had meant two suitcases and a shopping trip to ensure she had enough clothing to last the whole time. And now she had come to zip the cases up they barely met in the middle.

She had spent the last couple of days on her laptop gazing dreamily at images of Florence and reading up about the Accademia Gallery where Michelangelo's *David* was on display. She wanted to visit the Ponte Vecchio and wander through some of the beautiful neighbourhoods, hand in hand with her new husband, admiring the architecture and experiencing the real Florence. She couldn't quite believe she was actually going to be there, let alone as a newlywed. She considered getting another suitcase for all the souvenirs she would no doubt be purchasing.

All the RSVPs had been received and dealt with, and she and Harris had spent a whole evening working on the seating plan which, once completed, had been forwarded to Olivia along with a box of disposable cameras that were to be put on each table. She wanted as many photos as humanly possible so they could revisit their wedding whenever they wanted.

Bertie was of course coming to the wedding – he had the job of ring bearer seeing as he had done so well with the engagement ring, and a special tuxedo bib, like the ones Wilf and Marley had worn for Olivia and Brodie's wedding, had been obtained in readiness – and then he was going home with Jules and Reid to stay with them until Bella and Harris returned.

Everything was coming together now and with only a week until the big day the nerves had kicked up a notch. Bella was barely sleeping and her dreams were filled with bizarre incidents such as her forgetting to put on her wedding dress and walking down the aisle in her undies; and Bertie eating all the wedding cake and pulling all the table cloths off the tables when people were trying to eat, causing utter chaos; and Granny Isla being kidnapped by the mob; and, worst of all, being ditched at the altar.

On numerous occasions she awoke suddenly, sitting up and crying out into the darkness, after which Harris pulled her into his arms, doing his best to soothe her. But it kept on happening.

As they sat at the table after one such fitful night, she caught Harris watching her. 'What? Do I have jam on my face?' she asked, putting her slice of toast back on the plate.

He shook his head, reached out and took her hand. 'No, it's not that. You just... you look tired, sweetheart. I'm worried about you. These horrible nightmares need to stop but I don't know how to help. I don't understand why you're so stressed when everything is going well. We've got everything pre-pared. There's really nothing for you to worry about. You should be excited and looking forward to our wedding, not worrying about what could go wrong. I want you to enjoy the build-up, not feel anxious the whole time.'

She gave a deep sigh. 'I know. I know. I just feel this awful sense of dread that something bad is going to happen. I don't want to feel this way, but I can't seem to help it.'

'Tell you what. Why don't you go to Drumblair a couple of days early, and take Bertie with you? That way you can spend a couple of nights before the wed-ding with Skye and Liv. They wanted to throw you a wee bridal shower so maybe you should let them, even if it's just the three of you. What do you think?'

'But that would mean my girlfriends from Skye couldn't attend, and Granny Isla and my mum. Wouldn't they be upset about that?'

His brow furrowed. 'Hey, you're one person. You can't take on the worries of the world or you'll drive yourself mad. And you'd decided you weren't having a bridal shower, so they already know they're not in-vited to one. And I'm pretty sure they'll totally under-stand that you're spending time with your oldest friends.'

Bella nodded. 'Maybe you're right. But what about Granny, Tam and your mum getting to Drumblair?'

'Don't worry about them, either. Your mum and dad don't have room for them all in their car with Callum being at theirs, so I've already booked Rab's Cabs to take them the day before the wedding and he's coming to pick them up on Boxing Day to take them home. So actually, Isla and my mum could come to the bridal shower if you hold it the night before. And your mum and dad will be there by then too. Mum, Isla and Tam are booked into one of the holiday apartments at the castle, as are your folks and Callum, so it's all good, they're taken care of.'

Bella's heart tripped over itself. 'But what about everyone else?'

'Everyone else from Skye is sorted. They're all heading over after work on the day before the wedding too. Some are staying at the Glenmoriston Town House and some at the Kingsmills. They're not our worry though, sweetheart. They're all sorting themselves out, and not only that but they'd all be upset if they knew you were spending time fretting about them. So, there you go, that's a few less things for you to think about, eh? Why don't you go and give Olivia a call before you start work? I think she'll be happy to have you a couple of days early. And you're your own boss so no one to answer to there.'

He was right and she really did need to relax for her own sanity.

'And you're still planning on coming over on the morning of the wedding? Is that wise leaving it until the last minute like that?'

'Bella, darlin', it's only a two-hour drive. I'll set off at the crack of dawn and I'll come in the Jeep so I'm fine if it snows. I can bring my suitcase for the honeymoon and what I'm wearing for the wedding with me so it's all good. I've got it all straight in my mind. Another thing you can tick off your worry list.'

He was right. She was making mountains out of molehills. And she desperately wanted to enjoy the run-up to the wedding so maybe going to Drumblair early was a good idea. She still would have preferred that Harris came over the day before the wedding, so he at least had time to relax beforehand, too, but the police force was still experiencing staff shortages on the island, and he had a colleague coming down from Portree to cover while they were on their honeymoon, so he had a handover to do. He wasn't worried in the slightest, so Bella decided that she shouldn't be either.

* * *

Bella arrived at Drumblair in the rain on the morning of 22 December. Olivia had been excited to hear she was coming early and had immediately sprung into action to make arrangements for an afternoon tea party bridal shower at the castle for the next day. Mirren had already been enlisted to make cakes and shortbread. Luckily, she didn't have to be asked twice where hospitality was concerned; it was in her blood, and Skye was on decorating duty.

'The tables will already be set out in the picture gallery for the reception so we're having it in there,' Olivia said excitedly as she scribbled things on her iPad.

'Please don't go to loads of trouble, Liv. I'm happy with just a movie and some popcorn.'

'Nope. We're having afternoon tea with the fancy cake stands from the café. I've already ordered the sandwiches from Noah.'

Bella huffed. 'Wouldn't he rather be off just before Christmas?'

'No, he was happy to do it. He's a great guy. And he has a few leftovers from the café anyway so we're doing him a favour really because he hates waste.'

'The thing is, Liv, I don't want to get drunk the day

before my wedding. I want to meet Harris at the altar feeling fresh and hangover free.'

'That's fine. We'll stick to tea and coffee and a glass of alcohol-free fizz,' Olivia said with a shrug. She had thought of everything.

* * *

The afternoon of the 23rd rolled around quickly and Bella was ordered to stay away from the picture gallery until Olivia messaged her to say she could come through. It seemed an awful lot of fuss for half a dozen people. But nevertheless, she had made a special effort to look nice and had worn one of her favourite new dresses in midnight-blue that was fitted at the waist with a flowing skirt. It had a 1940s look about it and felt quite appropriate for an afternoon tea.

When the WhatsApp message arrived, Bella dutifully walked through the large, curved oak door into the gallery and was met with a chorus of, 'Surprise!' As well as her mum, Granny Isla, Maeve and Mirren, all her friends from Skye were there too. Jules, Caitlin, Millie, Morag and Ruby had all come to celebrate with her, and Sergeant Mel was there too. Skye adorned her with the obligatory *Bride to Be* sash and plastic tiara, like she had won a Miss World contest, and thrust a beautiful bouquet of flowers into her hand.

Feeling more than a little emotional, Bella hugged each of her friends in turn before glancing around the Drumblair picture gallery at the decorations. There were white pearlescent helium balloons, weighted down with silver love hearts, silver horse-shoe confetti had been sprinkled on each table, bot-tles of alcohol-free prosecco were on hand so they could still celebrate with a bit of fizz, and there was a large photo of Bella Blu-Tacked to a whiteboard easel, with a piece of white net attached to a magnet.

'Ooh, goody, we're going to play pin the veil on the donkey!' Isla said with a chuckle.

'Charming, thanks, Granny.'

Isla reached up and patted her cheek. 'You know I'm only kidding, dearie. You're going to be a beau-tiful bride.'

They were surrounded by the incredible paint-ings of Olivia's ancestors watching over them as they took their seats at the tables that had been laid out for them by Mirren and her assistant Cecily. Lots of familiar faces that Bella remembered from her child-hood visits to Drumblair were there, frozen in time in oil on canvas. She remembered Lady Freya, Olivia's mum, telling them stories about each of the people pictured and how they were related to Olivia. It was truly fascinating, and they were some of the most intriguing stories she had ever heard.

Olivia stood and clinked her glass with a fork. 'Good afternoon, ladies! Thank you for being here on this very exciting occasion where Bella waves goodbye to being a "singleton" and prepares to join the "smug marrieds" club.' The *Bridget Jones* reference made Bella giggle. 'You'll all be happy to know this is a man-free zone. Just us girls for a wee while.' The women cheered good-naturedly.

The waiting staff from the café began to bring the cake stands in and place them on each table along with pots of tea and coffee. Classical music played in the background as the women chatted and ate finger sandwiches, mini quiches and a selection of fresh cream scones and cupcakes.

'Look at us, eh?' Granny Isla said. 'We're the pineapple of sophistimacation.'

Bella giggled. 'I think you mean pinnacle, Granny, and sophistication.'

Isla took a big bite of her fresh cream scone, most of the cream ending up on her nose. 'Aye, that's what a said,' she mumbled.

Isla clinked her spoon against her glass. 'I'd like to make a wee speech if I may.'

The room fell silent, and all eyes turned to the purple-haired woman who suddenly looked like a rabbit in headlights. 'Ahem... Thank you for coming today to celebrate my beautiful Arabella's last day of being single. I just wanted to say a few words. But now I've got your attention my mind's gone blankety blank.' Everyone giggled. 'My granddaughter has always had a special place in my heart. We've always been such good friends, and she has looked after me since she moved in with me a few years ago. We had some fun times together and I can honestly say I am the luckiest old woman on earth to have such a special person in my life.'

Her chin trembled. She turned to Bella. 'You are the most important person in my life, dearie, aside from your brother, of course. And your dad. Oh, and your mum. Ooh, heck, and my new husband. And obviously Beau's quite important but he isn't really a person.' Giggles travelled the room. 'Sorry, I think I've drunk too much coffee, I think I need to start drinking decapitated instead.' Everyone laughed. 'What I mean to say is, Arabella, I've loved you from before I held you in my arms on the day you were born. And I'm grateful to have you in my life. I'd love to give you this necklace.'

Isla reached into her handbag and took out a velvet box. 'It was a wedding gift for me from your lovely grandad, God rest him, and I'd like you to have it as your something old.' She walked to stand behind Bella and fastened a white-gold chain around her neck with a heart-shaped pendant encrusted with tiny marcasite stones. 'It's not diamonds because we weren't well off, but it may as well have been for how much it meant to me.'

Bella touched the pendant where it sat perfectly just below her throat and tears spilled over from her eyes. She stood and pulled Isla into her arms. 'Thank you, Granny. It's perfect.'

* * *

The afternoon was wonderful and flew by. Olivia set her phone up on a table, set the timer going and took a group shot of the friends, and Bella felt herself relaxing. The worries of the previous week or so dissipated, leaving her shoulders where they were supposed to be instead of up by her ears. The feeling of impending doom had been replaced with a feeling of love and excitement. And at the end of afternoon, she hugged everyone goodbye and thanked them all, telling them she would see them tomorrow before retiring to her bedroom to get an early night.

Harris video called her at nine o'clock when she was in her pyjamas, sitting on the bed cuddling Bertie.

He was propped up in their bed at home, shirtless and ready for an early night too. 'How was it?' he asked.

'Great fun. We ate cake and drank tea; we played pin the veil on the bride and apparently, I'm wearing mine all wrong because judging by the efforts of the afternoon it should be worn on the nose or the left boob.'

Harris laughed. 'I mean, I'm all for breaking tradition, but I still think wearing it on your head would be best.'

Bella nodded. 'Yeah, I think that's what I'll probably go with.'

'Was it a nice surprise seeing everyone there?'

'It was brilliant. I had just expected a small thing, so it was really lovely. But I'm ridiculously tired now.'

'That's the worry wearing you out. You'll sleep like a log tonight, I bet. Well, that is if Bertie doesn't keep you awake snoring anyway.'

Bella giggled. 'It'll make a change from you snoring.'

Harris gasped and feigned shock. 'How very dare you?'

'Just think, the next time I see you it'll be at the chapel.'

'Speaking of which, I've sent you a link to a Spotify playlist I've put together for you for while you girls are getting ready. I think you'll like it.'

'Aww, you're so sweet, thank you.'

'You're welcome, sweetheart. I'll let you go and get some sleep. And I'll see you tomorrow at the chapel. Don't forget your lines though, eh?'

She tapped her chin and pursed her lips. 'It's... erm... I'll consider it, isn't it? Wait no... It's oh, go on then, if I must?'

He laughed. 'Goodnight, Arabella Douglas. Tonight's the last time you go to sleep with that name.' Her heart skipped at his words. 'I love you so, *so* much, and I can't wait to be married to you.'

'And I you. Sweet dreams.'

The call ended and Bella switched off her bedside lamp.

24

Bella sat with Skye and Olivia sipping mimosas and Isla drinking *decapitated* coffee, as the makeup artist put the finishing touches to her look for the important day ahead. Dougie had set a fire going in the grate, which was welcome seeing as it was a freezing cold and frosty Christmas Eve. She had sent Harris's Spotify playlist to Olivia so she could play it on her Bluetooth speaker as they prepared for the wedding. Bruno Mars was currently singing about wanting to marry someone as Olivia and Skye sang along and danced around the drawing room, champagne flutes held aloft and feet bare while Bella looked on, trying not to giggle, lest she be accidentally poked in the eye with an eyeliner pencil, and Isla chuckled as she observed them all.

They were temporarily dressed in their specially commissioned embroidered *Bridesmaid* and *Maid of Honour* robes that matched the *Bride* one Bella wore; they had been a special gift from Mirren and Dougie. Bertie was out walking with Brodie, Wilf and Marley in a bid to ensure the young dog was more calm than usual for the ceremony, seeing as he had an important role in proceedings.

From her seat by the window, which was the best place for natural light, Bella could see clouds in the sky that looked to be heavy with snow, and she wondered if she might get her wish for a white wedding in more ways than one. Only she just needed it to hold off until everyone arrived safely. And by everyone she meant Harris.

Skye and Olivia had presented Bella with some very pretty pearl and marcasite earrings as her something new. The blue garter she wore on her thigh hit two of the wedding traditions both on colour *and* the fact it was borrowed from Olivia and of course she wore her granny's gifted marcasite pendant as her something old.

The hairstylist had already been, and Isla, Olivia and Skye were primped and primed, ready to get dressed when the time arrived. Bella had let her blonde hair grow to below her shoulders in the lead-up to the wedding and today it was half pinned up with curled tendrils falling loosely to frame her face, and tiny diamantes and pearls scattered through the top and back. Her makeup was simple but enough to show up in photographs, and hopefully to last out the day. She loved how she looked and was feeling confident in her skin for the first time in a very long while. She simply couldn't wait to get her dress on and get to the chapel. And she couldn't wait to see Harris again.

Everything was on track; Harris had called at nine thirty to say he had been a little delayed but that he was setting off shortly, and the wedding wasn't until one so there was plenty of time. He'd assured he would already be showered and would only need to change when he arrived. It was now ten o'clock and Bella had relaxed a lot, but she was sure that the alcohol in the mimosas had had a hand in that fact. Bruno Mars finished singing and then it was the turn of Train and 'Marry Me'. Bella smiled as she listened to the lyrics. He'd clearly put a lot of thought into the songs he had chosen and each one so far had made her excited and happy.

'It brings it all back to me,' Olivia said with a sigh as she flopped onto the squashy burgundy sofa. 'I loved my wedding day so much and didn't want it to end.'

'You looked so beautiful,' Bella said, remembering the glow she'd had about her.

'You look gorgeous too, Bells,' Skye said.

'Thank you.' She turned to Skye. 'Anyway, when are you guys going to tie the knot, Skye? You've done it all back to front. The house and baby but not the wedding.'

'You know me, I like to be awkward.' She grinned. 'And don't you worry, I'm working on Ben. We both definitely want to get married but there's always something getting in the way. For example, said house and baby. But we'll do it eventually. Although seeing how stressed Bella's been, I might suggest we elope.'

Bella narrowed her eyes and tried to keep her mouth still as the makeup artist was at a critical point with lipliner. 'Erm... didn't you consider doing that before and your mum pretty much had kittens over the whole thing?'

Skye rolled her eyes. 'Oh yeah... I'd forgotten about that. Sod it though, it's my wedding. Or it would be... if it was happening.'

'Maybe you girls need to do what they do in

wrestling and tag team him into setting a date,' Isla said.

'Ooh, now you're talking, Isla. We need to hatch a plan,' Skye said, giggling. 'Anyway, what song have you chosen for your first dance at the reception, Bells?'

'You'll think we're weird because it's not your traditional first dance song and it's not a slow one either, but we've chosen the song that reminds us of when we first properly met. It's a song we both love and it's just... *us*.'

'Come on, Bella, to coin a Granny Isla phrase, *my suspenders are killing me*,' Olivia said with a giggle as she nudged Isla.

Skye almost choked on her drink. 'You really are a gem, Granny Isla.'

'Aye but you all thought I was joking,' Isla replied with a wink.

'So, go on then, Bells, which song is it?' Olivia asked.

'It's "Dog Days Are Over" by Florence and the Machine,' Bella said as she remembered the day when Harris took her to meet Neil the mechanic about getting Fifi fixed after she had hit a giant pothole. She had worn her long-sleeved Florence and the Machine top which had sparked a conversation about something they had in common, and Harris had guessed her favourite song to be 'Delilah', whereas his was 'Dog Days Are Over'. And after that, his favourite song quickly became hers.

'Oh, wow! I think that's a brilliant choice. It's different and that's a good thing,' Skye said.

'Oh, I do like Florence and her machine. That's what they call her songwriting partner, you know. But she's actually a human,' Isla added proudly. 'What are you having as your entrance music, hen?'

'I've chosen Pachelbel's "Canon in D Major",' Bella said. 'I know it's a common choice but it's a beautiful piece of music and I think it will be so lovely to walk down the aisle to. I've been imagining it for ages now.' Her heart skipped again, and a shiver of excitement travelled through her body.

'Ooh, yes, I agree. It's definitely the right choice,' Olivia said. 'A real classic.'

Olivia poured more mimosas into their glasses and Bella had a giggling fit. 'I'm going to be slurring my vows at this rate.'

'Believe me, you'll completely sober up once that chapel door opens,' Olivia told her.

'I can't wait to see Harris all dressed up waiting for me at the altar,' Bella said dreamily. 'It's like all my Christmases and birthdays have come at once.'

Mirren burst into the room without knocking, which wasn't like her at all. 'Have you heard from Harris?' she asked, her face pale and her eyes wide.

'Yes, don't worry, he's on his way. He was a wee bit delayed but I'm not worried,' Bella replied. 'He'll make it in plenty of time.' Then she noticed the expression on Mirren's face and her heart stuttered. 'Why? What's wrong?'

Mirren swallowed and shook her head. 'Oh... nothing... it's nothing.' She turned to Olivia. 'Olivia, perhaps could I have a quick word with you in the corridor?'

Olivia stood. 'Mirren? It doesn't look like nothing. Is everything okay? Has something happened?'

She nodded and forced a smile. 'I'm sure it's all fine.' And then almost immediately her face crumpled, and she shook her head. 'It's probably nothing at all but...' She sighed deeply and pointed at the TV. 'Switch on the news,' she said. The three friends shared bewildered glances. So, she repeated herself, getting agitated and wagging her hand at the screen in the corner of the room, 'The news, on the TV, switch it on.'

Bella sat upright, forcing the makeup artist to take a step back. 'What is it? What's wrong?' Her heart began to thud in her chest; a pronounced and quick *thump thump thump* which was no longer about excitement but dread. 'Is Harris okay? What's happened, Mirren?' Skye gripped her hand.

Olivia switched the TV on and flicked to the news channel. 'Oh,' was all she managed to say as she covered her mouth with her hand.

'— So just to recap, we've had reports of a vehicle fire on the Skye Bridge at the midpoint between Kyle of Lochalsh and Glentorrin. The road is closed in both directions and fire services and police are in attendance. There are not believed to be any casualties at this time,' the female newsreader was saying, and on the screen, as she spoke, was a scene of chaos. Police cars with their blue lights strobing could be seen blocking the traffic from entering the bridge at the Kyle of Lochalsh side, which meant no one was getting off it either. Crowds of onlookers had gathered to watch events unfolding. 'I repeat there are thankfully no casualties reported,' the newsreader reiterated as arcs of water and billowing smoke could be seen in the distance, 'but, as today is Christmas Eve, we have to warn you there may be a fair bit of disruption for the foreseeable future, for those hoping to access or leave the island, as the road will likely be closed for some time until the fire is completely extinguished, there is no danger to life and the damaged vehicle can be safely removed.'

'See, no casualties, which is good,' Olivia said as she looked across the room to Bella.

Bella felt the colour drain south from her face and she grabbed her phone and immediately dialled Harris's number. It went straight to voicemail. She tried again and the same happened, so she typed out a text:

Harris, are you ok? We've just seen that there's been a vehicle fire on the bridge. I'm worried about you. Please call me.

Skye walked over to Bella and put her arm around her. 'It said no casualties, Bells. He's probably driving. In fact, judging by the time he set off he should have passed the bridge by the time the fire happened. You know he won't answer the phone when he's driving.'

'She's right, hen,' Isla said. 'I'm sure he'll call you on the WhatsUp if he pulls over. Or he might just come straight here and not bother stopping.'

Bella's phone rang and she answered it immediately. 'Harris?'

'Oh... sorry, no, love, it's Mum. I was just wondering if he'd arrived yet.'

'No, Mum. We're still waiting for him.'

There was a brief pause where she could hear her dad mumbling something in the background. 'Okay... it's just that...'

'It's okay, Mum, I know about the fire on the Skye Bridge. We're hoping he was already across when it happened.'

'Okay, love. Keep me posted though if you hear from him.'

Bella nodded. 'I will.' She ended the call and slumped onto the sofa. 'What if he's stuck? What if he doesn't make it in time? Or... what if it's his car that's on fire?'

'Let's not think about that until we know more, eh?' 'Chapel of Love' began to play on Harris's Spotify song list and Skye reached down to Olivia's phone to stop the track. 'He'll be here, Bells.'

Time ticked slowly by whilst they sat and waited for news. Bella's mum and dad had joined them, as had Tam, and of course Maeve, who was worried about her son. Mirren rushed about making everyone cups of tea and handed out shortbread to keep everyone going and pretty much give them something to do to occupy their time and Dougie kept the fire stoked, poking it frequently as if it was the only thing he could do to feel useful.

Bella kept ringing Harris in the hope he would answer. He didn't.

* * *

Twelve o'clock arrived and still there had been no word from Harris. The makeup artist had gone, and the rest of the wedding guests had arrived. Everyone had been relocated to the dining room for more space. Everyone was standing around in their wedding finery talking in hushed whispers as if they felt it disrespectful to speak any louder.

Bella, her two best friends and Granny Isla sat still dressed in their robes, silently wondering what to do while the other members of the family and their friends waited with them. Bella's knee bounced up and down in a rhythm of its own as she peered around the room, taking it all in in a bid to keep her mind occupied. As the wedding reception was taking place in the picture gallery at the other end of the castle, the dining room had already been decorated in readiness for their Christmas lunch the day after, and a stunning garland of greenery with red velvet ribbons and pinecones was draped across the large marble fireplace. The fresh smell of pine wafted through the air, filling the space with the inimitable fragrance of Christmas. There was a huge Christmas tree in the corner with piles of gifts wrapped in shimmering paper beneath it, the lights twinkled, and Bella found herself staring at them, entranced, as she thought back to the last Christmas she had spent with Harris; the Christmas he had proposed to her in front of their families. She missed him terribly, even though it had only been a couple of days since she left their home, and the current situation only made things worse.

Harris's best friend and best man to be, Neil, came over to speak to her. 'Bella, love, d'you want me to go pick up my bike and go see if I can find 'im? I can bring 'im back pillion if he's stuck on't bridge. I've got a spare 'elmet.' His deep voice and Yorkshire accent thick and familiar.

Bella reached out and touched his arm, grateful for his offer. 'Thanks, Neil, I really appreciate the offer, but let's just wait until we hear from him. I don't want to send you all that way if it's not necessary.'

He nodded. 'Aye, all *reyt*, love. But just say't word an' I'll go.'

There was a knock on the door and Olivia went to see who it was. 'Oh, hi, Esme, is everything okay?'

Olivia's PA stepped sheepishly into the room. Olivia had mentioned earlier that she hadn't been due to work Christmas Eve but had heard what was happening and had run over from her cottage in the grounds to offer any help she could.

'Sorry to bother you, Lady Olivia,' Esme said, 'but the photographer is wondering if she can take shots of the bride and bridesmaids getting ready.'

Skye placed a hand on Bella's arm. 'Maybe you should get your wedding dress on, Bells. Let's have some photos done, eh? You need to be ready for when he gets here. Because he will get here.'

Bella burst into tears. 'What's the point if my groom isn't coming? You say he'll be here, but he hasn't been in touch so I'm not sure what to think.'

Her mum and dad enveloped their daughter in an embrace. 'Come on, love, don't think like that,' her dad said, his voice wavering, evidently hating seeing his daughter in distress, and even more so on her wedding day.

25

Another ten minutes passed, and everyone was chattering worriedly amongst themselves so that a low hum was all that could be heard. Bella had taken to pacing the floor, still wearing the robe with *Bride* emblazoned on the back. She'd had her nails done and was trying really hard not to bite the skin around them as she usually did when stressed.

Her phone rang and she almost dived on it, fumbling in a hurry to answer the call as everyone in the room seemed to collectively hold their breath. 'Harris? Harris, is that you? Are you okay? Where are you?' she asked in a rush of panicked words.

'Aye, darlin', it's me. I hope you don't mind me not

video calling but I know I'm not supposed to see you before the wedding,' Harris replied. There was a simultaneous sigh of relief as Bella nodded at the room to confirm it was him. She sniffed and he paused. 'Hey, are you okay? You sound upset.'

A sob escaped from Bella's chest. 'Oh, Harris, I've been so worried about you. We saw on TV about the fire on the bridge and I was terrified it was your Jeep. Or that you'd be unable to get here, and we'd have to delay the wedding.'

'Oh, dammit. I was hoping you wouldn't see that. I hoped you'd be too busy drinking champagne and listening to my playlist. I knew you'd worry. That's why I didn't call you because I knew I'd have to tell you I was stuck. But it's not my Jeep, so don't worry.'

'I was hoping you might have missed it, but you didn't answer when I called so I panicked.'

'Aye, I would have missed it if I'd been able to set off when I thought I was going to. The thing is, after the first delay which was a phone call about something that really could've waited, I was leaving just as an old guy pulled into the car park at the station. He was driving from Aberdeen to see his daughter who lives up at Waternish, he's supposed to be spending Christmas at her new house and hasn't been before, but he'd somehow gone in a circle, taken a few wrong turns and got totally lost, then ended up back in Glentorrin. So, I gave him the directions he needed and drew him a map and sent him on his way, but that meant I was delayed leaving *again*. And that resulted in me getting stuck at our end of the bridge because the fire had just happened. I heard the sirens and wondered what was going on. I knew the police officers working the cordon at our end so I went to see if I could do anything, more fool me, and ended up helping them to redirect people. Turns out it was an engine fire on an old diesel camper van. Although who wants to spend Christmas in one of those old things? The smell was rancid, and the fumes were travelling for miles, so it wasn't safe for anyone to cross.'

'But you're not injured or anything?'

'No, I'm absolutely fine, sweetheart. I recognised the firefighter in charge as that woman who came to get you out of the lift when you were trapped with that American numpty, and I was explaining to her that I was on my way to get married. She spoke to her guys, and they gave me some breathing apparatus and then escorted me across past the fire, so I was safe. Anyway, I've just pulled over to get a bottle of water because I'm fair *drouthy*, and then I'll set off again. I'll be there at ten to one, which leaves me a few minutes to get a quick wash to rid myself of the smoke. Because I absolutely stink at the moment. Tell Brodie I'll need to borrow some aftershave. I know he has the good stuff.' He laughed. 'But *nothing's* stopping me from marrying you today, Bella Douglas, do you hear me?'

Bella laughed as tears of relief spilled over. 'I hear you. I'm just glad you're okay and will get here.'

'Hey, stop crying! I don't want a blotchy, puffy-faced bride,' he said laughing. 'Now go on and get that dress on and get your makeup redone because it sounds like you need to. And I'll see you as soon as you walk through the chapel door, okay?'

She nodded and laughed. 'Okay.'

'I'll be the one in the kilt that fits this time. And Bella—'

'Yes?'

'I love you.'

She beamed. 'I love you too.'

When she ended the call, the room erupted in cheers and applause. Maeve hugged her, and then her mum and dad and granny followed suit. Everyone was relieved but no one quite as much as Bella.

'Right! Everybody get yourselves down to the

chapel so we can get this bride ready to be wed!' Olivia shouted and the dining room began to empty, everyone expressing their relief as they left. Once everyone had gone, Bella and her bridesmaids were left alone, they made their way upstairs to Olivia and Brodie's bedroom where the dresses were hanging, ready to be worn.

The bridesmaids' dresses were a rich deep green colour with billowy long sleeves, which was very apt for the season, they each had Donaldson tartan shawls on account of the winter temperature, and their bouquets were a mix of seasonal evergreens and berries interspersed with gypsophila.

Bella gasped when she saw them and her eyes welled with tears once again. 'You all look so beautiful.'

'Ah ah ah!' Olivia said, holding up her hand. 'No more tears!'

Bella's bouquet had arrived from the florist in Drumblair too and it was stunning; filled with Christmas roses and evergreens, it looked every bit the part for a festive wedding.

'Let's get that music back on,' Olivia said as she hit play once more and 'Chapel of Love' began again from the beginning, but this time they all sang along, even Isla, and Olivia retouched Bella's makeup using her own.

'It might not look as good as the first time around, but you'll still look beautiful,' Olivia told her.

'Let's get some champagne down us. I think we need it now, we've lost that pre-wedding buzz,' Skye said, producing a bottle she had brought up with her along with three glasses.

'Aye, I'll partake of a wee glass too. That decapitated coffee is fair boggin,' Isla said with a shudder. 'I'll be drinking the proper stuff again when I get home.'

The photographer came in to take some photos of them getting ready, and once Bella was dressed, they made their way to the central staircase for some more pre-wedding shots. Jack Johnson's 'Better Together' was the next song to play as the photographer snapped away and posed Bella, who couldn't help the smile that had made its way across her face.

* * *

Bella stood in front of Olivia's full-length mirror and couldn't believe her eyes. 'Liv, you are a genius,' she said as she fought back happy tears. Her lovingly created floor-length lace and satin dress fit perfectly and was finished off beautifully with the Donaldson Clan tartan sash in green, red, blue and black; a very festive-looking fabric. All that was left now was to travel the short distance to the chapel and marry the love of her life.

Dougie had polished up Lady Freya's old Rolls-Royce that had been in one of the garages for years. He had kept it running ever since she'd passed away and polished it regularly in her memory. And even though the walk down to the chapel by the loch wasn't too far, Dougie insisted on driving them down, so their dresses didn't get spoiled.

'You look stunning, Bells,' Skye said, dabbing at her eyes.

'Don't cry or you'll set us off too,' Olivia said, nudging her. 'But she's right, you do look stunning.'

'My beautiful Arabella,' Isla said, cupping her face in her hands.

There was a knock on the door and Olivia opened it. 'Hey, gorgeous, I just wanted to let you all know that the eagle has landed.' It was Brodie. He stepped inside the room and caught sight of Bella. 'Wow! You look amazing. Harris is going to flip!'

Bella laughed. 'Is he okay?'

Brodie nodded. 'Completely unscathed and smelling fresh as a daisy now he's washed the smoke off and borrowed my cologne. Just a heads-up, too, it's started to snow. I'll see you soon.'

He left and Bella gasped, making a dash for the window to open the curtains. Sure enough, feathery, glittering flakes were floating from the brilliant white sky overhead and settling on the ground beneath them, blanketing everything in a smooth covering like icing on a wedding cake.

'I got my wish!' Bella said as she stood there. Isla, Olivia and Skye joined her to gaze out at the view as the snowfall got faster.

Skye linked her arm through Bella's. 'This place always looks so magical when it snows. I used to love coming here in winter when we were kids.'

'I know, the snowball fights were rather epic,' Olivia said. 'Unless Kerr was involved. He was far too competitive.'

'Aye, him and his cronies were a wee bit too aggressive for us. Although I think we gave as good as we got,' Bella said, remembering how the snowballs stung even through her padded coat as they hit her arms.

'We sure did. We're no shrinking violets. Do you remember the time we built snowmen and raided your mum and dad's wardrobe for the accessories?' Skye said, giggling.

'I sure do. I was grounded for a week after that for using my mum's pure silk scarf and dad's best tie.' Olivia laughed. 'Kerr took great delight in taunting me for the whole week when he was going out to play but Mirren used to sneak me mugs of hot chocolate to my room so it wasn't so bad.'

'Mirren's hot chocolate was always the best,' Skye said dreamily.

'It still is in my opinion,' Olivia replied with a smile.

'It's coming down pretty fast out there, lassies,' Isla said.

Skye shivered audibly. 'Bells, you're going to be freezing. We have our shawls but I wonder if you should wear a coat. We don't want you catching pneumonia.'

Olivia gasped. 'Ooh, I've just remembered. I have the perfect thing for you to wear until we get to the chapel, Bells.'

'Haha! Chapel bells,' Isla said, giggling. Olivia, Bella and Skye turned to look at her, shaking their heads but smiling. 'What? I thought it was funny... and topical.'

Olivia walked to her wardrobe and opened the double doors before pulling out an ivory satin hooded cape, embellished at the hem with crystals and pearls. It was almost as if it had been made to accompany Bella's dress.

Bella's eyes widened as she looked at the exquisite item. 'That's perfect! Where on earth did it come from?'

'Believe it or not, I made it years ago as part of my university portfolio. I've kept it all this time because I loved it and couldn't bear to part with it. I must have known, eh? You can take it off just before you go in.'

Skye shivered. 'I'm glad we've got the Donaldson tartan shawls to wear because it really has dropped chilly.'

'We've made sure the heating is on in the chapel, so it'll be nice and toasty in there,' Olivia said.

There was a knock on the door. 'Come in!'

Bella's dad walked into the room and stood there glassy-eyed, shaking his head. 'Well, look at you. You're a vision, Arabella. An absolute vision.'

'Thanks, Dad. I think we'd better get going.'

* * *

The snow had slowed a little by the time they reached the chapel, and once Bella had stepped out of the car she clung to her dad's arm, afraid of slipping. Isla, Olivia and Skye walked on ahead, their green dresses and tartan shawls a striking contrast to the glistening white of the snow.

They stopped at the door and Bella removed the cape, passing it to Olivia before she and Skye approached the door and, as if by magic, it opened.

Bella waited for Pachelbel's 'Canon in D Major' to begin but as Skye and Olivia walked into the chapel another, very familiar tune began to play. Bella was confused at the change of song but when she realised it was 'Adore You' by Harry Styles she laughed and shook her head. As Mr Styles sang about walking through *fire*, she made eye contact with Harris and completely understood the reason he had changed the music.

He looked wonderful in his kilt and jacket. There was something innately sexy about a man in a kilt, but there was something even better about *her* man in a kilt. He was so handsome, and of course, incredibly sexy.

Harris beamed at her, shaking his head as she slowly walked towards him and when she reached him at the altar, she caught sight of his silver St Christopher sitting on top of his tie, glinting in the lights of the candles, and she smiled. It was as if Harris's grandad was there with them in spirit.

After her dad stepped aside, Harris whispered,

'You look stunning, Bella.' His eyes were glassy with emotion and her own eyes began to sting a little.

She whispered her reply, 'Thank you. So do you. Nice kilt, by the way. I hope it stays up.'

He chuckled and whispered back, 'Me too. Oh, and I hope you don't mind the change in song. It sort of felt quite fitting after the events of this morning. And your friend Mr Styles says it far better than I could. But I mean every word he's singing.'

She smiled. 'It's absolutely perfect.'

'Just like you,' he replied.

The celebrant began. 'Ladies and gentlemen, welcome to Drumblair Chapel on this beautiful Christmas Eve. We're here to today to celebrate the union of Harris and Arabella.'

A dog barked from somewhere at the back of the chapel and after a scuffle Bella turned to see Bertie running down the aisle towards them wearing his tuxedo bib, his tongue lolling out of his mouth. They both crouched to greet him, laughing as he wagged his tail and then sat like such a good boy beside Harris, his tail swishing on the stone floor like a sweeping brush. A little velvet pouch hung from his collar, just like it had on the day Harris proposed.

'I think our four-legged ring bearer would like us to hurry up,' the celebrant said, and a rumble of laughter travelled the room. Bella returned her attention to Harris to find his gaze was fixed on her. He reached out and took her hand and she knew this was it.

'Are you ready for forever?' he whispered.

'Absolutely,' she replied.

26

Bella gazed up at the Botticelli masterpiece *The Birth of Venus* and in a split second totally understood what Reid had meant about it being an emotional experience. Tears of happiness welled in her eyes, and she couldn't quite believe she was here. Tuscany, and Florence in particular, had been where she had dreamed of visiting since she had seen images of the architecture online. She had been captivated by the place and now, thanks to her new husband, here she was, experiencing it for herself.

Harris slipped his arm around her shoulder. 'Are you ready to leave?'

She didn't take her eyes from the painting. 'Even

though we've been here at the gallery for two hours and this is the third time I have visited this painting, the emotions are just as raw each time.'

'She is beautiful,' Harris said. 'This place is incredible. But we need to go if we're going to catch the Cavalcade.'

As if being snatched from a trance, Bella turned to him. 'Oh, gosh, yes. We can't miss that.'

The winter sun was low in the sky, and it wouldn't be long until it made its descent towards the horizon and Florence was already bathed in a warm orange glow in spite of the chilly temperature. The horse-back rider at the front of the procession was dressed in the most sumptuous silks in rich, vibrant colours. As they followed the procession from Palazzo Pitti, they saw people dressed in Renaissance costumes of red, gold and blue. It was like a painting come to life. Bella had learned that the participants' clothing had been inspired by the fresco in the Medici Palace Chapel that had been painted in the mid-1400s. They had visited the Magi Chapel the day before and had been awed by the outstanding example of fifteenth-century artistry.

As they walked, the atmosphere was humming with chatter and excitement as men with wicker baskets handed out sweets to the children. Music was being played on accordions, guitars and even bagpipes, which made Bella think of home. Huge flags were being waved, and every face held a smile.

As the winter sun began its descent, candles were lit and even though it was still technically daylight, they took on the mantle of the warm glow that the sun had passed on. In spite of the chill in the air, Bella had never felt warmth like it. Harris held her hand and every so often he gazed down at her, smiling, his abundant happiness evident for all to see.

The parade ended in the Piazza del Duomo, and they were greeted by the angelic sound of a children's choir serenading them with festive songs. Had they been at home, Christmas would have been over by now, but here they got to extend the experience and were able to witness the wonderful living nativity as the wise men placed gifts before the Christ child. Bella had tears in her eyes as she watched everything play out before them.

* * *

Later that evening, they enjoyed a divine meal at one of the bistros at the Piazza Santo Spirito with melt-in-the-mouth steak and gnocchi in a rich, creamy sauce. Both happy and full of good food, they sat for a while enjoying a glass of chianti and the *movida* on a heated terrace as they watched the evening revellers laughing and singing. The centre of the piazza featured a beautiful octagonal sandstone fountain which people stopped by to take photos and selfies, just as they too had done earlier.

Afterwards they took a wonderful moonlit walk along the river back to Hotel Pendini and their room which overlooked the Piazza Della Reppublica and the skyline of Florence beyond. After a long, languorous shared shower, Harris decided to forego room service and instead went to the bar to acquire some drinks, and while he was gone Bella stood at the Juliet balcony to look out. There were still a few people in the square below making the most of the dry evening and Bella could just about hear their chatter, but more prominently a string quartet were playing Mozart's '*Eine Kleine Nachtmusik*' and the beautiful melodic sound floated through the air, sending shivers down her spine. The sun had set now, and the navy-blue sky overhead was filled with thousands of tiny specks of glittering light. She inhaled deeply and tried to commit the moment to memory. After all, that was the point of being there.

Their room was the epitome of luxury, with stunning antique furniture and the most beautiful cream wallpaper with ferns and foliage painted all over it in shades of pale green. It was like something she would've chosen for one of her own designs. The main feature of the room was the huge brass bed that felt like sleeping on a cloud. But the view was the best part. Harris had promised that one day they would return in the spring or summer to experience the place in the sunshine. But he had made such a wonderful choice that being there at that precise moment was the closest thing to perfection Bella had experienced or could imagine.

She wrapped the fluffy white robe around her, not minding the feel of the cool breeze on her skin, and thought back to the shower they had shared earlier. She pulled her bottom lip between her teeth and smiled at the memory, her face flushing a little. She never wanted this honeymoon to end.

Harris returned to the room with a bottle of prosecco and two glasses, and she turned to see him walking in. Her heart swelled as his mouth tilted up in a delicious smile. He shook his head and remained on the spot for a moment, just staring at her.

'What?' she asked, tucking her hair behind her ear.

He sighed. 'You... there... now... I don't think I've ever seen a more stunning sight. Well, apart from watching you walk down the aisle towards me.'

She felt a flush of embarrassment, or desire, or a mixture of both travel upwards from her chest. No one had ever looked at her the way Harris did. No one had ever made her feel so beautiful. He placed the glasses and the bottle down and walked slowly towards her. He slipped his hands into her hair and kissed her as if it was the first time. She pulled him inside and closed the door to the balcony before letting her robe slip to the floor.

***

Bella's eyes fluttered open as a crack of daylight streamed in through the curtains and she rolled over to see Harris lying on his back with one arm above his head and the other resting on her hip. She snuggled up to him and he instinctively moved to wrap her in his arms. She inhaled the familiar scent of his skin and placed a kiss on his bare chest. She'd had vivid dreams overnight that had changed the way she thought about certain elements of their future. She just had to work out how to tell him.

'What's wrong, sweetheart?' he asked, eyes still closed as he placed a kiss on her forehead.

No time like the present, she thought. 'Can we talk?'

He pulled away to look at her, his eyes now open and focused. 'Aye, of course. What is it? Are you okay?'

She nodded. 'I've been thinking... well, actually, I've been dreaming.'

'And?' A crease of worry formed between his brows.

'Maybe we don't have to wait that long.'

'For what?'

She chewed her lip for a moment. 'To start a family.'

He raised his eyebrows. 'I'm sorry, what? What's brought this on?'

She pushed herself up onto her elbow to look down into his eyes. 'I dreamt last night that we were out walking in Glentorrin and... you were pushing a pram, and I was holding the hand of a small child. I've never felt so serene and calm as I did in that dream. It felt like a sign.'

He stared at her for a few seconds, and she began to wonder if perhaps she'd said the wrong thing. After all, it wasn't so long ago that she'd said she wasn't ready, so she probably sounded crazy saying a dream had changed her mind. But it was the truth. She could only hope that he didn't hate the idea.

She tried to find a way to explain things better that wouldn't make her sound like a crazy person. 'I know I sound like I've got a slate loose, but all I can think about now is little Harris and little Bella, or whatever combination they arrive in. My job is pretty flexible anyway and we have the space in the house. But if you hate the idea and you're not ready that's fine, too, of course I would never expect—'

He pulled her down and stopped her words with a kiss and when he pulled away again his eyes were glistening. 'So, we're doing this?' he asked, almost in a whisper.

Bella's eyes welled with tears, and she laughed. 'If you definitely want to.'

He nodded. 'I definitely do.'

Her heart flipped in her chest. 'Oh, my word. We're going to try for a baby.'

He beamed up at her. 'We are. I love you so much.'

'And I love you,' she told him as she pulled the covers over their heads and kissed him once more.

* * *

MORE FROM LISA HOBMAN

The next book in The Scottish Highlands series is available to order now here:
https://mybook.to/SkyeBook5

ACKNOWLEDGEMENTS

Firstly, I would like to thank Rich, Gee, my mum and dad, and my bookshop business partner and close friend, Claire, not only for your unwavering support, but for keeping me supplied with snacks, hugs and encouragement and for allowing me the space I need when I am in *Panic! At the Deadline* mode! (See what I did there?) I appreciate you all more than you can possibly know.

A huge thank you to Lorella and the team at Lorella Belli Literary Agency for believing in my stories and always being there when I need you. Your expertise and knowledge have enabled me to do what I love for another year, and I am eternally grateful.

Much appreciation goes to my editor, Caroline, CEO and founder, Amanda, and the whole flipping fabulous team at Boldwood. Working tirelessly behind the scenes, you continue to go from strength to strength and it's so exciting to be along for the ride. Long may it continue!

Finally, thanks to you, my incredible readers. Without you I would simply be a woman in a beautifully decorated office (thank you Rich and Dad), making up people and talking to folks who only exist in my imagination! You give me the courage to carry on making up these stories and characters and you take them into your hearts, which is something I don't think I will ever get over. I hope you enjoy this one too.

All my love,
Lisa

ABOUT THE AUTHOR

Lisa Hobman has written many brilliantly reviewed women's fiction titles – the first of which was shortlisted by the RNA for their debut novel award. In 2012 Lisa relocated her family from Yorkshire to a village in Scotland and this beautiful backdrop now inspires her uplifting and romantic stories.

Sign up to Lisa Hobman's mailing list for news, competitions and updates on future books.

Visit Lisa's website: www.lisajhobman.com

Follow Lisa on social media:

[facebook icon] facebook.com/LisaJHobmanAuthor

[instagram icon] instagram.com/lisahobmanauthor

[tiktok icon] tiktok.com/@lisahobmanauth

ALSO BY LISA HOBMAN

The Skye Collection Series

Dreaming Under An Island Skye

Under An Italian Sky

Wishing Under a Starlit Skye

Together Under A Snowy Skye

The Highlands Series

Coming Home to the Highlands

Chasing a Highland Dream

A Highland Family Affair

Shooting Stars Over the Highlands

Snowy Surprises in the Highlands

Standalone Novels

Starting Over At Sunset Cottage

It Started with a Kiss

A Summer of New Beginnings

What Becomes of the Broken Hearted

Boldwood

Boldwood Books is an award-winning fiction publishing company seeking out the best stories from around the world.

Find out more at www.boldwoodbooks.com

Join our reader community for brilliant books, competitions and offers!

Follow us
@BoldwoodBooks
@TheBoldBookClub

Sign up to our weekly deals newsletter

https://bit.ly/BoldwoodBNewsletter